CREDO'S FIRE

Book Three of the Alex Wolfe Mystery Series

ALISON NAOMI HOLT

CHAPTER 1

I stared into deep pools of velvet brown surrounded by the longest, lushest eyelashes I'd ever seen. She held my gaze, beckoning me to cross that line. I stepped back a pace. "You know emus are mean, right?"

My partner, Casey, nodded, "Yup."

"I mean, not mean all the time, just mean like when you try to stuff 'em into the back of a van or something." The emu continued to stare at me, not an ounce of fear crossing her round, inquisitive face. I looked back at the growing ranks of patrol officers who'd come to watch us capture this six-foot escapee from someone's backyard. "C'mon, one of you guys give us a hand. These things are strong."

Every one of them, to a man, shuffled their feet and backed up a fraction of an inch.

"Marlin? Look, you're six foot, she's six foot. What could be so hard?"

Marlin's a buff, handsome African American cop who'd never backed down from a fight—until now. "Sorry, Alex. I saw an ostrich tear a man apart with its feet on the Animal Channel and I'm not goin' near that thing. They said their legs are some of the strongest of any animals, and that those toes can rip metal wire fences."

I walked over to where he was standing and reached up to put my arm across his shoulders. "Well, you see, that's just the thing. This is an emu, not an ostrich. There's a big difference."

Marlin carefully peeled my arm from around his shoulders and headed for his car. "No way, Alex. I'm gettin' while the gettin's good. See you around." I watched his departing back, then turned to glare at the others who either looked at the ground or just grinned.

The van from the local humane society pulled up just as I walked back to where Casey stood stroking the emu's head across a short chain link fence. The fence enclosed our complainant's small back yard which held plastic lawn chairs, a portable barbeque grill and, incredibly, a wandering emu. I looked over my shoulder at the van and sighed. My first impression of the driver did nothing to assuage my fear that Casey and I were on our own on this one. A little man slid out of the driver's side and when his feet finally hit the ground, the top of his Philadelphia Phillies baseball cap came to about the middle of the side view mirror. He walked over and held out his hand to Casey who shook it casually. She and I both looked to the passenger door hoping that someone around six foot five with huge biceps would emerge to help us out.

Casey raised her eyebrows. "Please tell me you didn't come alone. This is gonna take more than just the three of us."

The driver, apparently named "Pete" judging by the letters stenciled above the right pocket of his shirt, raised his hands and backed away. "Three of us? Oh no, I'm just the van driver. I don't do animals. My boss said the cops had an escaped emu they needed brought to the facility, so here's the van." His head swiveled between Casey and me. "You load it, I drive it. Any more 'n that and you guys are on your own."

Casey fingered the embroidery on a bright yellow pillowcase the anxious homeowner had lent us to put over the animal's head to keep it calm. I reached up and scratched my forehead, "I'm gonna kill whichever commander decided detectives need to work two days a month in uniform."

"It's all part of the job description, Alex. Budget cuts and all that. Patrol needs help, we're it."

I swept my arm back towards the ever-growing crowd of police officers. "Yeah? Then why can't patrol help us?"

The van driver opened the rear doors and moved a few items to make room for the emu. He grabbed a rope and handed it to me. "Here, you're gonna need to tie her legs together so she doesn't kill you with those claws."

With one last glance back at the onlookers, who now included a cameraman from the local media, Casey and I pushed open the little gate and entered the fenced back yard. The emu took a few steps toward us, curiously studying our hands as if looking for a treat. There was no fear—on the part of the emu anyway. I reached out and hesitantly stroked one of the wings while Casey spoke soothingly to the bird, worried more about the emu's feelings I'm sure, than about the damage it could do to us. "Easy girl, you'll be all right, we're not gonna hurt you." She moved slowly until she stood next to the big body, which came up to about the middle of Casey's chest. "Okay, Alex. I'll take the head, you sweep her legs out from under her and we'll go from there. Let's try to do it slowly to keep her from panicking."

A glance down at the clawed, three-toed feet made me hope my life insurance was up-to-date. "Jesus." I took a shaky breath and bent over, slowly circling my arms around stout legs that resembled thick, solid branches. "Okay, slowly, on three. One, two, three!" I tightened my grip her legs at the same time Casey tried to slip the pillowcase over her head. Just as I'd expected, the pillowcase went flying and so did I. With one flick of just one enormous leg she'd sent me sprawling while Casey was left holding the neck of a very pissed off bird.

With the emu bucking like a bronco and Casey hanging on for dear life, I lunged for the legs making sure to lead with my body instead of my face and head. A huge claw whipped forward and raked the inside of my thigh, tearing my uniform pants from crotch to knee. I managed to get my arms around both legs and lifted enough of her off the ground so Casey could gently direct the head and body sideways to the ground. The emu raked me again with her claws, luckily this time only catching the side of my boots instead of my leg.

Casey called out a warning. "Grab the legs down low, Alex! You can't let her rake you like that!"

3

"No shit, Einstein! Look what she did to my leg!" Blood dripped from a long, luckily shallow gash on the inside of my thigh. My heart rate felt like it had tripled and my words came out more of a snarl than the jovial wisecrack I'd intended. All three of us were laying on the ground by this time, the emu still trying to free a leg and flailing her head wanting to tear a hunk out of Casey's face. The van driver collected the pillowcase from the low hanging branch of the tree where it had landed and threw it at Casey who managed to catch it with one hand while still controlling the bird's head with the other.

I slid further down the legs, pinning one foot between my knees and the other between my arm and my body. Even holding her like that, she was still jerking me around as though I were a ragdoll. Suddenly, all movement stopped and I looked up to see Casey holding closed the opening of the pillowcase that was now covering the emu's head. I frantically looked around for the rope to tie the legs. It lay about two feet away, curled around my butt print where I'd landed on my first attempt at "doing it slowly to keep her from panicking."

As I lay there considering my options, our friend Jack Dougherty came running over. He must have driven up during my "fly like a butterfly, try not to pee" imitation. "Shit, how come nobody's helping you guys? You're crazy doing this with just the two of you." Jack grabbed the rope and helped me pin the legs together so we could bind them. Both Casey and I were too winded to give Jack any kind of explanation and once the legs were secure, we lay in the dirt trying to catch our breath.

Finally, Casey nodded toward the van. "Okay, now all we need to do is get her in there."

I studied the height of the floor on the van while gently stroking the body of the big bird. "Well, she's about 140 pounds, most of it in the middle. You still need to control the head and I have to keep the legs and feet under control."

Jack called over to the quickly thinning group of officers who'd been hooting and hollering at our impromptu rodeo just a few minutes earlier. "I need two of you losers over here, now!" Two of the newer officers hustled over. Jack moved behind the bird and squatted down. "Help us get her into the van." As soon as we lifted, the emu began bucking again. Casey ended up inside the van with the emu's head flailing in her lap and I ended up on top of the bird with my legs clamped around its thighs. Before we knew what was happening, Jack had slammed the rear doors shut and yelled at the driver. "Get 'em to the compound and I'll pick 'em up from there."

Once the doors closed and the outside noise subsided, the emu quieted and I rested my head on her feathery body. "Shit."

Casey reached over and ruffled my hair. "Look at the bright side, Alex. We're gonna be on the five o'clock news looking like idiots. What more can a person ask for?"

I reached up and pulled a small feather off my tongue. "Did she get you?"

She stuck a finger deep into a hole in her dark blue uniform shirt. When she pulled it out, blood covered the tip of her finger. "Just a little bit." She motioned to my leg with a flip of her chin. "I like your new air conditioning. Is the cut very deep?"

"Nope, but the pants are shot, thanks to our lady here."

The news cameras were waiting for us when we pulled into the back lot of the Humane Society. Jack opened the rear doors of the van and helped us carefully prop our girl up on her two bound feet. I untied the rope expecting her to try to kick me again, but she just stood there. We kept the hood over her head and kind of steered her to the awaiting pen. Once inside, Casey carefully removed the hood and we both stood back, ready for anything.

She waited a second, slowly taking in her surroundings and then she began checking out the trees and grass in her new enclosure. Our Emu, it seemed, had more curiosity than anger programmed into her pretty little head and when Casey approached to give her a parting, "no offense" pat, the emu reached down and gently pecked at the badge pinned to her uniform shirt. Casey turned to me with that look I know only too well. Translated, it meant, "I want to take her home."

I laughed. "What, to go with your five goats, four pigs, three donkeys, and two horses, now you need an emu in a pear tree?"

She stroked the long neck. "Well, if the owner doesn't show up and they can't find a home for her, I'll take her." We walked from the enclosure to where Jack waited for us in his patrol car. I searched the lot for the media but apparently a cooperative Emu hadn't been an interesting conclusion to their story.

As we neared his patrol car, Casey and I both sped up, racing each other for the shotgun position since neither of us wanted to sit in the back where drunk prisoners threw up or left a load of lice or fleas. I reached the door handle first but Casey shoved me towards the rear of the car. She quickly pulled open the door, stopping short when she saw Jack's gear bag securely strapped into the passenger seat.

Jack sat in the driver's seat and leaned towards her, stretching his lanky chest over the center computer console. "Hey, you mind sitting in the back? I have all my stuff here and it'd be a hassle to have to move everything twice." Casey made a face and stared into the back window. Jacked laughed. "Don't worry, I power washed it this morning." The back seats in our patrol cars are made of molded, hard plastic and when things get filthy, a good power cleaning at the local carwash does wonders.

We gingerly climbed in, pulling the doors shut after us. I immediately felt claustrophobic with the steel grid partition in front of my face and no door handles on the doors. "God I hate riding back here."

Jack glanced in the rearview mirror as he drove us back to our car. "I know, no fun. Hey, I've been meaning to ask, has either of you been to the E.R. lately?"

Normally, Casey and I end up at the emergency room at least once a week interviewing victims or suspects in one of our cases. We've been partners in the Special Crimes unit for a little over a year, investigating kidnappings, home invasions, cold cases and basically any offbeat crime the department felt needed special handling. We both shook our heads as I thought back to the past couple of weeks. "No, we've mostly been working on a cold case from back in the eighties, a fifty-year-old weight lifter who disappeared without a trace. Why do you ask?"

He rubbed the back of his head and I watched a light shade of red start at his collar and slowly creep up his neck to his hairline. "I dunno, no reason." He reached down to turn up the volume on his police radio.

Normally, it was hard to shut Jack up. He loved to talk about his kids and their sports, or how well his wife was doing in the art world, so it was really unusual for him to stop talking without someone jabbing him in the ribs to remind him to let someone else get a word in edgewise. I prodded him a little. "So, what's goin' on at the E.R.?"

His hesitation spoke volumes and Casey and I exchanged looks. Like a dummy, I unbuckled my seatbelt and slid forward to get a better look at his face. Not two seconds later, a black Chihuahua ran in front of our car. Jack slammed on the brakes and I ended up with my face plastered against the metal partition. Casey quickly unbuckled her seatbelt and turned around to sit with her knees on the seat, worriedly staring out the back window to see if we'd hit the dog. When she saw him run back the way he came, she let out a sigh. "I thought we got him. If these stupid people can't keep their pets off the streets they shouldn't own 'em."

I peeled myself off the screen. "I'm fine, thanks for asking."

"Seatbelts are a wonderful thing, Alex." Jack smiled as he pulled up next to our vehicles and came around to open our doors. I quickly jumped out of our portable prison, wiping myself off wherever my pants had touched the seat.

Not one to be deterred by a face plant, I cornered Jack before he could slide back into his seat. "Jack, what's wrong at the E.R? Is something going on with Maddie or Marcos?" Maddie was our slightly overweight—okay, our generously padded friend who currently wore her hair in a modified rainbow Mohawk and who regularly changed her animal sculpted nose rings to please her "ever changing animal within," whatever that meant. She and Marcos, our hunky, cross-dressing Adonis, were both nurses in the Emergency Room and if something was going on with them, I wanted to know about it.

Jack reached up to scratch his head, then nervously crossed his arms over his chest. "Well, it's just that..." His face returned to that unusual shade of red I'd noticed earlier, and I waited patiently, knowing he'd eventually spit out what was bothering him. "Look, I'm not gay or anything, so I don't want you to get the wrong idea about what I'm saying, but, well, I don't think everything's okay with Marcos. I don't mean I'm watching him or anything....I mean I'm not interested in him or.....shit, I shouldn't have even brought it up."

I rolled my eyes. "C'mon, Jack, you can still care about a gay guy without being gay yourself. He's our friend. Period. End of story, and if something's wrong, we need to help him."

Casey was leaning against the trunk of the car listening. "He seemed okay about two weeks ago. Terri and I ran into him at the Fourth Avenue Street Fair. What makes you think there's a problem?"

"You just need to stop by and take a look at him, that's all. I can't explain it, it's just an impression I've gotten the last couple of times I've been to the E.R. He doesn't look or act like the nutcase I'm used to seeing. I thought maybe you two could figure out what's going on."

I felt a breeze blowing through the hole in my pants so I reached down to close the flap. "No problem. We can go by after a quick stop at the station so I can get a new pair of pants."

Jack laughed. "Good thing she didn't reach a little higher or you'd be on your way to see Marcos right now with blood pouring out of your femoral artery. I'm gonna ream some ass in de-briefing tonight. Those assholes should've jumped in and helped."

Casey shook her head. "No, don't say anything on our account. With too many people clustered around her she might have gotten hurt. We could've used one more person, but it wasn't a big deal."

Jack shrugged as he slipped into the driver's seat. "Ok, well take care, ladies. I'll see you at the next call."

We watched him back out of the driveway, then got into our patrol car and drove to the station to change. When we walked into the locker room we ran into our Sergeant, Kate Brannigan, who had just changed out of her uniform. She looked down at the gaping hole in my pants, flicked a glance to the tear in Casey's shirt, then nodded. "Well, I don't need to ask as I'm sure I'm going to see it on the six o'clock news."

She pulled open the door and paused before stepping into the hallway. "In fact, you might want to watch the national news tonight since I just got a call from one of my network connections asking for your names and work assignments." She caught and held my eyes for a moment, lowering her chin and raising her eyebrows in her typical "Is there anything I should know about?" look.

I raised innocent eyebrows and shrugged which elicited a sigh and a resigned shake of her head. She turned to Casey, "Anyway, you two need to change into your regular work clothes. There was a fire out at the Rillito Racetrack this morning and Rick Longoria just called asking us to take the scene. He and his squad are at some advanced arson training in Michigan, so, Casey, you're going to take the lead and Alex, you're going to help her."

I reached over and held the door for her. "Okay, but I don't know much about arson, boss. That's pretty technical stuff."

Kate nodded. "I know. I mentioned that to Rick, and he said the fire department investigators will handle the actual arson. You're only interviewing potential witnesses and racetrack employees. He said if you come up with anything of interest, he or Martin will follow up on it when they get back."

I let the door close behind her and walked over to where Casey had already begun the tedious process of removing her gun belt, patrol boots, Kevlar vest, uniform pants and shirt. I did the same, then started the whole operation in reverse after first shaking out my tan Dockers to get out most of the wrinkles and pulling on my white Polo Shirt. I threaded my belt through the loops in the pancake style holster I used for plain clothes work, transferred my Glock from my uniform holster into it, took my badge from the breast of my uniform shirt and hooked it onto the badge holder I wore on my belt. The whole process was second nature, and while I didn't really think about what I was doing, it still took a fair amount of time to complete.

Casey finished tying her shoes, threw her torn uniform in her locker and headed for the door. "I'll meet you up the office. I have a few phone calls to make before we head out."

As she opened the door to leave, my friend Ruthanne walked in. "Hi Case, how's that new goat? He seemed pretty feisty."

I turned to stare at Casey, who'd promised me she'd stop rescuing every wayward animal that came her way. "What new goat? You got a new goat? Casey—"

Ruthanne grimaced as she realized her mistake. "Uh oh."

Casey disappeared through the door and I glared at Ruthanne. "You took another homeless goat out to her place again, didn't you?"

Ruthanne shrugged. "She's just fostering it for me until I can find it a permanent home. I didn't have anywhere else I could take him and his asshole owner's gonna be rotting in prison for a long, long time." Her shoulder length brown hair was pulled back into a ponytail which swished back and forth as she punctuated her words with a not so convincing shake of her head.

"So? You're a cop, not a zoo keeper."

"Well, the pound was on its way to pick him up since the asshole's going to do thirty years in federal lock-up, and the goat kinda found its way into the back of my car, and I kinda left before Animal Control got there." She shoved her hands into her pockets.

"You know she can hardly afford to feed the ones she already has."

"She's fostering it..."

"Bullshit. You and I both know that once it's at her house she can't let go. You gotta stop doing this shit, Ruthanne."

"Well, I can't bring any more of 'em to my house..." She looked up with a calculating expression. "...unless I started bringing them to you?"

"Forget it. Goats, pigs, horses, camels, and any ungulate for that matter are specifically forbidden in my neighborhood. Specifically...so don't even think about it." I threw the rest of my uniform stuff into my locker and slammed it shut.

Crossing her arms, Ruthanne chuckled as I pulled open the locker room door. "Ungulate?"

I grinned as I walked out, "I'll ungulate you if you don't stop foisting your rescues off on my partner." As the door closed on her laughter, I reached over and pushed the button for the elevator, which is directly across the short hallway from the women's locker room. The locker rooms are in the basement of the main police station along with several detective units, which are housed to the left as I faced the elevator. To the right is a set of double doors leading to the large cavernous bay where most of the SWAT equipment is kept.

When the elevator doors opened, Captain Beulow stepped out, his lip curling into a sneer when he saw me standing there. Beulow is a pear shaped man whose sunken chest and rounded shoulders top a bulbous bottom that should have been impossible to stuff into our tailored uniform pants. But here he was in all his cellulitical splendor, his pants zipper bulging at the seams... no thanks to his, I'm sure, very tiny manhood. There was no love lost between us—in fact our relationship could be described as adversarial at its best and fetid at its worst—so I silently stepped onto the elevator and turned to press the button for the second floor. When I looked up, I caught the malevolent glare Beulow threw over his shoulder as he walked away. I matched him stare for stare until the elevator doors closed, feeling the rancor that twisted my gut every time I saw the man.

I stepped into the office and Sharon, our secretary, called out a cheery hello as I pulled down the arm on her M&M man and retrieved the piece of candy that had rolled out onto his little tray. I returned her greeting, popped the chocolate into my mouth and headed back to where Casey and I had our desks. Our office held three different detective units in one big bullpen setting. An aisle split the office into two sides. Child Abuse is on the left, the Special Crimes Unit on the right, and Domestic Violence is buried in the back opposite the lieutenant's office. The sergeant's cubicles are in a glassed-in area on the front, left side of the room. Our desk space shares a common wall with the Lt.'s office and the entire North side of the room is made up of a lower three foot wall with massive plate glass windows on top looking out over the lovely fire department parking lot.

Casey had the phone up to her ear, and as she saw me approach, she turned away so I couldn't hear what she was saying. Shrugging, I pulled open my desk drawer and took out my digital recorder, a camera and an extra couple of pens which I tossed into my canvas briefcase before zipping the top and placing the whole bag onto the center of my desk.

I waited a few minutes, staring at the back of Casey's head while she finished her conversation. After a few minutes, I reached over my desk and tapped the top of her workspace with my pen. "Hey Case, Kate said we needed to get out to the racetrack."

She held up one finger, indicating she didn't want to be disturbed. I sat back and waited, wondering who she was talking to. A commotion near Sharon's desk caught my attention, and I watched as Nate Drewery, one of the detectives in our unit, and Jimmy Weatherby, a patrol officer I'd met a few months ago, dragged a protesting foul-mouthed arrestee through our offices and back to the interview rooms. I didn't pay too much attention until I heard the suspect call out my name.

"Hey Wolfey, I screwed your mother to the wall last night. Then my brother screwed her too."

When I focused on his face instead of the full sleeve of tats on his left arm, I knew exactly who they'd brought in. It would have been difficult to forget the eyeballs that bulged from their sockets or the chubby fish lips surrounded by several days growth of his brown, scraggly beard. I'd always considered it a miracle that his eyelids actually fit all the way down over his black, toady eyes.

"Yeah, she was real nice, I fucked her up real good." He jerked his hips back and forth, making little kissy noises as they pushed him into one of the interview rooms and shut the door. I could still hear his muffled obscenities and smiled at Nate as he came walking back to my desk.

Nate motioned to the door with a toss of his head. "A friend of yours?"

"Hardly. He's one of those who should have been culled from the herd at birth. What'd he do this time?"

He shrugged. "Don't know. Kate just told me to meet Jimmy by the garage elevator and help bring the guy to the interview rooms."

I nodded. "The arson, then. I wonder what he did to get himself arrested. He's not exactly the arson type."

Casey hung up the phone and tuned in to our conversation. "What exactly is your version of the arson type?"

"Well, I guess somebody who has a history of setting fires, abused as a kid, pulls the wings off flies, you know, that type. Leslie's just a stupid wannabe tough guy who comes from a quiet, middleclass neighborhood.

Both Nate and Casey turned to look at the door where all parts of my anatomy were being dissected in detail. Casey raised her eyebrows. "Leslie?"

"Yeah, he's a midtown kid who tries to be one of the—" I made little quotation marks in the air, "tough guys." He lived in my beat when I worked patrol. I've actually scraped him up off the sidewalk more times than I've arrested him. His general M.O. is he pisses somebody off, they pound him into the ground. A couple of times I got there in time to pull the other guys off him. It wasn't until the last time I rescued him that I realized my rescue actually pissed him off more than the bullying." I shrugged again. "Now, every time he sees me he turns into that foul mouthed cretin you just hauled in. He may be a jerk, but I just don't peg him as an arsonist."

Nate shrugged. "No wonder he said his name was Otto. Damn, in my old neighborhood you name a guy 'Leslie' and he'd lose his teeth before he was two."

I stood up and stretched, motioning to Casey. "Anyway, Kate said to meet her at the racetrack. I think we need to get going."

Casey gathered several papers from her desk and shoved them into her briefcase. She checked to make sure her tape recorder was still in the little pocket on the inside of the lid, then shut the case and snapped the locks. "Let's go then."

CHAPTER 2

We pulled into the huge, mostly empty parking lot of the Rillito Racetrack less than twenty minutes later. I spotted Kate's metallic blue Ford Taurus and pulled in beside it. Casey opened her door and stepped out but before I'd unbuckled my seatbelt, she leaned back in and lowered her sunglasses. "Here comes the media. I wonder if they're following us around to try to fill up their headline slots on the five o'clock news."

Anytime the media shows up I try to keep a low profile. Two times in one day was a little much for my comfort zone. The news van stopped in the center of the parking lot long enough for the cameraman to hop out. I watched him in the rear view mirror as he set the bulky camera on his shoulder, aiming first at the main racecourse on the right, then slowly panning left in order to get a good overall shot of the scene. Since the racing season hadn't opened yet, the only vehicles in the lot belonged to either police, fire or racetrack officials. I got out and took a good look around, halfway expecting Kate to poke her head out of one of the burned out stalls to tell us what she needed. Once I followed Casey into the nearest horsebox, I understood why she hadn't.

Kate was kneeling next to the remains of a human hand sticking out of the dirt. Another man I assumed was the fire department's arson investigator knelt beside her. I carefully backed out so as not to disturb any evidence—well, any evidence that hadn't already been destroyed by fire, hundreds of gallons of water, and ten pairs of turnout boots worn by all the firemen who'd tromped through the scene dousing the flames or checking for hotspots.

Casey backed out as well and we took a minute to check out the overall scene. She let out a low whistle. "Man, I'd love to have a shed row barn like this. I could keep all my critters in one place instead of having to cobble together different houses for each separate breed." Unlike most families, all of Casey's "kids" came equipped with either four feet or feathers.

I nodded sagely even though I wouldn't know the difference between a shed row barn and a storage shed. We walked over to one of the other buildings that hadn't burned. There appeared to be about three individual freestanding barns. I studied the one we stood in front of, feigning interest in their design as Casey pointed out various features with unadulterated lust in her eyes. She reached over and pulled back a latch on one of the upper doors. "These are called Dutch doors. The upper half with the metal bars is designed so when you open it, the horse can look out over the courtyard while the lower wooden half stays shut and keeps your boy where he's supposed to be." Grabbing my arm, she maneuvered me into the doorway. "See those boards? They line the entire stall from the ground up to about five feet so the horses can't kick each other when they're in neighboring enclosures. Then they've got poles up to about twelve feet. They need to be that high so the horses don't hit their heads if they rear up for some reason."

I grinned at her enthusiasm and stepped back in order to look down the row of double doors. All of the barns consisted of about forty stalls, twenty on one side and twenty on the other. The doors to the horseboxes faced out into a central courtyard, and the rear wall of each stall backed up to its twin, which faced in the opposite direction.

Casey could have probably gone on for several more minutes, but I'd seen enough and when I turned back, she followed. We walked to the burned out hulk of the first building, scanning the ground and surrounding areas for any clues to what might have happened. Most of the flammable material had been consumed by the fire, and what was left lay in ruins. I reached up and nudged one of the upper swinging doors on the first stall, causing it to squeak loudly while it moved around on its rusted hinges. The bars were blackened by smoke while the lower wooden half had been burned completely away. The walls, what remained of them, had fallen sideways into the boxes and portions of the roof had collapsed.

Once again we looked into the horsebox where we'd first found Kate. She was standing to the side now, and we were able to get a better view of the scene. The hand, which I assumed belonged to a body buried somewhere in the rubble, had a shovel resting under it. My guess was that one of the firemen had realized at the last second what he'd unearthed and had quickly abandoned his efforts to sift through the pile looking for hotspots. Kate swiveled in place trying to get a good overall view of the scene. As she turned toward the door, her gaze came to rest on me, and then on Casey. She stood, wiping her hands against each other in an effort to clean off the soot. "Did you guys see the lieutenant on the way in?"

We both shook our heads. Kate took out her notebook, wrote something in it, then pointed the pen at me. "I'm expecting him, so look sharp." I dug my hands into my pockets while Kate stared at me. I liked our lieutenant well enough but he tended to get uptight whenever he saw me around. He's a by the book kind of guy, and I'm more of a fly by the seats of my pants kind of girl. I think I make him nervous.

Kate pointed toward our cars. "Alex, I want to widen our scene. Get a new roll of tape and extend the perimeter to include all the barns on either side of this one." She motioned to the partially skeletonized hand with her chin. "This body's obviously been here a while, and we're going to have to dig around in each of the stalls to see if we come up with any more."

I nodded and returned to the parking lot, popped the trunk of my 2012 Ford Taurus, and pulled out a roll of yellow crime scene tape. The two-year-old Taurus was actually an improvement over the last car I'd been assigned. At least this one had less than 100,000 miles on it and the previous owner hadn't been a three pack a day chain smoker. Sure the rules said no smoking in our work cars, but tell that to the thirty-year veteran I'd inherited my previous car from.

I heard the sound of tires on gravel and turned to see a black Jaguar sedan pulling into the lot. Since I didn't recognize the vehicle, I walked over to tell whoever it was that this was a crime scene and they needed to leave. I smiled when I saw Gabe, my muscle bound friend who also just happens to be a mafia bodyguard, open the driver's door and step out. He carefully buttoned his black suit coat before stepping up to the rear door and pulling it open. Another friend, Gianina Angelino, the head of the Angelino Crime Family, stepped out of the car and surveyed the scene.

I smiled at the woman who'd given me a racehorse several months earlier. "Is that a new car? What happened to the Lincoln?"

Gia returned my smile before turning and reaching into the car to retrieve something I couldn't see. As usual, she looked stunning when she bent over in her black designer jeans, her slick leather boots covering her calves up to the back of her knees. It never ceased to amaze me how sensuous a woman in her mid-fifties could look and the word just slipped out. "Wow."

She straightened without turning. "You better not be referring to what I think you're referring to, Alex."

"Nice car."

Gabe's dimple appeared and I watched him slowly shake his head. Gia stepped away from the door and Gabe shut it, taking up his customary position slightly behind and off to the side of his employer. I watched as Gia retrieved an ornate metal cigar case from the front pocket of her double-breasted car coat. My mouth gaped as she flicked up the lid and took out one of her signature cigars. She casually held the cigar to her lips while Gabe held a lighter for her. Once she had her cigar lit and had taken in a long, slow breath of smoke, she glanced up to see me staring at the cigar case. "Alex, please close your mouth, that's hardly attractive."

"Is that gold? Is that entire case gold and are those diamonds and rubies all around that lion? And is that real silver in the lion's mane and whoa, a unicorn with sapphires on its horn?"

Another small smile played across her features as she looked down at the case. "For future reference, although I doubt you'll ever heed my advice, it's considered gauche to remark upon the quality of a person's effects." Eyebrows raised, she waited for me to acknowledge what she'd just said.

Not wanting to appear gauche, I crossed my arms and held my breath for a second before my curiosity got the better of me. "Yeah, but are those real gems? And is it real gold?"

Staring at me for a minute, she answered at the end of a deep, but, I was hoping, amused, sigh. "Yes, this is our family crest that dates back to the sixteenth century. The lion represents our claim to royalty, some Duke related to the Habsburgs or some such nonsense, and the unicorn represents courage and strength." She glanced over at the barn. "Now if you're through admiring my cigar case, I need to go see what's left of my barn."

She stepped forward and I blocked her way. "Oh, whoa, sorry but you're gonna have to wait 'till we're through. I was just putting up some more crime scene tape."

Gia stepped around me and started toward the barn again. "It's my barn, Alex. I'd rather not wait for the investigation to be complete before I can assess how much damage the fire may have caused."

I stopped her by clasping her arm just above the elbow and felt a huge, meaty hand almost rip my arm from its socket. Gabe pulled me back and stepped between me and Gia, following her as she made her way across the parking lot. I shook out my arm, circled around them and stepped in front of her again, halting her forward progress. "Like it or not, Gia..." Gabe began to step forward and I pointed my finger at his 44-inch chest and said testily, "Gabe, stay." He bristled and Gia held up her hand to call him off. I turned back to her. "As I was saying, like it or not, this is a crime scene, and you're not invited."

I heard footsteps crunching in the gravel behind me and looked over my shoulder to see Kate approaching. She stepped up next to me. "It's okay, Alex. Ms. Angelino, it's good to see you again." She smiled and pointed at Gia's cigar. "I'm sorry, but I'm going to have to ask you to put that out. We don't need any more evidence added to our already complicated crime scene."

"Of course." Gia returned Kate's smile as she handed the cigar to Gabe, who proceeded to grind the tip into the palm of his hand, glaring at me while he did so. I rolled my eyes at his implied threat, secretly relieved when the corners of his mouth quirked up just a tiny bit.

Kate half turned and pointed behind her. "I understand these stalls are traditionally assigned to you during the racing season."

The fact that this was Gia's barn finally registered in my tiny little brain. This barn that had a body buried in one of the stalls. I blinked, and my heart suddenly pounded out an additional fifty beats per second. I took a shallow breath as I remembered a man dying in a small room under the race course stands and Gabe saying "Won't be any trouble...unless you make it trouble." I turned wide, almost panicked eyes to Gabe, who gave a tiny shake of the head.

I casually turned my back to the two women and opened my eyes super wide, asking Gabe the ten million-dollar question. He grinned slightly and turned his attention back to Gia and Kate. I stepped into his line of sight and glowered at him with all kinds of directed meaning.

Kate's voice cut into my mounting panic. "Alex."

I took a deep breath, carefully morphing my features into country casual, then turned to face her. "Yeah?"

Both women looked at me as though waiting for an answer, and I stared back at them hoping my mounting dread and consternation weren't plastered all over my face. Kate's eyebrows lowered as she cocked her head. "Earth to Alex, you can take the cotton out of your ears now."

"What do you mean?"

Kate took a deep breath. "I've only asked you the same question three times now. Have...you....put...up...the tape like I ordered you to?"

The last part of the sentence came out much louder than the first, and I toyed with the idea of telling her she didn't need to yell, but then thought better of it. "No, ma'am, but I'd be happy to get right on it." I stepped around behind her, then motioned with my chin for Gabe to follow. He didn't. When I realized I couldn't exactly drag him to my car by his wavy black hair, I retrieved the yellow roll of tape from my trunk, tied one end to the metal push bars on the front of my car and began walking around all of the barns, slowly reeling out the tape and winding it around sign posts or corral boards as I went.

As I walked, tiny vignettes played out in my over active imagination. Kate handcuffing me, Gabe going down in a shootout with the cops—wait, I am the cops—me sneaking Gabe out of an interview room and into my police car to take him to a waiting taxi in Puerto Vallarta. I couldn't believe this was happening. By the time I returned to the push bars, my overactive imagination had Gabe lying on a Mexican beach in a bathing suit rubbing oil into his overly muscled forearms while I languished in prison doing Sudoku puzzles.

Staring down at my shoes didn't help calm my nerves, so I glanced up and saw Casey and an older man walking across the parking lot. They had obviously just come from the main part of the racecourse. Casey carried three shovels, and the small Latino walking beside her was pushing a green wheelbarrow with what looked to be some more shovels, two rakes, a pitchfork and a push broom sticking out over the edge. The man smiled at something Casey said before lowering the wheelbarrow onto its stand so he could wipe his brow with a blue and white checked handkerchief.

Casey saw me and held up the shovels. "You ready to dig, Alex?"

My stomach turned sour when I thought about finding more bodies buried in the Angelino's barns. Glancing back at Gabe, I wondered exactly whose hand was sticking up and how long he or she had been there. Gabe flashed me an unconcerned grin, which helped steady my nerves until I noticed several detective cars pulling into the lot. Kate must have called in the reserves to help with the search.

I walked to where Casey and her new friend were waiting and took one of the shovels from her. "I thought we were gonna interview people. I don't want to dig. I hate finding bodies. I don't want to find any more bodies, okay?"

Kate, who must have followed me over to where Casey had brought the tools, stepped up beside me and motioned for the newcomers to gather around. While we waited for everyone to wander over, she turned to me. "You were going to interview people up until the point this became a homicide. I called Jon Logan and he's coming out with his homicide dicks to take over that part of the investigation. So, whether you want to dig or not is a moot point."

I leaned into the handle of the shovel and sighed. Once all of the detectives had assembled, Kate stepped into the middle of the pack and took out her notebook. "Okay, listen up. When the firemen were checking the debris for hot spots they found a body buried in a shallow grave. I need you to break up into teams of two. Each team takes ten stalls and digs around checking for anything suspicious. You don't need to dig too deep unless you find something that would lead you to believe there might be a body. Leave the stalls that sustained fire damage until the arson investigators are through with their investigation. I don't think you'll find anything, but if we don't check and someone else does and locates a second victim, well, then we screwed up, and you all know how I hate screw-ups." She paused to let that sink in. "Any questions?"

Nate, who must have left Jimmy to watch Leslie at the main station, spoke up. "Can you tell how long the body's been there?"

"No, and I'm not going to guess. Any other questions related to what your assignments are?"

"How old's the vic?" Nate again.

"I don't know and since it's not your case, you don't need to know. Okay folks, let's get—"

"Can you tell if it's male or female?"

Kate gave him "the eye" usually reserved for me, but he didn't catch it. Her lower jaw jutted forward and her eyes closed slightly, all very clear Kate signs if you know how to read them. Some of the more seasoned detectives exchanged knowing looks before grabbing their shovels or rakes and heading out to claim their barns.

Nate opened his mouth to ask yet another question that we obviously hadn't had time to know the answer to, so before he could dig himself any deeper, I stepped up, put my arm around his shoulders and pointed to Kate. "Nate, notice the glare in the eyes, the way her pen starts tapping harder and harder on her thigh and, most importantly, the way the vein in her neck is beginning to pulse more rapidly than normal? Do you know what all that means?"

It took a second, but the penny finally dropped. "I need to shut up?"

"Precisely."

"Got it. Thanks."

I stepped back a few steps. "Don't mention it."

Kate growled as she turned and headed to the burned out barn. I watched her go, then turned to Casey. "Hey, I'll meet you in the second barn, okay? I need to take care of something first." Casey glanced over at the Jaguar, then nodded.

Shouldering my shovel, I walked back to where Gabe leaned against the hood of the Jag and Gia stood by the trunk talking on her cell phone. Gabe watched me walk up, his typical deadpan expression locked firmly into place. The slight breeze kicked up a tiny dust devil next to the car and the two of us stood silently watching it for a second. Several questions came to mind, but one in particular roared to the fore. Taking a deep breath, I leaned close and spoke in a slightly strangled stage whisper. "I need to know now if that's who I think it is."

Bushy Italian eyebrows lowered into a scowl and he answered in the same hushed tone that I had used. "Do I look stupid to you?"

I whispered back through gritted teeth. "I'll answer that when I know the answer to my question."

Sounds of barn doors rolling open broke the silence and I waited impatiently for him to answer. I watched him blow out a long, slow breath before he turned to face me head on. He put a beefy hand on my shoulder and leaned down into my face. "If I ever buried a stiff," He paused and gave me a meaningful look. "And if I have it ain't none of your business, do you really think I'd bury it in Ms. A's barn?"

"Who's the dead guy then?"

He shrugged. "How should I know?"

"Alex." Gia had finished her phone conversation and strode over to us. "We don't know who's buried in my barn, but I guarantee you I intend to find out who put him there and make absolutely certain they never have the opportunity to do it again." On that ominous note, Gabe stepped past me and held open the rear car door. Gia seated herself in the back seat.

After he'd closed the door, I grinned up at him. "Well, if you suddenly remember who the crispy critter is, give me a call, okay?"

Gabe walked around the hood to the driver's door. "When I find out who buried a carcass in Ms. Angelino's barn or who set fire to the place, well," He shrugged. "Let's just say you won't be needin' to worry about no court costs." He undid the buttons on his coat before lowering himself into the driver's seat and pulling the door shut behind him.

CHAPTER 3

All of the barns were lined up in a row, one right after the other. When I finally found Casey in the third one down from the arson site, she'd already checked two of the stalls and was starting on the third. She leaned on her shovel as she watched me carefully step around the loads of manure she'd managed to pile outside the doors of the first two horseboxes. "Glad you could make it."

When I'd first approached the barn area, the smell hadn't been too bad, but the closer I got to the freshly turned stuff Casey had unearthed, the more I knew this was not where I wanted to be. I buried my nose in my elbow. "Ugh, that's awful."

Casey took a deep breath. "I don't know, Alex, I think there's a certain," she rubbed her chin and stared up into the rafters, "je ne sais quoi, to the odor."

"Je ne sais quoi?" I scuffed the manure with my toe, watching little puffs of desiccated meadow muffins waft up into the air. The top layers of the stalls had turned to mud since the fire had set off the sprinkler system in all three of the barns, but the deeper she'd dug, she'd obviously unearthed loads of dry stuff layered underneath. The idea of digging into decades worth of horse droppings was far down on my list of things I wanted to do for the day. "Hey! You hungry?" I checked the time. "Will you look at that? Lunchtime already! I'll be happy to do a food run. Whatcha feel like?"

Casey chuckled as she began digging around in the dirt again. "You don't smell it after a while. Bring your shovel over here and start poking around for a soft spot. We can go to lunch whenever Kate says we're done."

I sighed and then with growing disgust, gingerly stepped into the stall. Deciphering her digging pattern wasn't too difficult; put your shovel in the dirt at the front left of the stall, dig a couple test holes, move two steps towards the rear, and repeat until every foot of the stall had been checked for cadavers. Eventually, the stink stopped before it reached my brain thus allowing me to speak without a Donald Duck accent—you know, the way your voice sounds when your nose closes itself off from the back of your throat?

Anyway, we had two stalls left to dig up when we heard first one, then several people yelling "Stop him! Grab him!" Just as we turned towards the voices, a determined looking Asian ran around the end of the building and headed down the gravel runway separating our barn from the next one over. As he ran toward us, I sized him up, thinking it shouldn't be too hard to stop a short, compact man in his mid seventies wearing a three piece business suit and burgundy oxfords. Casey and I quickly stepped in front of him and blocked his exit.

The guy skidded to a halt, picked up a short piece of a two by four and held it out in front of him. I thought he was going to try to attack us with it, but instead he tossed the board in the air, let out an ear splitting yell, leapt up so that his head almost touched the ground and kicked the board so hard it splintered into several different pieces. He then landed back on his feet, staring at us to see if we'd understood his message.

Casey swore under her breath. "Shit." Apparently she spoke his language.

A few seconds later, Kate followed him around the corner which seemed to galvanize him into action. He charged straight at us, obviously expecting us to step aside after his little board splitting demonstration so he could make his escape.

"Oh hell no." I stepped in front of Casey and swung my shovel straight for the guy's chest, hoping I'd land a lucky blow and knock him three ways to Sunday. Instead of slowing down or ducking, he hit the handle with the edge of a closed fist, snapping the wood in two before it came anywhere near his face. I stared dumbly at my shovel as he ran past, only remembering at the last minute to stick my foot between his shins to try to trip him up.

To my surprise, instead of going down, he somehow tangled his leg in mine and sent me flying without really even slowing his forward momentum. After finishing with me, he barreled into Casey who grabbed him around his chest in a bear hug apparently intending to wrestle him to the ground. He immediately exploded out with both arms, easily breaking her hold and pushing her just enough for her to lose her balance and fall backward into our carefully placed piles of horseshit. He leapt over her and instead of stopping short when Nate and Ruthanne ran around the back of the barn, he again leapt into the air and punched both of them square in the chest with his two feet.

The two detectives went flying and the Asian disappeared around the far corner without a backwards glance. By that time, I was on my feet and pissed that he'd managed to make fools out of five members of our department. Kate continued after him but Casey and I picked ourselves up and were fast on her heels. The guy could fight, there was no question about that, but fortunately for us he wasn't a very fast runner. I'd been a sprinter at the University of Arizona and I easily passed Kate and then began closing the gap. He must have heard me charging after him because he called over his shoulder in heavily accented English, "I don't want to hurt you. Just let me go."

"No fuckin' way!" When I got close enough and was able to grab the shoulder of his coat, he somehow shifted his weight and tangled his arm in mine. He pulled just enough to loosen my hold and sent me flying head first into the dirt. I skidded like I was sliding into third base and without missing a beat, was back on my feet and close on his heels before he'd even been able to run ten more steps. I grabbed the back of his coat again, fully intending to pull him down to the ground. When I managed to wrap my fingers in the folds of the material, he spun to my left, somehow wrapping his arm around my forearm and holding my wrist pinned under his arm so that he was able to hyperextend my elbow. He'd stopped our forward momentum and there was no doubt in my mind that with just the slightest movement he could very easily break my arm.

Kate jogged up and stopped, bending over and bracing herself with her hands on her knees trying to catch her breath. Casey, also breathing heavily, took up a position to her right while Nate and Ruthanne circled around behind us. Several other detectives who had finally caught up filled in the circle until there was nowhere for the man to escape. Casey held her arms out to her side, palms up. "Hey, take it easy. You don't need to break her arm."

Nothing in my officer's training had prepared me for a fight with a martial arts expert so I just stood there in a halfway crouch, waiting to see what would happen next and hoping against hope the guy had really meant it when he'd said he hadn't wanted to hurt me.

When Kate's breathing had slowed enough to allow her to talk, she straightened up and walked slowly towards us. "Okay, just relax. I don't even know why you were running from me. Look, there's no way you can get through us all. Just let her go and let's talk." I loved the way Kate naturally took charge of her surroundings. No one, including the man twisting my arm, even questioned that she was the one who would handle everything. We had all just waited for her to catch her breath, then knew she'd sort through everything when she was ready.

The man sighed. "Unfortunately, I could easily escape your ring of officers, however, all or most of you would be seriously injured in the process."

Being bent over at the waist with my arm leveraged up behind me, I had to crane my neck up so I could see Kate. "Don't worry boss, I've got everything under control here."

The man laughed softly, then addressed Kate. "You are in charge here?"

"Yes."

"Then I would like to speak with you alone, just the two of us."

Thinking quietly for a second while she studied the man, Kate tapped the side of her leg with her fingers, obviously trying to decide if she could trust the guy who had one of her detectives wrapped up in a casual arm lock. Finally, she nodded and motioned over her shoulder with her thumb. "All right, everybody back to the barns, I'll be fine here."

Everyone except Casey started back the way they had come. Kate half turned. "You too, Casey. Alex will be along in a minute."

I raised my head again. "Bull shit. I'm not leaving you here alone with him."

Kate chuckled, obviously amused. "And just what do you plan to do if you have to rescue me? Keep his hands tied up while he twists you in a knot?" She motioned to the man. "Please let her go now so we can talk."

The man released my arms. I turned towards him, and to my surprise he brought his two palms together in front of his chest and bowed to me. "You are a most worthy opponent."

I crinkled my forehead. "What? I never even came close to stopping you."

He lowered his chin, holding my gaze with sparkling black eyes. "My Grandfather was a Su Suk Kwan Jang Nim in the art of Hwa Rang Do." My complete lack of comprehension must have shown on my face because he took pity on me and translated. "He was a seventh degree black sash in the martial art, Hwa Rang Do. He was one of ten in the world at that time. I studied under him for many years, and that is why you were unable to stop me."

I raised my eyebrows. "Oh..."

"However, success is not always the end you believe it should be." There was something in the way he settled his stance that reminded me of the way my high school history teacher settled in to tell us one of his spellbinding tales of the unfortunate wives of Henry the Eighth or about the exploits of one of my distant ancestors, the ferocious, and in my overactive imagination, incredibly handsome, William Wallace.

When my father had told me I was related to Wallace, I'd walked into class the next day and bragged to my classmates about the gallant and noble blood running through my veins. That is until our teacher got to the part where Wallace was condemned as a traitor to the king, emasculated while he was still alive, hanged, disemboweled, beheaded and quartered. I think that was maybe my first inkling that being a hero wasn't all it was cracked up to be. I remember thinking that I wanted my bowels to remain right where they were, thank you very much King Eddie the first.

Oddly enough, even though his stance was similar to my history teacher, the little oriental went even further, crossing his arms and tilting his head towards me just like that teacher had whenever he started a story. "When I was a small child, my grandfather would spar with me. I was always very impatient with myself because I could never best him." His easy smile appeared again. "But I never gave up trying. At the end of each sparring match, we would go and sit for two hours by the side of the river where we would watch the water roll by." He closed his eyes and took in a deep breath, obviously enjoying the memory before he opened them again and looked at Kate. "My apologies for the delay, but there is a lesson here that would be good for this one to hear."

Kate motioned toward me with a flick of her hand. "Be my guest. I'd love it if someone could break through that stubborn streak of hers and teach her something new for a change."

"Ah, it is precisely that stubborn streak that makes her such a worthy opponent." I raised my eyebrows to Kate, intending to rub in the fact that at least somebody appreciated my stubborn streak. She rolled her eyes and the man turned his attention back to me. "I stopped you four times in four different ways, yet you continued to pursue me." He paused a beat before continuing. "Do you know why my grandfather and I sat quietly by the waters of the Bukhan River?"

I stared at him before slowly shaking my head. "No"

He smiled again. "Neither did I. For two years, our lessons would end by that river. I was often impatient and didn't understand why we were there, but neither would I dare question my grandfather about his teaching methods. One day, as we sat watching the water roll by, I finally understood. I turned to my grandfather and said 'The rocks under the water are smooth.' That was the last day we ended our sparring by sitting next to the river."

He cocked his head to the side, waiting to see if I understood. Being taught a lesson by someone I had been chasing minutes before wasn't something I was used to. Usually if I had to chase someone, there'd be a fight, I'd win, and the bad guy would go to jail in handcuffs.

The difference here was this man didn't seem like a bad guy, and he definitely wasn't in cuffs. "You sat every day for two years, two hours a day, never speaking to each other? Never, not once?"

He shrugged. "That was his way. It was a lesson in patience as well as in observation."

I studied him for a while as I thought about the rocks. "So, you said you liked my stubborn side. I can guess about the rocks. The water that's softer than the rocks ended up being stronger in the end because over time it wore the rough edges off the rocks and made them smooth."

He smiled and inclined his head to acknowledge my words. "Just so."

I turned to Kate, a huge shit-eating grin on my face. "You do realize boss that if you're the water and I'm the rock, it takes years and years and years for the rock to become smooth."

Shaking her head, Kate pointed toward the barns. "Go."

Casey and I took one last measuring look at the man. I nodded in a kind of Americanized version of an oriental bow. When our eyes met again, I smiled. "I wish I had taken the time to learn how to fight the way you do." I shrugged. "Maybe someday."

He dipped his head. "Just so."

When Casey turned and headed back towards our barn I stared at the little oriental for a few seconds, then reluctantly followed.

CHAPTER 4

When we'd finished digging up all of the stalls without finding any more bodies, Casey, Nate, Ruthanne and I headed to the Sleepytime Café to grab some lunch. When we walked in, Maureen, our usual fractious waitress pointed to a table in the corner. "Sit over there and I'll bring you your iced teas. Anybody want anything different this time?" We all dutifully shook our heads as we slid into the Naugahyde booths.

When our iced teas arrived, I took six little blue packets from the container next to the salt and pepper, tapped them on the table to get all the grains to the bottom of the packages, simultaneously tore open the ends on all the packets and dumped the white powder into my drink. It was more than just a habit for me. I'd call it a ritual where everything had to occur in the correct order or the tea just wouldn't taste right. The others had all been watching me, and when I picked up my knife to stir the contents Ruthanne held out her hand to Nate. "Ha! I told you, every single time."

Nate shook his head. "Not yet."

I had no idea what they were talking about, so I picked up the straw Maureen had left next to my plate, grabbed the end of the wrapper and pulled it off about ¼ of the way from the top. The bottom part came off next and I crumpled the paper into a little ball before sticking the straw down through the middle of the ice.

Nate scratched his balding head before he reluctantly pulled out his wallet, retrieved a very wrinkled dollar and placed it into Ruthanne's outstretched palm. "How can someone fix their tea the same way, every single time?"

Casey chuckled and put about five spoonful's of sugar into her tea. "You guys are betting on Alex's drinking habits now? You used to just bet on how long it would take her to piss off Kate during an investigation."

Ruthanne pocketed the dollar. "Hey, speaking about somebody being pissed off, have any of you guys been to the E.R. lately?"

Casey and I exchanged glances before shaking our heads. Up until that moment I'd forgotten about our conversation with Jack and I was sure Casey had as well. Just as I was about to ask if she was talking about Marcos, a family of four walked through the back door. At least I assumed they were a family since there was an adult male and female with two teenagers in tow. The father, a barrel chested man in his mid forties, looked our way. When his gaze went to the badge affixed to my belt I knew we were in trouble.

There's rarely a day goes by where Casey and I are left to ourselves during our mid-shift lunch break. Honestly, I don't mind helping people, but that's what I do for a living, help people, ten hours a day, four days a week, and it's nice every now and then to take a break without someone coming up to tell us about their Uncle Harry who worked with the Atlanta P.D. or to ask for directions or for help or for anything else for that matter. I sighed when the four of them made their way to our table and the father pointed to my badge.

"Policija?"

His question took me by surprise since I had assumed he was an American. "What?"

The oldest boy, who looked to be about 19, pointed his index finger at me like he was holding a gun. He was a nice looking kid; clean-shaven with short blonde hair and a ready smile. "Policija?" He pointed his make believe gun at my badge. "Policininkai...šeiva." He pulled the trigger on his gun. "Pow, pow?"

I nodded. "Police, yeah, I'm police." I shrugged at Casey and Ruthanne while the family moved into a huddle and began speaking in a language I'd never heard before. The young man was apparently appointed as the designated communication specialist because after about a minute of highly agitated discussion amongst themselves he turned to me and began speaking, punctuating every other sentence with wild gesticulations obviously meant to give me a hint as to what he was trying to say.

"Mano vardas Petras." He pounded his chest and then repeated himself. "Petras." Turning to the older man, he quickly patted him on the back. "Tai yra mano tėvas, Donatas." He pointed to the woman, "Mano mama, Danuta." And then to the other teen, "Mano mažasis broils, Antanas."

Not understanding a single word, all I could do was shrug. Casey pointed to the young man. "Petras?" She must have said the right thing because all four of them started vigorously nodding their heads. She pointed at the father. "Donatas?" Once again the family of bobble heads nodded in unison. "I think he's introducing everybody. I'm not sure what language he's speaking, but that much was pretty obvious." She held out her hands palm up. "How can we help you?"

The young man must have thought she understood what he was saying because he took off on an agitated monologue that although it sounded somewhat Slavic, communicated absolutely nothing to us. "Mano mažasis roils sako jis pamatė moters dūris vyro šioje alėjoje atgal ten, bet kai mes nuėjome ieškoti, ten buvo niekas ten." He pointed toward the back door of the restaurant then motioned for us to come with him.

Maureen walked over carrying four laminated pieces of notebook paper that served as the restaurant's menu. "Do you folks want a booth or a table?"

The mother shook her head. "Ačiū, bet mes čia ne valgyti. Mano sūnus pamatė kažką, o mes manome, kad policija turėtų žinoti apie tai."

Maureen's eyebrows pulled together in a frown. "Jūs esate iš Lietuvos?" All four nodded again and Maureen looked over at us. "They're Lithuanian. I think she's saying they need you for something." The four of us had our mouths hanging open as we stared at our waitress who we all knew probably hadn't made it through the sixth grade let alone attended Lithuanian night classes. She must have realized what we were thinking because she plunked her meaty hands on her hips in her typical "don't mess with me" stance. "What? My grandparents were from a little village in the southern part of Lithuania called Matuizos. They didn't speak any English and since they were my babysitters..." She shrugged, expecting us to fill in the blanks.

My estimation of our surly friend rose a few notches. "So, what do they need? Can you ask if it can wait 'cuz I'm starving. All I had for breakfast was a packet of noodle soup."

Nate wrinkled his nose. "Noodle soup? Who the hell eats noodle soup for breakfast?"

"Everything in my fridge went bad when the power went off the other day. I've been eating cupboard stuff 'till I can get some time to go shopping." I motioned to the little family with my chin. "So what do they need?"

Maureen chatted with them a while, every now and then inserting an English word when her brain apparently couldn't dredge up the right Lithuanian equivalent. After a few seconds, she looked over at me. "Well, the kid there says he saw a woman stab a man in the alley but when the family went to look, the alley was empty."

Just then, a very loud and obnoxious biker yelled at Maureen from across the restaurant. "Hey, Maureen. Need some more of this battery acid you call coffee if you're done with the fuckin' bacon over there." His girlfriend apparently thought he was hilarious because she held the end of her nose up with her thumb and started snorting like a pig.

I ran my hand over my mouth, stared at the ceiling and counted to ten. Kate had told me I couldn't piss anybody off any more and I was trying super hard to do what she wanted. Really.

Bolstered by his girlfriend's reactions, the moron just had to take it to the next level. "You don't remember me, do you, Wolfe? Well I remember you. I was talkin' to a couple a bulls the other day. Real pals of yours." He stood up and sauntered our way. I groaned thinking how much I just wanted to get something to eat and get back to work. His face looked familiar, but I just couldn't put a name to the face. When he reached our table, he pushed aside the little family and stood beaming down at me. A smile spread across his face, a gap showing where one of his left incisors had gone missing. "They said you was a real asset. I told 'em they was off by a couple a letters."

As I slipped out of the booth and glared up at the guy I suddenly remembered where I'd seen him. "Tucker Jordan. Bad ass without a dick." I had to crane my neck to look him in the eye because he was a good foot taller than I was and about two hundred pounds heavier. He was a basically harmless biker without a gang whose idea of polite chitchat included hurling insults back and forth with whomever he was conversing with at the time. I pointedly lowered my gaze to just below his overhanging belly where something was missing after most of his balls had been shot off by one of his previous girlfriends. He blushed three shades of red.

Since he'd shut up, I relented, smiling to show there were no hard feelings. "So what happened to Suzy? I heard the two of you got back together after the, ah, incident."

His grin widened, and he pointed back towards the lady who was still sitting at their table. "I got two of 'em now. Suzy and Connie." He raised his eyebrows in a stab at meaningful communication. "If I'da known how much better the plumbing was gonna work after losin' certain parts, I'da pissed Suzy off way before I did."

Everyone at our table groaned and I held up my hand. "Okay, Tuck, way too much information. I'm getting ready to eat here and some really gross images are forming in my head."

"Yeah, I knew who you was when you walked in and I thought I'd give ya a shout."

Connie called over to him. "Hey Lover Boy, your seat's gettin' cold." She stuck out a pouty lower lip and patted the bench seat he'd vacated.

Shrugging, he started back to his table. "Gotta run. See ya 'round, Wolfe." When he slid into his seat, Connie snuggled up close and gave his ear a little nibble.

I turned back to the little family and sighed. "Shit. Okay, Maureen, can you ask them to show me where he saw the stabbing?"

Maureen translated and I was quickly hustled out the door by Petras and Donatas. The mother and second son followed on our heels. We went down an alley behind the diner until we came to a dumpster that had been tipped on its side with what seemed like a years worth of dirty diapers, beer bottles and other trash-strewn all around. For some reason, the kids in this neighborhood seem to feel an overwhelming need to lift up the only dumpster assigned to this particular area and dump it onto its side. Sometimes during a slow, boring night, the midnight beat cops will set the dumpster upright and then take bets to see how long it'll take the kids to notice and dump it over again.

As we walked through the trash, the younger son started jabbering, then grabbed my arm and pulled me further into the alley. Convinced that the only way I was ever going to get my lunch was to humor the kid enough to satisfy him that I'd done my duty, I let him drag me along. As with most alleys in Tucson, this one was bounded on both sides by whatever material the homeowners had used to fence in their back yards and in general ran the length of about a football field. Here, the types of fences ranged anywhere from concrete blocks to bricks to chain link to wood and the occasional woven wire fencing usually reserved for goats or sheep.

When we reached about the fifty-yard line, the boy stopped walking and released my arm. Stepping around behind a large, hard plastic trashcan, he began pointing at a spot on the ground, motioning for me to come closer so I could see his exciting find.

The hairs on the back of my neck began to tingle, and without me really knowing why, my alarm bells went off. I always listen to the little gnome that sits on my shoulder and right about then I felt the little guy start jumping up and down and waving his arms. I tried to shut him up by telling myself this was a nice touristy family and my little gnome was just being paranoid. A glance over my shoulder quickly changed my mind.

The other three members of the family had spread out in a semicircle blocking my way back to the restaurant. I put my back against the block wall that bordered this part of the alley and pulled my radio from where it was hanging at the back of my belt. "9david72 to 73." My right hand drifted down to my Glock and I rested it there while I waited to hear from Casey.

Two more men jumped over a fence from someone's back yard blocking the alley in the other direction. "9david73 to 72. Are you okay?"

"Negative, I need back-up, now."

"What's your location?" The tone of her voice told me she'd left the restaurant at a run. I had just enough time to yell, "Alley behind the knocked over dumpster—" before I had to clock the father in the head with my radio. He'd come after me holding a hood of some kind and had tried to whip it over my head like Casey had tried to do with the Emu. Before I could get on the radio again, the other two men lunged at me. I punched the first guy in the mouth and elbowed the second in his solar plexus, which bent him over enough to allow me to step around and drive my fist into his kidney. The others all jumped on me, pulling me to the ground just as Casey slid around the corner of the alley in her Chevy Impala. I heard her gun the engine and held onto my Glock so none of my attackers could pull it out of its holster. At the sound of her arrival, all of my attackers left me in the dirt and sprinted down the alley away from Casey and her car.

I saw Ruthanne's car fishtail around the corner at the other end of the alley and watched as everyone, including the father who'd picked himself up off the ground, jump over fences and disappear into the neighborhood. Casey jumped out of her car and ran up to where I was pushing myself to my feet.

I'd seen the guy I'd punched jump the fence into a back yard and I took off at a sprint, grabbed the top of a chain link fence and pulled myself up. "Let's go!" Using a move I'd learned in elementary school, I leaned over the top of the fence, grabbed the wire on the other side and kicked my feet over my head so that I ended up standing on the other side of the fence facing forward.

Movement at the far end of the yard caught my attention. The man leapt up onto a doghouse at the other end and climbed over the fence. Casey and I hit the doghouse at a full run, propelling ourselves over the chain link where we landed easily in the grass of the house's front yard. The guy must have stumbled on his way down because he was just picking himself up off his knees and getting ready to run. Casey shoved him in the middle of his back, then landed on top of him as they hit the ground. I grabbed his right wrist and twisted it behind him and she slid off to do the same to his left. I reached behind me to grab the pair of handcuffs I keep tucked in the back of my pants but came up empty handed. "Shit. I lost my cuffs somewhere."

Casey pulled out her cuffs and slammed the ratchet down on the man's wrist causing the metal arm to swing around and engage on the opposite side. She did the same with the other arm and then pulled him to his feet. We began walking him back to the alley where she and Ruthanne had left their cars. As we walked, Casey started shaking her head. "The handcuffs are probably in the alley. So, what? Are you trying to set a record for how many foot chases we get into in one day?"

"Yeah? Well why the hell were they trying to grab me? Who did I piss off in Lithuania?" As we passed the dumpster, we saw Ruthanne and Nate rounding the other corner with one of the "sons" in tow. A Patrol car had pulled in behind Casey's Impala and she loaded our prisoner into the back seat and told the officer to take him to the main station. My handcuffs had landed in the dirt near where I went down. I picked them up and shook tiny stones and debris from inside the ratcheting mechanism. I spun each cuff several times to make sure they were clear before replacing them in their customary position at the small of my back.

The patrolman with the suspect backed out and Kate pulled in to take his place. Eying my dusty clothes as she walked over, Kate grimaced as she gingerly held her hand to the small of her back. When she saw that I'd noticed the gesture, she shook her head. "I tweaked my back a little bit when we were chasing Mr. Myung. How about you? Are you okay?"

Trying to brush all of the dust and dirt from my pants and shirt was turning out to be a losing proposition. Thankfully, I hadn't put any more holes in my clothes because my supply of work pants and shirts was dwindling to a paltry two department issued polo shirts and two pair of Dockers. "Yeah, I'm fine and before you ask, I have no clue what just happened or why."

Casey left off brushing the dirt from my back and stepped forward. "Mr. Myung? Did you end up arresting him?"

"No, and before either one of you ask, what we talked about is confidential."

Both Ruthanne and Nate walked up after depositing their prisoner into the back of a second patrol car that had responded to the scene. Ruthanne grinned. "He's on his way to Juvy. So, how many times do you plan to do a face plant in the dirt today? I think this makes three if I'm counting correctly."

Smiling back at her was about the only answer I had right at the moment. Kate bent over to stretch her back, and when she stood up, she looked straight at me. "Care to enlighten me?"

There wasn't much I could say. "Well, we were just about to order lunch at the café when this family came in. At least they looked like a family; mother, father and two sons. They said the youngest son had seen a lady stab a man back here in the alley, but when the family came to look, nobody was around." I walked over to the trash barrel to look at where the boy had pointed just before everything went to hell in a hand basket. "The kid walked over here and was pointing down at something. That's when the gnome showed up and the family blocked me in on this side and two guys jumped over the fence and blocked me in from that side."

Kate crinkled her forehead. "The gnome?"

"Yup."

Casey chuckled. "She says a gnome shows up and sits on her shoulder whenever something hinky is about to happen." She scratched her head. "And to be honest, I haven't ever known him to be wrong."

After she'd thought about that a minute, Kate shrugged and motioned for me to continue. I walked to where I'd been jumped and picked up the discarded hood. "The dad came at me and tried to throw a hood over my head." I unhooked my radio from my belt and held it up. "I clocked him with my radio."

Kate shook her head and said with a sigh. "Does it still work?"

I clicked the button a few times and heard the reassuring static and the voice of the dispatcher saying. "Unit calling?"

"9David73, sorry about that, just checking my radio." I looked at Kate. "Yeah, it still works. Then they all jumped me and when Casey and Ruthanne came around their respective corners, everybody took off running. We chased 'em and caught two: One of the men who jumped over the fence to block me in and the oldest boy."

Ruthanne held up four fingers. "There's only four reasons to put a hood on somebody." She put down three and held up her index finger. "One, the person being hooded is ugly as shit."

"Hey!"

She laughed, "Okay, that doesn't apply here. Two," She held up two fingers in a peace sign. "They're about to hit a piñata." Her eyebrows rose up in a question mark. "Probably doesn't apply either?"

I shook my head.

"Three, they're gonna kidnap somebody, and four," All four fingers were raised again, "Their hands and feet are handcuffed to the bed posts, they're smiling at you and you're gonna..."

"Stop." Kate raised her hand and interrupted Ruthanne mid-sentence. "Thanks for the analysis, Ruthanne, but don't you have somewhere else to be?"

I shrugged. "I kinda wanted to hear Ruthanne's version of what happens next."

Nate nodded enthusiastically. "Me too."

"Can we get back on topic? And Nate, I think you have other things you could be doing as well." Kate watched as the two of them walked to their car with Ruthanne happily explaining to Nate her viewpoint of reason number four. When they'd finally driven off, Kate ran her hand through her blonde bangs, thinking through everything that had happened during the day. She nodded when she finally made up her mind about where she wanted things to go from here. "The assault detectives will be taking this case until we can figure out exactly why those people wanted you. The homicide dicks are handling the burned body and the arson squad will follow up on the arson when they get back. In the meantime, I'm heading to the station to interview some guy named Otto who we caught poking around in one of the barns right after we arrived."

I nodded. "Leslie." When she looked puzzled, I shrugged. "The guy's name is Leslie Schuman. You know how some guys are has-beens?

Well he's a never-was. He's just some loser who likes people to think he's tough."

She nodded before turning and heading for her car. "Leslie it is then. It's getting late. You two head to the station and give the assault guys your version of what happened, and stay alert. We don't know if they wanted you in particular, Alex, or just a cop in general."

Casey and I watched as she backed out of the alley and drove away, then I followed Casey to her car. "I checked with Megan this morning. She and her cowboy friend are definitely coming for dinner tonight. Are you and Terri gonna make it?"

Megan is my crazy, lifelong best friend who really doesn't understand the meaning of the words, "You probably don't want to do that." She's my former childhood playmate and college roommate who will do anything on a dare and usually pulls me right along with her no matter how outrageous the act.

Casey's friend, Terri, is a patrol officer who works in Team Two. Our police department divides the city up into six teams. Team Two encompasses the Northwest part of town. She's also Casey's live-in girlfriend who just happens to cook the most wonderful desserts in town.

"We'll be there. Last night she was making some chocolate cheesecake cups to bring with us. I had one for breakfast and it was absolutely..." She closed her eyes and breathed deeply, making my mouth water just thinking about it.

Until I'd tasted Terri's fresh lemon creme pie in a gingersnap crust I'd never have believed a dessert can be almost as wonderful as a good orgasm. Now, I'm a believer. "I think I'm gonna just eat cheesecake all night, and you guys can eat my lasagna. It's the one thing I know how to make, now that I know I'm not supposed to use the smoke alarm for a kitchen timer..." I heard Casey groan as I headed back to my car. It had been a super busy day and I was anxious to get our interviews over with so I could head home, grab a hard lemonade and start cooking.

CHAPTER 5

Casey and Terri were the first to arrive. I tried to grab one of the cheesecake cups when Terri walked through the door but she swatted my hand away. "You can't eat these yet. You have to let the calories fade away for a while. I told Casey that this morning but she snagged one when I was in the shower."

Casey walked into the kitchen and put her six pack of beer into the fridge. "I told her I was doing her a favor. If I get fat, that'll make her look skinnier. And, I ate it standing up. It's a known fact if you eat food standing up all the calories go to your feet and then you walk 'em off."

Terri put the cheesecake in the fridge next to the beer. "Well keep your mitts off until after dinner. You can grab seconds after everyone else has eaten their fill."

Just then, Megan and her new cowboy boyfriend, Tony, came walking through the front door. Megan took off her jacket and threw it over the back of my couch. "Keep her mitts off what?"

Terri closed the fridge door. "Dessert, and that goes for you too. Mitts off."

Tony headed for the couch and both Megan and I admired how his tight little butt fit into his well-worn Wrangler 501's. Megan grinned at

42

me, raising her eyebrows with all kinds of directed meaning, then followed Tony and put her arm through his to direct him toward the kitchen before he could plant himself on the sofa. She held up an aluminum foil covered bowl. "Well, my cowboy made a very manly dish called Sausage Stuffed Peppers. He says it's a manly thing to cook because he uses Longhorn Spicy Sausage."

I pulled the lasagna out of the oven and brought it to the table. Everybody ooohed and aaahhed until Megan lifted the lid to the garbage and starting rooting around. "Okay, where is it?"

I shrugged. "Where's what?"

"The frozen lasagna box. I know it's here somewhere."

"I have no clue what you're talking about. This is a family recipe that's been passed down through generations."

Megan let the lid drop. "Yeah, but I happen to know you can't cook anything but Captain Crunch and I also know it's Mrs. Stouffer's family recipe instead of yours."

I sighed innocently and held my hands out wide. "Think what you want, but I have been toiling in the kitchen ever since I got home." Tessa, my rescued hunting dog, chose that minute to come traipsing into the room carrying what was left of the Stouffer's lasagna box, with Jynx, my little Papillion Chihuahua mix, jumping up trying to grab it out of her mouth.

Everyone started laughing when Tessa walked over and dutifully sat at my feet, happily wagging her tail and waiting to be praised for returning the box to me. I guess she figured I must have misplaced it under the covers of my bed where I'd tried to hide it from Megan's prying eyes. I smiled as I took the proffered box, then motioned everyone to the table. "Well, let's all sit down and bless Mrs. Stouffer's grandmother for her wonderful recipe. Everybody dig in!"

Tony was new to our group and since the rest of us had known each other for years we all wanted to make him feel comfortable. Casey took a bite of the stuffed peppers then pointed at Tony with her fork. "Where'd you learn to cook these? They're wonderful."

I could tell he was pleased but when he just shrugged and continued eating, I thought I'd give it a try. "So you're a rodeo cowboy, right? What's your specialty? What do you ride?"

Megan piped up. "Me!"

I glared at her and tried again. "Do you ride bulls? What's that like?"

"Yup." He forked another pile of lasagna into his mouth.

Obviously a man of few words. Casey looked over at me, then gave it one last effort. "Alex and I worked a case at the Pima County Rodeo this year. Maybe you heard about it.

"Yeah."

Not wanting to overtax his brain with too much stimulation, I thought I'd give him an out. "I can tell you're a man of a few words."

He raised his gaze to mine and grinned a little boy grin that was sexier than hell. "My granddaddy had a saying. 'Never miss a good chance to shut up', and I don't."

The conversation finally got going when Megan asked Casey to tell us about the little goat she'd just adopted. Apparently, he was a mini pixie La Mancha and wasn't any bigger than a medium to small dog. Casey regaled us with his antics while we ate and when everyone had cleaned their plates, Terri jumped up from the table. "Okay, I think we'll move on to dessert." She went into the kitchen and brought out the wonderful, delicious, mouth-watering cheesecake cups. Everyone ate at least one, with most of us opting for two while Casey and Megan both scarfed down three.

I have no clue how Terri could make something so absolutely perfect without Mrs. Stouffer's help. She had somehow managed to make chocolate cups shaped like paper baking cups. She filled them with some kind of cheesecake mousse that was to die for, and as if that wasn't enough, she topped the whole thing with an incredible berry concoction. My guess is they were about fifty thousand calories each, so I had just eaten one hundred thousand calories in one sitting. When we'd finished our dessert, we waddled into the living room and pulled out the board games.

We were well into our third game of Pictionary when my cell phone rang. I didn't recognize the number so I stepped into my bedroom in order to be able to hear over the shouted guesses and cheering. I recognized Maddie's voice right away. "Hey Alex. Sorry to bother you so late but it's about Marcos."

I suddenly remembered what Jack had said and immediately felt guilty for not stopping by to check on Marcos. "Yeah, Jack mentioned he'd noticed a change in him lately, but I haven't had time to stop by to see him. What's up?"

"It wouldn't have mattered even if you had come in. He didn't show up for work tonight. We're scheduled for a midnight shift, nine to nine. He's two hours late and I can't find him. He's not answering his phone and none of his friends know where he is."

"Has something been bothering him? Is he sick? Did he get one of those dreaded diseases we're always teasing him about?"

She laughed quietly. "No, I wouldn't wish an STD on anyone, but I almost wish helping him was as easy as throwing some antibiotics his way. You know that guy he met about two or three months ago? Jason something?"

"Yeah, he moved into Marcos' condo, right?"

"Right. Well, about a week and a half ago, Marcos and Jason were coming home from a night out. When they got home, two officers were waiting for them. Marcos said they read Jason his rights and when he refused to answer their questions, they arrested him."

The yelling from the other room had risen several decibels so I walked over to close the door. I peeked around the corner in time to see Megan circle her left breast with the magic marker. Casey jumped up and accused her of cheating right about the time the door closed. "Sorry Maddie, the gang's all here and they're a little loud. Now why was Jason arrested?"

"They're accusing him of raping some woman. Marcos hasn't been able to visit him yet, and the judge set the bail pretty high. Marcos is shitting himself worrying about what's happening to Jason in there."

I pulled in a deep breath. "Do you think he did it?"

"Marcos doesn't think so. I've only met Jason a few times. His work schedule is the exact opposite of ours so the only time we can get together is the rare occasions when our days off coincide."

I'd never met Jason so I didn't really know what to think. "Off the top of your head, Maddie, without thinking, would your first impression be that he might be capable of something like that or not?"

"Well...the cops have brought in a lot of rapists to the E.R. over the years. Some guys, I say, yeah, absolutely I believe he's enough of an asshole to rape someone, but other guys, you'd never guess they could do something like that. Jason definitely fits into the second category. Anyway, Alex, the problem is I can't get off work to go look for Marcos. Do you think you can go find him? I'm really worried about what he might do."

Sighing inwardly, I nodded even though I knew she couldn't see me through the phone. "Of course I'll go. Have you called the gay bars where he usually hangs out?"

"Most of them. Those were the first calls I made after I tried his cell. Nobody's seen him."

"Okay, I'll let you know if I find him." I hung up and returned to the living room, sorry I had to break up all the fun. Fortunately, they'd just finished the last game and it seemed like everyone was getting ready to call it a night.

Casey walked over to my desk where all the jackets were piled and retrieved her brown suede coat. She shrugged it on before finding Terri's jeans jacket and helping her into it. "Everything okay?"

I knew Marcos wouldn't mind if I told everyone what was going on since we were all friends and generally didn't keep secrets from each other. Well, all of us except Tony who didn't know Marcos and therefore wouldn't care what I had to say one way or the other. I filled them in on what Maddie had told me.

When I finished, Casey was quiet for a moment. I saw the muscles in her jaw ripple, a sure sign that something was bothering her. She turned to look at Terri, who smiled. "I know you're dying to go with her. I'll drive the car home and maybe Alex can drive you home when you're done."

I shook my head, "No, that's okay. You live an hour away from here and it'd just be easier if the two of you went home together. I can—"

Megan put her hands on her hips. "Go by yourself? No way am I gonna let you have all the fun." Megan grabbed Tony's dark brown Carhartt jacket and cowboy hat and threw them to him. As he caught both and juggled his hat to his head, she unceremoniously pushed him toward the door. "I'm a woman on a mission, Lover, so you're gonna have to get home on your own tonight."

To his credit, Tony showed his pearly whites in a playful smile before tipping his cowboy hat in a gentlemanly gesture of goodwill. "Much obliged for the evening, ladies." He winked at me. "You take care of my little sugar britches, now, ya hear?" He pulled Megan into his arms and the two of them kissed so long I thought I'd have to get some type of debonder to pry them apart.

When they finally came up for air, Tony nodded at everyone once more before letting himself out the door. I watched him go, then turned back to Megan. "Sugar Britches?" I stuck my fingers down my throat and pretended to gag.

Megan reached into her pocket, pulled out a stick of gum, unwrapped it and threw it into her mouth. "Jealous?"

I shrugged. "He is kinda cute. Not too bright, but cute."

"I know what you mean. The other day he told me 'A rolling stone is worth two in the bush.' So I said, 'A bird in the hand,' and he just looked at me like he was waiting for me to finish my sentence." She laughed and wiggled her eyebrows. "But you know, that ain't what I'm keepin' him around for…"

"So you're using him for his cowboy parts. I'll bet he hates that."

"Well, he's not complaining, if that's what you mean. In fact, when he was talking about the rolling stone, he wanted to make sure I knew he's not the marrying type. He says traveling the rodeo circuit isn't good for serious relationships. That was right before we…." The blood rushed to her face and she fanned herself with the palm of her hand. "Well, let me just say I'm definitely going to miss him when he leaves to ride some other lady bronc."

As I started collecting dirty plates from the table, Megan motioned to her dog, Sugar. "Get the napkins, Shug." I watched her brown lab methodically walk from place to place gathering the used napkins and walking them one by one to the trash. My metal can has a pedal at the base and when someone steps on the pedal, the lid pops open. Each time she brought a napkin to the can, she stepped on the pedal and deposited the napkins into the open garbage pail.

"That dog is absolutely amazing. Do you think I can train Tessa to do stuff like that?"

"Alex, Tessa is smart enough to learn anything anyone wants to teach her. You're the one I'd have problems with. Ninety percent of dog training is trying to get the owner to do what they're supposed to do. The dogs are super eager to learn. But the owners..." She stepped over and knocked on my head with her knuckles. "The owners not so easy."

When Sugar had deposited the last napkin into the receptacle, Megan called her back over to the table. "Watch this. It's something new we've been working on." She pointed to one of the plates. "Stack 'em, Sugar." The dog's chocolate brown eyes stared at Megan for a second. She looked at the plate, then back at Megan who gently pushed the plate across the table toward another plate. "Stack 'em."

Sugar obligingly put her nose to the side of the plate and pushed it in the same direction Megan had. A chair blocked her way so that she couldn't move the plate as far as she needed to. When I stepped over to shove it out of her way, Megan put her hand on my arm. "Give her credit, Alex. She's smart enough to know how to move a chair out of the way." As though she understood what her mom had said, Sugar put a paw on the side of the chair and pushed it until it hit the kitchen wall. Returning to her assigned task, Sugar stretched up and put both paws on the table. One paw blocked the second plate from moving while the other rested on the table. Looking over at Megan, her eyes almost seemed to ask what she was supposed to do now.

Megan pointed to the first plate. "Slide it, Shug. You can do it. Slide it." Sugar nudged the plate with her nose until the rims of the two plates were touching. Then, to my astonishment, she popped the edge of the first plate up with her left paw and Megan pushed the other plate under it. When the first crashed down onto the second, Megan bent down and hugged her girl. "Aren't you the good girl! Look at that! You're such a good girl." Picking up the plate, she examined it carefully. "No cracks." She grinned at me. "We're working on finesse. Not quite there yet, but at least I don't have to buy you an expensive new plate for your collection."

"Yeah, these are genuine Wedgewood bought with stamps from the local grocery store." I caught Tessa staring at me and leaned down to stroke her soft white ears. "We could do that, couldn't we girl?" When she didn't answer, I walked over to the hall closet to get my jacket.

"Anyway, let's leave the dishes until we get back. I'm kinda anxious to find Marcos. It's not like him to miss work without calling in."

We walked out the door and Megan turned to the three dogs. "You three stay here, we'll be back." My white Jeep wrangler was parked in front of my house and we climbed in and zipped up the windows. The weather had turned unseasonably cold and since we were both Arizona born and bred, the mid fifties tended to chill us to the bone. Megan buttoned up her denim jacket while I tried several times to start my cranky engine, which roared to life on the third try. I patted the dashboard before shifting into drive and heading off down the street.

CHAPTER 6

The first two bars we stopped at only welcomed men, and we felt out of place and under-dressed at both. When we entered a place called The Backdoor, we hit the jackpot. This particular bar catered to both the gay and lesbian crowd. People of all shapes and sizes from all walks of life were sitting around tables drinking beer or hanging out at the mahogany bar that stretched the entire length of the back wall. Megan and I slipped into an opening at the far end, careful not to jostle anyone out of their place. The bartender, a beefy tattooed man with two hoop earrings in his left ear, checked us out before setting a Bloody Mary down in front of a patron. When he looked up again I caught his eye. He held up one finger telling me to wait while he took several more orders and mixed a variety of drinks.

After handing the last glass to a waiter, he walked over and laid both of his huge hands on the bar in front of us. The ring on his right index finger had an oversized ruby cut into a two-tiered, flat-bottomed triangle, but what really piqued my interest was the coiled tension that lived just behind his calm exterior. Megan pointed to the blue concoction he'd just given to the waiter. "I'd like one of those, please."

The bartender studied her a minute. "That's an Alaskan Iced Tea. I always put some extra Cointreau in to add a kick. You sure that's what you want?"

Megan and I both answered at the same time.

"Yes."

"No." I jabbed her in the arm with my elbow. "No. We might have a long night ahead of us and I don't want to have to carry you around everywhere we go."

She jabbed me back. "Yes. I'm a big girl who happens to be able to hold her liquor."

The bartender nodded, then looked at me expectantly. I shook my head. "Nothing for me, thanks."

I knew there was no arguing with Megan without causing a major scene so I swiveled around to survey the room. There was a live band playing in the corner and I watched several couples slow dancing around the dance floor. By the time Megan's drink arrived I'd figured out two things; one, Marcos wasn't there and two, there are plenty of gay people with two left feet. Bowing to the inevitable, I swiveled back around, pinged Megan's glass with my fingernail and asked the bartender, "So what's in these things anyway?"

A look of serious professionalism came over his face. "There's definitely an art to mixing it just right. I mix Rum, Gin, Vodka, and some Blue Curacao, along with about two ounces of sweet and sour mix. All that gets poured over ice and I top that with a lemon lime soda." He leaned in close and whispered. "What makes mine so good is the real lime juice I squeeze on top." He nodded at me. "An entire lime. I ain't kiddin' you." He spoke with an odd mixture of educated man about town versus leather garbed biker dude. "And, like I said, I add extra Cointreau just before I set it out."

His hands rested on the bar top again while he checked me out. Staring at me with half closed eyes, he crossed his arms and announced, "You're a cop."

It wasn't a question so I just raised my eyebrows. "So?"

"So why're you here? Nothin' funny goin' on and some of these people, maybe some judges, maybe some politicians or Indian chiefs, don't need their names drug through the blender, if you know what I mean."

It seemed a lot of people were mixing their colloquialisms these days and it took me a minute to sort out what he'd just said. "Oh, right. I'm not here to make trouble for anybody. I'm trying to find a friend of mine, Marcos Quiroz." He continued to stare at me so I thought I'd take a stab at breaking the ice that had apparently formed between us. "So, how did you know I was a cop? What gave it away?"

He snorted while shaking his head as though it was obvious. "You haven't stopped looking around since you got here. Nobody walks behind you without you watchin' out of the corner of your eye and you always turn your head to the other side to make sure they've kept walking and didn't stop behind you where you can't see 'em." He made a fist and held it up for me to see. "You checked out my ring and I could tell you were looking at it as a potential weapon instead of as just a nice piece of jewelry since I got it so conveniently situated on my pointin' knuckle."

I smiled at him, impressed with his observation skills. I decided to give him back what he'd just given me. "What's your name?"

"Gus."

"Well Gus, turnabout's fair play. You were in the military. Your hair's down to your shoulders but your bearing is straight and strong. You act like you're just pouring drinks, but actually I've watched you catalogue every person in this room and take note of when they move to a new location. Your tattoo says .338 Lapua Magnum, which tells me you were a sniper either in Iraq or Afghanistan. And," I raised my right eyebrow and nodded toward his hand. "you know as well as I do why you wear that big ass ring on your index finger."

He glared at me for a minute longer, but eventually a big smile slowly spread across his face.

I smiled back. "And...I'm gonna go out on a limb on this one, but my guess would be you were assigned to the 28th Infantry Division since your ring looks like it's the shape of a red keystone."

From the way his mouth dropped open I knew I couldn't have surprised him any more if I'd actually told him the name of his drill sergeant in boot camp. He closed his mouth, shaking his head in wonder. "How hell did you figure that out?"

I allowed myself a small, triumphant grin. "When I was in patrol, my partner was obsessed with military trivia. When we were on mids and things got slow, he'd start reeling off all kinds of trivia about weapons and bombs, military history, and certain characteristics of individual units." I pointed to his ring. "like knowin' that rock you're wearing was designed specifically for the 28th. I studied up a little bit and eventually got good enough to trip him up every now and then." I shrugged. "It helped pass the time."

The guy on the stool next to me chimed in. "Hey, I got one for ya. What did an enemy have to be for a U.S. soldier to call him a "believer" in 'Nam?"

Surprised, I turned and really looked at the man. Up to that point, he'd just been a body taking up space. Physically, he had the build of a forty or fifty-year-old casual weight lifter, but the crags in his face and full head of Gray hair told a different story. He held out his hand to shake. "Name's Single, Single Darden. I was eavesdropping on your conversation." He shrugged and looked a bit sheepish. "Kinda hard not to."

I shook hands, then answered his question. "Dead."

He laughed. "Bingo!"

Megan sidled out from behind me, cocked her hip and gave the guy her "come hither" look I knew only too well. Give her a drink, especially a strong one like the Big Blue she currently held in her hand, and any man within striking distance was fair game. "Single? That's your name? Your real name?"

The guy grinned. "Yup. After two sets of twins and one set of triplets, my parents were so happy when I popped out alone they decided to name me Single." His smile faded a little when Megan took a long, slow, sip from her Alaskan Iced Tea and then provocatively ran her tongue over wet lips, never taking her eyes off the guy during the whole process. The man shifted nervously. "What're you lookin' at me like that for? You do know you're in a gay bar, right?"

"How do you know I'm not the prettiest cross dresser you've ever seen?" She giggled and I rolled my eyes and pushed her back to my other side where she belonged.

I plucked the almost empty glass out of her hand and handed it to Gus. "Here, I think she's had enough for now." I turned back to my neighbor, "Okay, since you've thrown down the gauntlet, what's the oldest American military uniform item in continuous use?"

"Shoot, give me a hard one, will ya? That's a gimme for an old jar head like me."

"Well then, what's the answer?"

He stuck out his chest and ran his fingers down the middle of his shirt. "The gold buttons on the Marine Corps Dress Blues."

I thought a minute. "You want something hard, huh? Okay, who was the real life sniper in Saving Private Ryan and what type of rifle did he use?"

Single ran one hand through his hair and punched me on the shoulder with the other. "Damn, you got me on that one."

Gus had moved off to mix another drink, but he must have been listening to our banter because he gave the answer over his shoulder. "Don't know the real guy's name, but in the movie he used a Springfield 1903, probably an A4."

I nodded. "Good answer since the sniper wasn't based on a real person."

Single let out a guffaw. "A trick question! No fair." He downed about a quarter of the beer in his mug, wiped the foam from his lips, and swiveled to face me. He studied me a minute, then seemed to make up his mind. "I heard you asking questions about Marcos. Whatcha want him for?"

"Are you a friend of his?"

"Maybe. Depends on your answer." He took another sip and watched me over the rim of his glass.

"Some other friends have been worried about him, and they asked me to come find him to make sure he's okay. Have you seen him?"

Single looked at Gus and raised an eyebrow, silently asking if Gus thought they could trust me. Gus studied me again, shrugged and nodded slightly. Single nodded back, set his beer on the counter and motioned for Megan and me to follow.

I grabbed Megan's arm after she tripped and nearly did a face plant on one of the pool tables. She pulled out of my grasp and walked with exaggerated dignity behind Single, her back stiff with the concentration only an inebriated soul can muster. In her case, she was only tipsy, but I needed to remember to keep her away from any of Gus' Alaskan Iced Teas in the future.

Single led us through a door in the back of the bar which in turn led us to a stairwell with stairs going up onto a well-lit second floor landing. Several pieces of very colorful, extremely erotic art hung at various intervals along the stairwell wall. The scenes grew more and more festive, and a lot more crowded, as we ascended. We paused at each painting, mesmerized by the bright colors and imagery depicted in each scene.

At the top of the stairs, as we stopped in front of an image of a human-animal orgy, Megan reached out a hesitant finger and lightly touched the glass. "These oils are incredible, and look at how the artist used the matte glass to scatter the reflected light." She moved her hand in a circle. "See how the images are kind of blurry? He did that with the glass. It's a great technique a lot of artists use." Shaking her head, she took a small step closer to try to read the signature that was scrawled along the bottom edge of the painting. "I can't believe these paintings are hung in a back stairwell of a gay bar."

Believe it or not, before she opened her own dog training school, Megan had earned her masters degree in art history. Her mother happens to be one of the foremost experts on Medieval and Byzantine art, and she passed along her passion to her oldest daughter. Single, who had continued walking down the hallway, stopped and came back to where we were standing. "Gus did those. Pretty good, huh?"

Megan turned to stare at our self-appointed guide. "Gus? No way." She took a step back in order to be able to see all four paintings and mumbled quietly to herself. "No f'in way..."

"Yeah, he did these about fifteen years ago. You should see the paintings he did right after he came back from Iraq. He doesn't show 'em to many people, but I got to see 'em once when I took some food to his house after he'd got himself shot by some bar fly. Now those pics are some pretty insane stuff." He turned and once again started down the hall.

We followed, but out of habit I glanced behind us, mentally calculating the distance to the doorway at the bottom of the stairs just in case anything happened. My little gnome hadn't made an appearance, but my senses went on high alert as we passed several closed doors on either side of the hallway where various grunts, groans and the occasional high pitched squeals came cascading out accompanied by a rhythmic thumping emanating from door number three.

In front of me, Megan, whose head seemed to be on a swivel as she listened to the various noises, walked past an open door on her right. She stopped mid-stride, took two steps back and leaned into the doorway. When I stepped up to the door to move her along, I glanced in to see four very naked, well-oiled people writhing on a mattress that was strategically placed on the floor in the middle of the room. Several other people clothed the exact same way were sitting around the mattress watching the entertainment with unconcealed lust written on their faces.

By the time I'd catalogued all this in my mind, Megan had inched into the room and was gaping at the erotic tableau. I grabbed her shoulders, turned her around and escorted her out into the hallway. "Ooookay, why don't we just follow Single to see if we can't find our buddy, Marcos."

Megan shook her head as if to clear it. "Was that a blow up doll? Four live people and they still need to use a blow up doll? Jesus, shouldn't we close the door or something? I mean, Jeez..."

Single, who had turned and was patiently leaning up against the wall with his arms crossed over his chest had a silly grin plastered on his face. "No, darlin'. Half the fun for them is either being watched or watching. Everybody'll take a turn on the mattress at some point."

He turned and continued down the hall. Megan glanced over her shoulder at me, her wide, smiling eyes telling me just how very much she was enjoying our little hunt for our elusive friend. When we passed another open door neither one of us could help looking inside. Once again Megan stopped and this time I ran right into her. Megan stage whispered. "This one's right out of some of the hard core romance novels I read when I'm lonely at night."

"Megan, TMI." I glanced at Single who was once again waiting patiently for us at the end of the hall.

Megan stepped into the room, which was empty except for the medieval contraptions bolted into the wall and/or stretched across a king size bed. She playfully reached for a cat o' nine tails hanging from a peg near the door. I quickly grabbed her hand and pulled it away. "Whoa, think about it a minute Megs. Do you have any idea where that thing may have been in the last few days, or weeks, or months for that matter?"

She looked quizzically at me for just a heartbeat before the dim bulb in her brain suddenly got brighter. Her mouth formed an "O" and she promptly scurried back out the door. "Ew, ew, ew, ew, ew..." She walked gingerly down the hall holding her hands up near her shoulders so as not to touch anything, anywhere, ever again. "Ewwwww, you mean they don't sterilize everything after each use? Oh that is so gross. Marcos wouldn't be in any of these rooms, would he? If he is, I'm not touching him. I'm not touching him, or any of his stuff ever again. In fact, I'm out of here."

I blocked her exit, putting both of my hands on her shoulders and turning her until she faced the door where Single was waiting. Megan gave him her wrinkled nose, 'that is disgusting' stare down.

Single shrugged, "Hey, I don't work here and I don't play with the toys neither, just in case you was wondering." He looked from me to Megan, who still wore an expression of disgust and disbelief plastered across her face. "Well I don't." Mumbling to himself, Single turned and knocked quietly on a bright red door next to where he'd been waiting. He listened for a few seconds, then knocked louder. When no one answered, he reached down to try the knob.

The door was locked and as Single called out again, Megan leaned around his shoulders trying to get a preview peek at whatever was happening inside. I grabbed her and pulled her back, shoving her a little behind me and to the side of the door. She tried to push back. "Alex! Why should you get the first peek?"

Without turning to look at her, I eased her behind me once more. "Because if we're interrupting something illegal and someone panics and takes a pot shot through the door, I'd rather you weren't standing in front of it asking to be shot."

Single looked over his shoulder. "Nah, this ain't that kind of place."

I held his gaze. "Uh huh. Didn't you say Gus was shot by some barfly? I assume that happened in this bar, right?"

The big man blinked, nodded once as he acknowledged the truth of what I'd said and stepped to the side of the door. "Hey Ernie, you in there?" He yelled through the door then spoke to us over his shoulder. "Ernie lives here, permanent like. He's an old friend of Gus' from his sniper days."

Just as I had decided it was a lost cause and was turning to leave, the door was jerked open by a six foot two masked Cat Woman holding a multi-stringed fetish whip. "Ernie's necktie's tied a little tight right now. Whaddya need?" Her gaze moved from Single, to me, to Megan who had slipped out from behind me and was craning her neck at an impossible angle to try to see around the door and inside the room. The woman smirked, stepped out into the hallway and pulled the door shut behind her. "I don't mind you watchin', Red, and neither does Ernie, but you gotta pay for the privilege."

Megan quickly stepped back, a brilliant shade of pink snaking up her neck, fanning out on her cheeks and continuing up until it disappeared into her bright red hair. I took a step forward. "We're actually just looking for a friend of ours, Marcos Quiroz. You seen him around?"

She looked at Single who lifted a shoulder. "Gus said to help 'em, an' they seem all right to me."

Sighing, she pulled off her mask and ran a hand through her lush, auburn hair, slowly giving her head a toss to loosen strands that had become matted by the strings holding the mask in place. "So why is a cop asking around about Marcos? What's he to you?"

There it was again. She knew I was a cop without me saying a word about my line of work. "What? Do I exude cop pheromones or something? How does everybody around here know I'm a cop?"

Cat Woman rolled her eyes. "Puleeze, just look at you."

I scrunched my eyebrows, insulted by the way she'd said "puleeze" as though the fact that I am a cop would be obvious even to the most uneducated moron. There was a mirror hanging down the hall a few doors away so I walked over and stepped in front of it, taking a few moments to take a good long look. I didn't see anything out of the ordinary, just me. Nothing screamed, "Cop! Fuzz! Narc!"

The woman ushered Megan over and planted her next to me. "Now, look at her, then look at you." Megan's merry eyes exuded unbridled excitement along with a touch of innocence and a big dose of naiveté. I looked back at myself. Compared to Megan, my eyes had about as much emotion as Sgt. Joe Friday on Casey's favorite sixties television show, "Dragnet." I turned and glared at the unmasked Cat Woman who simply raised one eyebrow to emphasize the obvious.

We stared at each other a minute until I let a smile slowly creep across my face. "Okay, you win. If I ever go undercover, I'll definitely come to you for lessons."

Chuckling, she shook her head. "The only lessons I give are when someone's looking for a naughty schoolmarm or a mother superior with very long stick. Look, Marcos was here about an hour ago, but his friend Drew took him back to his place to try to dry him out. You know The Septin Apartments on Roger Rd?"

I nodded.

"He's in apartment 210. Tell Drew Anita sent you, otherwise he'll never open his door."

Anita cocked her head towards Megan who was looking a little puzzled. "What's the matter, Red? You look like you can't figure out why there's a round pizza in a square box with triangle slices." Amusement crinkled the corners of her eyes as she studied my best friend.

Nodding, Megan pointed to Anita's red door. "I thought this was a gay bar. If you're in there, shouldn't Ernie's name be Earnestine?"

Anita barked out a laugh, obviously surprised by Megan's question. "I suppose you'd be right if Michael wasn't in there as well."

The confused look on Megan's face amused Anita who glanced over at me and winked. Once again, realization hit Megan a little late. When she'd figured everything out, a huge grin spread across her face. Nodding slightly she whispered, "I definitely have to read some more books."

I winked at Anita. "Thanks. I owe you one." I looked back at her door. "Don't you think you should maybe check on ol' Ernie? I'd hate for anything to happen to him while he's learning how to tie a Windsor." Anita chuckled and let herself back into the room as Megan, Single and I trooped down the stairs and into the bar. Gus was busy filling drink orders so Megan and I slipped out the front after handing Single a twenty and telling him to buy some drinks on us.

Single followed us out and stuffed the bill back into my pocket. "Listen, Marcos is friends with just about everybody in here. He's a good man and so's his boyfriend Jason. You wanna help? Then figure out why Jason is in jail for a rape he didn't do."

I shook my head. "I don't know anything about Jason or what exactly he's been charged with. Right now all I care about is finding Marcos and making sure he's okay."

Stepping closer, he tapped me on the chest with a stubby finger. "Marcos won't be okay, not any of us'll be okay until somebody figures out the truth about Jase. He got railroaded by somebody in your shop. You wanna help, then that's what you do."

"Yeah, well, I already got into trouble a while ago investigating somebody else's case, so it's not really an option for me to pull Jason's ass out of the wringer. I'm happy to check on Marcos, but that's about as much as I can do." I took a step back. "Look, I'll see you around, okay?" I held out my hand as a gesture of good will. Single just stared at it before slowly raising his gaze and glaring at me. Lowering my hand, I glared right back. "What?"

"You know what." If I didn't know better I'd say he almost sounded petulant. Marines can't sound petulant, can they?

"Look, other detectives get testy when you act like they aren't doing their jobs right. You just need to let them finish their investigation and let the justice system work."

Single let out a particularly obnoxious snort, his lips curled in distaste. "I didn't figure you for a coward, but I guess first impressions ain't always right."

He started back into the bar and I grabbed his arm and jerked him back. Well, I tried to jerk him back but actually neither his arm nor his body moved more than an inch. He still had pretty solid muscles for a guy his age. "Coward? If I'm the coward here, why aren't you out stompin' around for justice and fair play? Who the hell are you to call me a coward?"

Megan inserted herself between us, obviously trying to fend off my runaway mouth before my temper got the better of me. "Uh, Alex…"

Single slowly rounded on me, the muscles in his jaw rippling. "Twenty years in the Corp, that's where I 'stomped around' for justice. For the gooks in 'nam? Fuck no." He spat on the ground, missing my shoe by inches. "For my brothers and sisters, for the ones the brass don't give a shit about. Brass is brass is brass, no matter what fuckin' uniform they wear. They need a scapegoat, you think it's gonna be one of them get's shafted? You think they care about some pussy ass homo on the street gets his self arrested on some trumped up, candy ass charges?"

He jabbed his finger into my chest again. "No fuckin' way Jason would rape some dame, which means to me the guys on your department, they fucked up and you're a fuckin' lily-livered coward if you just walk away."

The neon sign above the door bathed his back in greens and reds as I watched him walk into the bar. The door slammed shut behind him. As we turned to leave, Megan and I had to step to the side to allow two men to pass. The taller one, wearing tight, white dress slacks and a Gray suit jacket sped up and held the door open for his friend. He reached up to straighten the paisley blue silk pocket square tucked into his breast pocket and as he did so my attention was drawn to the unusual wedding ring he wore on his left ring finger.

What made the ring unique were the six colored gemstones that were tastefully mounted on the head. I recognized the red ruby, the blue sapphire, and the green emerald, but I couldn't identify the yellow, orange or violet gems that made up the rest of the inverted triangle. Glancing down, I checked the other man's hand and sure enough, the same rainbow colors shone brightly in the reflected light of the bar.

The first man noticed me looking and put his arm around his buddy's shoulders before flashing me with a mouthful of perfect teeth under joyful, sparkling eyes. "Married two months ago in Connecticut. He's a full-blooded member of the Mashantucket Pequot Indian tribe. They've been recognizing same sex marriage since 2011." He kissed the top of his much shorter friend's head. "You should have seen him, he looked absolutely spectacular in his tribal costume and I swear half the tribe turned out to wish us well."

"Oh wow!" Megan reached out and grabbed the tall man's hand. "I wanna congratulate you, too! Mazel tov! " She pumped his hand several times, then grabbed the other man in a huge bear hug. " That is so cool! Congratulations!"

Both men beamed. I watched her friendliness and enthusiasm envelope them, marveling yet again at her easygoing, innocent way with people. Thinking back to my face in the upstairs mirror, I tried to put a little extra animation and cheer into my voice as I reached over and shook each man's hand. "Congratulations. You guys make a great looking couple."

They both thanked us and as the tall one ushered his husband inside, he threw that huge, megawatt grin over his shoulder one more time before the door completely closed behind them. Megan and I grinned at each other and headed out to the parking lot. "Mazel tov? You're not even Jewish and they sure as heck didn't look like Jews. What's up with that?"

"Well, I don't know any Indian words for congratulations and Mazel Tov just kinda slipped out. It didn't seem to bother them any." She climbed into the passenger seat and fished the keys out of her purse. I'd given them to her to hold when we went inside because I hated having extra bulges in my pants pockets and she was the only one of us who ever carried a purse. Once I'd climbed behind the steering wheel, she handed me the keys and pointed forward. "Onward, Jeeves, to our next destination! I love doin' this detective stuff."

Traffic was light, and I shook my head as I pulled out onto the street. "We aren't doing detective work. This is completely off duty and we are just out looking for a friend." I stopped at a red light and reached over and grabbed her chin so I could turn her head towards me and look her in the eye. I enunciated very clearly to make sure she understood. "I am off duty. I am not acting as a detective right now and neither are you, capisce?"

She slapped my hand away and laughed. "Okay, okay, we're two broads out cruising the gay bars looking for a friend. I get it, I get it. Don't worry about me... I'm just sitting here with my mouth zipped shut." She mimed turning a key on her lips, opened the window and threw out the key.

My cell phone rang with Casey's distinctive ring. I grabbed it off the center console. "Hi, what's up?" Neither one of us were much for standing on formalities since we'd worked together for the better part of a year and a half now.

Casey got right to the point. "I can't sleep. I'm worried about Marcos. You find him yet?"

I held the phone in front of me to look at the time. "Case, it's one in the morning. I thought you'd be in bed by now. We have a pretty good lead on where he's staying tonight. Megan and I are headed there now to check it out. I'll text you when we find him and we know he's all right."

"Thanks. I should've come with you. My old Catholic guilt's kicking in, I guess."

"You needed to get Terri home and honestly, I think Megan's glad you didn't come 'cuz she'd might have missed out on all the fun."

Megan yelled across the console. "I saw a bunch of nudies doing some real creative bouncing on a blow up doll! I definitely gotta get me one of those!"

Casey laughed. "Sounds like the type of place our Marcos would hang out, all right. Text me when you find him so I can get some sleep, okay?"

"You got it. I'll see you in the morning."

I could hear Terri snort in the background. "It is morning, Alex, and I have to get up in three hours to get ready for my early shift. Make it snappy so Casey stops pacing around the house and cleaning the stupid bird cages."

I looked at my phone. "Bird cages? You clean bird cages at one in the morning?"

"Only when I'm nervous and can't sleep. Sometimes, when I'm really upset, the bird cages are cleaner than my kitchen, and that's sayin' a lot." Casey disconnected just as I was turning into the Septin Apartments' lot.

As I pulled into a parking space, I looked around at the worn down complex and knew why the address had sounded so familiar. It was a two-story building with the doors facing out toward the trash-strewn parking lot. Gray stucco covered the walls, most of it weathered and peeling with gaping holes showing through to the chicken wire used to build the framework under the stucco. Four by three foot windows were framed in to the right of each door and rusted metal sections of fence lined the walkway along the second floor landing.

Looking towards the second floor, black memories of an arrogant bastard's head blowing apart from a SWAT sniper's bullet filled my mind. The man had taken a woman hostage, and had been holding her captive inside the apartment with a mattress pushed up against the window. I'd been on the hostage negotiation team then, and when negotiations had broken down and it was obvious the bastard was going to kill the women, I'd heard the incident commander give the SWAT snipers the go ahead to take the man out if they got a clear shot. I was watching the apartment through binoculars in order to give the lead negotiator whatever information I could gather. I vividly remember seeing the man's head appear above the mattress as he peeked out the window, and then the sudden red spray that misted out when his head disappeared.

I shook my head to clear it and noticed Megan watching me. Sometimes I think we've known each other so long she can actually read my thoughts and as she stood with me next to the jeep, her gaze traveled between me and the second floor apartments and back to me again. For once, she didn't have any smart aleck remarks. She reached up and put her hand on my shoulder, once more looking out across the parking lot. "It's okay, Alex. Whatever you're seeing's not there anymore. C'mon, let's go find Marcos and get the hell out of here."

A thin layer of clouds drifted over the moon, partially blocking whatever light we might have used to make our way through the parked cars. The streetlights in this neighborhood had been broken out years before by roaming bands of disgruntled teenagers and the city had given up trying to replace them after about the tenth or fifteenth time the light fixtures had been destroyed. I pulled out my cellphone and activated the flashlight app which gave us enough light to get to the apartment stairwell without barking our shins on twisted metal fenders or broken taillights.

As we reached the stairs, I tried to remember what room Anita had said Drew rented. "Did she say apartment one ten or two ten?"

Megan tilted her head to the side and sniffed the air. "What's that smell?"

Drawing in a deep breath in this neighborhood could be problematic due to the wastewater reclamation plant that had plagued the area with a continuous stench for the last fifty years. "It's that wastewater treatment plant. You know, the one you smell whenever you pass Prince Road along I-10? I hear they're gonna close it down, but only God knows when. Try not to breathe through your nose, although nothing really helps get rid of the stench."

"Ugh. You take me to the loveliest places." She grabbed my arm and pulled me up the stairs. "Two ten. She said two ten so lets get there and get the hell out of here before my nose hairs curl and burn."

All of the windows we passed had the curtains pulled shut, and two ten was no exception. I stood to the side of the door opposite the window and pounded on it with the flat of my hand. After a few seconds, I saw the curtain pull to the side and then fall back to its original position. No one came to the door, so I pounded on it again. "C'mon Drew, open up. We're looking for Marcos."

Megan chimed in. "Anita sent us. You know, the Cat Woman? Tall, masked, great breasts, carries a nasty looking whip?"

I sighed. "Megan."

She raised her eyebrows. "What? She does."

The door opened to a bleary eyed, bare chested young man wearing nothing but boxer shorts and black socks. His body was covered in hair and tattoos, and lined up across his chest were a series of seven raised, red lumps about the size of small plumbs, each with a black, circular nipple protruding from their centers. He rubbed his eye with the palm of his hand. "Whaddya want? It's what?" He turned and looked back into the room. "One fifteen in the morning. I gotta go to work in a few hours."

Megan stared at his chest. "Are those implants?"

The guy looked down, then back at Megan who tilted her head and looked a little closer. She reached out and poked two of the nipples. "Except for that one and that one I guess. Those are real, right?"

The guy pulled his arms into his chest and backed away, an incredulous look on his face. "What the fuck, lady, do I get to poke your nipples too?" The underside of his arm had a 3D image of flesh being pulled back to expose a series of gears and pulleys and some kind of hinged duct with multi-colored electric wires running out of it.

When Megan saw that particular tattoo, she grabbed his arm and turned it to get a better look. "Oh cool, look at this, Alex! Is that great or what?"

I stepped in between Drew and his assailant and pried Megan's fingers off his wrist. "Megan! Leave the poor guy alone." Drew backed further into his apartment and tried to close the door. I stuck my foot against the bottom edge to hold it open. "I'm sorry about that, she gets a little excitable. My name's Alex and we're friends of Marcos. Anita said we might be able to find him here. He missed work tonight and that's not like him. Is he here?" I was hoping I sounded a little less crazy than the woman who was peering around my shoulder trying to get a look at the rope tattoo encircling his waist with the end hanging down into his jockey shorts in a very provocative location. When I saw where her eyes were headed I pushed her back hoping she wasn't going to reach around and pull the guy's underwear out so she could get a look at the end of the rope.

Drew also saw what had grabbed Megan's attention and quickly covered the waistband of his boxers with one hand while continuing to cover his seven nipples with the other. He turned a somewhat panicked expression on me and put his weight against the door trying to push it shut. When my foot didn't budge, he took a deep breath, raised his hands in surrender and sighed. "Look, just let me get my clothes on and I'll come right back, okay?"

I nodded but kept my foot against the door. He stepped into the apartment and I watched him disappear into his bedroom. If I'd been there on police business, I wouldn't have let him out of my sight, but since we were here as Marcos' friends, I didn't want to be accused of trespassing where I hadn't been invited. I stared nervously at the bedroom door until he emerged pulling a dark blue polo shirt over a pair of perfectly ironed and creased blue jeans. He pointed back through the door. "Marcos is passed out in there. I had to practically carry him up the stairs and I can guarantee he won't be conscious enough to talk to you."

Wanting to be absolutely sure Marcos was okay, I pointed at the door. "Do you mind if I just go take a peek? That way I can tell Maddie I saw him and he's fine."

Drew swept his hand toward the door. "Be my guest."

Megan started to follow and I put my hand on her chest. "Wait here, and keep your hands to yourself." She put her hands on her hips, obviously miffed. I started for the door Drew had indicated and he crossed his arms over his chest and stepped up close behind me, all the while glancing over his shoulder to make sure Megan wasn't coming anywhere near him. I opened the door and stepped inside, taking a minute to let my eyes adjust to the dark.

Drew reached over and flipped on the light. "Here, I guarantee the lights aren't gonna wake him up."

Marcos was curled up on a pullout sofa snoring contentedly. After checking to make sure he was in one piece, I took a quick moment to look around. I guessed this was Drew's office because he had a full-sized mahogany desk pushed into one of the corners with a dark portrait of George Washington perfectly centered above the desk. I walked over and examined the portrait, which, to my untrained eye, seemed very old and very valuable. The wooden, gilt frame was almost as much a work of art as the painting. Ornate filigree stretched from each corner reaching about a quarter of the way down each edge. The two layers of edging had been meticulously carved with a repeating pattern of darker lines and swirls.

To the right of the desk were four framed medieval coats of arms, each one more colorful than the last. "Spencer, McCallum, Armstrong, Buchanan. Are these some of your ancestral roots?"

Drew nodded. "I'm a Spencer, my mom's maiden name is McCallum, my paternal grandmother was an Armstrong, and her mother, my great grandmother was a Buchanan. I've traced my roots back to fifteenth century Scotland and England."

A narrow floor-to-ceiling bookcase took up another corner of the room. I walked over and pulled out a leather-bound book and read the title out loud. *"The Life of Nelson, The Embodiment of the Sea Power of Great Britain by Mahan. Volume One."* I checked the book next to it, and sure enough, there was Volume Two. The entire bookshelf held books with titles relating in some way to past military battles or to some great military leaders or strategists.

I've been in a lot of rundown, skanky apartment complexes but I've never, ever seen anything like this room in any one of them. I replaced the book and started running my finger down a row of bindings. "*The Life of Lord Kitchener*, by Sir George Arthur, *The Birth of Britain* by Winston S. Churchill, *Mahan on Naval Warfare*." Shaking my head I continued on around the room. "Drew, this is crazy. You live in a pretty rundown apartment complex. What the hell are you doing with these kinds of books and a desk that looks like it should probably be in a museum?"

Drew shrugged. "I'm a military historian. I was completely broke when I was getting my PhD and this is where I lived. Almost everybody who lives here are my friends now, so last year when I finished at the University, I just decided to stay." A shy smile played on his lips. "Plus, there's the fact that a PhD in military history just about guarantees I'll be broke the rest of my life." He pointed to a second bookshelf on the opposite wall. "I supplement my income by doing genealogy for people who are too busy to do it themselves. Most of it's online these days, but I can never pass up a bargain on family histories or heraldic devices."

Megan, who of course couldn't possibly do what she was told, wandered into the room. She walked straight to the portrait of George Washington and began to study it. "Where did you get this?" She sounded suspicious and turned to glare at our host.

Drew walked over to study the portrait as well. "My great-great-great-something-or-other bought it and passed it down through the generations."

Nodding, she reached out and gently flicked the canvas with her fingernail. I didn't expect to hear anything, but a solid "tink" accompanied her gesture. My curiosity piqued, I stepped closer to get a better look. "A wooden canvas?"

She nodded. "Uh huh." She turned to Drew. "Do you even know what you have here?"

Drew shrugged. "Well, it's just an old painting as far as I know, but that's about it. I've kept it around because I love historical artifacts and the military." He made a sweeping gesture toward the portrait. "Voila, I kill two birds with one stone."

Megan's eyes shot up into her bangs. "Saying this is just an old military picture is like saying Margaret Thatcher was just some old lady." When Drew didn't respond, Megan's voice rose several octaves. "Let me put it this way. The first seven presidents of the United States were painted by the same man. He usually painted the faces and his two daughters would normally fill in the rest of the portrait. The other six portraits are hanging in a climate-controlled environment under extremely tight security at the United States Naval Academy. The artist's name was Gilbert Stewart."

Drew shook his head. "No way. This one's not even signed."

"He never signed his work, and he always painted on a wooden canvas. Look, there are two things I know. One, I can train any dog to do just about any thing. Two, I know art, and I know that your painting should not be hanging on that wall, in this shithole of an apartment complex."

Drew rested his hands on his hips with his eyebrows climbing up into his hairline. "Excuse me? Did I invite you into my..." He held up two fingers on each hand and wiggled them, "Shithole of an apartment? No, I did not. Did I ask you to criticize my home or give your exalted opinion of the art hanging on my walls? No, I did not. Did I look like I wanted your oh so intellectual opinion of my painting?" He waited a minute for Megan's answer. She silently returned his glare, and he once more answered the question himself. "That would be fuck no, I did not."

I'd been swiveling my head between the two of them, and when I saw Megan take an aggressive step toward Drew I stepped in between them. Megan reached around my shoulder and poked a finger into one of his seven nipples as she spoke. "First of all, Marcus is our friend, and if you hadn't invited us in, Alex would have broken the door down to get in here to find him."

I gasped and turned quickly to Drew. "Not true! I never..."

Megan pushed me aside. She was really on a tear now. "Second, a shit hole is a shit hole is a shit hole." She hit three of the nipples on that one. I grabbed her around the waist and started pulling her toward the door, apologizing as we went.

She pulled away from me and before I could grab her she had her nose practically touching his. "And finally, it's my oh so intellectual opinion that you're an idiot for keeping a national treasure on a wall where the cockroaches have to skirt around the priceless artwork framing said national treasure to get to the other side!"

Drew strode over to the office door and jerked it open. "Out! How dare you come in here using your police powers to harass and insult me when all I did was bring a good friend home to try to dry him out."

I waved my hands back and forth in front of my face. "Whoa, whoa, whoa, whoa! I never said I was a cop, I never insinuated I had any police powers and...wait a minute, how did you know I was a cop?"

He just glared at me. "Oh puleeze." He pointed at the door again. "Just get her out of here before I make an official complaint with your department."

Megan started to open her mouth and I quickly covered it with my hand and dragged her through to the living room. I had to literally pick her up and carry her out the front door onto the stoop where Drew slammed the door on our retreating backs.

I set her down and had to restrain myself from shoving her down the stairs. "What is the matter with you? Didn't I tell you I am completely off duty and this has nothing to do with the police department or with detective work?" I took the stairs two at a time and when I reached the sidewalk I steamed toward my jeep. I've been mad at Megan before, frustrated, embarrassed, and many other emotions too numerous to list, but this was the first time I'd been absolutely livid with her. After two steps, I spun around to face her and she had to sidestep to keep from running into me.

"Alex, you don't underst—"

I cut her off with a swipe of my hand. "I understand all right. I understand you just assaulted a man, several times I might add, insulted him, called his home a cockroach infested shithole, and then proclaimed that if he hadn't complied with our request to see Marcos I would have abused my police powers by breaking into his home to try to find a friend of mine whom he had benevolently dragged home from a bar because he was too drunk to get home by himself!"

At least she had the grace to look slightly chagrined. "I guess maybe I should stay away from Alaskan Iced Teas when we're out not doing police work, huh?"

I just gave her a disgusted shake of my head and stalked the rest of the way to my jeep. If she hadn't been fast enough, I just might have driven away and left her to stew a while in the middle of the parking lot. She jumped up into the passenger seat and reached over her shoulder to pull the shoulder strap on her seatbelt across her chest. "But really, Alex. I'm serious when I say that's a national treasure he has hanging on his wall. I can't believe some war historian with seven nipples has custody of one of the most valuable historic artifacts of the eighteenth century."

I just shook my head, still steaming and unwilling to cut her any slack. When I didn't answer, she reached over and punched my arm. "Hey, but we found Marcos...that's good news, huh?"

I turned and glared at her, then reached into my console to turn up the radio.

She tried again. "Look, if he calls the department, just tell Kate it was all me. Just tell her I'd had too much to drink and had verbal diarrhea." When I didn't respond, I heard her mutter "Well fine, then." She reached into her purse and pulled out her cell phone. I figured she was going to call Casey and let her know we'd found Marcos."

"Hello, Kate? Megan here. How're you doin'?"

I jerked the jeep to the curb and grabbed for her phone. "What the hell, Megs? Give me that damn phone!"

She straight armed me away and continued talking. "Look, I know...what?" She listened a minute. "Well, I know it's two in the morning, but—"

I lunged across the console and pinned her to the seat, grabbing the phone out of her hands and pushing end before I unzipped my window and threw her cellphone out into the street. "What the hell has gotten into you? It's two o'clock in the morning and you're calling Kate to tell her about something that she may never hear about anyway?"

Megan screamed, shot out of the jeep and ran into the street. She barely missed being flattened by a yellow cab driver who had to stand on his breaks and jump the curb to avoid hitting her. She stood in the middle of the street staring in the direction the cab had come from. Her terrified expression reminded me of a scared rabbit mesmerized by oncoming headlights. I quickly got out and began motioning for traffic to go around while she searched for her phone. When she found it, we both climbed back in and sat quietly staring out the windshield. She finally whispered "Jesus, Mary and Joseph."

I took a deep breath and nodded. My cell phone rang with Kate's siren ring. As I pulled it out of my pocket I looked at Megan and put my finger to my lips. She nodded, closed her eyes and leaned her head back into the headrest, one hand over her heart and the other clutching her cell phone with a white knuckled grip. I punched the answer button. "Hello?"

Silence greeted me on the other end. "Kate? Hello?"

Still nothing. I looked at the display to make sure I was still connected and then waited for Kate to say something. After about a minute, she growled, "Do you know what time it is?"

I quickly checked the time on the phone. "Um, looks like a little after two, boss. Is that all you needed?"

Silence. Then, "Are you and Megan still alive? Because the only reason I can see calling me at two in the morning is if there was some life threatening event where you need me to respond immediately because if there's not, I'm going to have to kill you myself tomorrow morning when you get in to work."

"Well, Maddie at the E.R. was worried about Marcos who didn't show up for work so she called me and Megan and I volunteered to go look for him and while we were looking for him—we found him by the way—but while we were looking for him Megan had an Alaskan Iced Tea and..."

"Alex?"

"Yes?"

"It's two in the morning and you're babbling. Save it for tomorrow."

"Ya but—" I checked the display again and saw that she had hung up.

Megan crossed her heart with her finger. "I promise never to have another Alaskan Iced Tea as long as I live." I nodded until she added. "Unless I can get my cowboy to take me to one of those upper rooms in Gus' bar. Now those look like a hoot!"

My cheerful Megan was back and since I had very nearly caused the death of my best friend, I smiled back and drove home, thankful that my crazy sidekick was still very much in one piece.

CHAPTER 7

When I walked into the office the next morning I avoided looking at Kate as I walked past her desk and headed back to my workstation. I had texted Casey that we'd found Marcos before climbing into bed, and she nodded at me as I walked up and dumped my briefcase onto my desk. "You look wiped. Judging from your text, you didn't get to bed until about five hours ago."

"Yeah, and then Megan spent the night because she didn't feel like driving home at that time of the morning. She refused to sleep on the couch and climbed into my bed and promptly fell asleep. I couldn't wake her, so I climbed in bed and thought I could get to sleep even after she kicked me in the back and whapped me on the nose but then Sugar climbed into bed with us with Tessa and Jynx not far behind." I flopped down into my chair.

She leaned forward over her desk and spoke in a whisper. "I did some asking around about Jason, Marcos' friend. Guess who Jason's father is."

I shook my head. "Who?"

She looked around to see who was nearby, then leaned closer. Before she could say anything, Kate stood up and started walking our way. She stopped and leaned against the metal column near our desks. "So, did Megan make it home all right?"

I nodded.

She smiled. "Those Alaskan Iced Tea's are deadly."

That was the understatement of a lifetime. I raised my eyebrows in agreement, silently sighing with relief that Kate was in a good mood this morning.

She turned to Casey. "I heard you were asking around about Marcos' friend, Jason, this morning."

Casey shifted uncomfortably in her chair. She raised her eyes to me, then nodded in answer to Kate's question without looking directly at her.

Kate nodded slowly as though weighing something in her mind. She leaned on Casey's desk and waited for Casey to meet her eyes. "Be. Careful." She turned to look at me, then walked back to her desk.

Casey let out the breath she'd been holding and silently nodded to herself.

I watched Kate until she was out of earshot, then asked quietly, "What was that about?"

Casey continued to talk in a quiet voice. "Jason's full name is Jason F. Beulow."

"So?" Then it hit me. "Jason Frederick Beulow?"

"Shhhh." Casey swung around quickly to make sure no one had heard. I looked over at Kate who was glaring at me over her reading glasses. "Didn't Kate just tell us to be careful? I guarantee that doesn't mean blaring out Captain Beulow's name right now."

I lowered my voice. "Marcos is dating Beulow's son?"

Casey nodded. "Estranged son."

"And he's been arrested for rape? But Beulow's the commander of the Sex Crimes Division. That makes for kinda awkward, doesn't it?"

"Yeah. C'mon. Ruthanne was gonna see what she could find out and we're supposed to meet her down in the locker room in five minutes."

We took the elevator to the basement and walked into the women's locker room to find Ruthanne sitting on the bench reading through a case report she held close to her nose. I flicked the paper with my fingers. "You need glasses or what?"

"Yeah, I left mine on my desk. I just have those dollar store ones, but without them everything's pretty blurry." She waved the paper at us. "The case report on the rape Jason is accused of. They said he slipped the victim some Ruffies then raped her in the women's room of the bar they were at."

Casey took the report and read it over before handing it to me. I sat down and read through the narrative, then flipped the report over so I could see who the arresting officer had been. "Looks like Arnold Keswick took the initial report from the woman who claimed she was raped." I took the other paperwork from Ruthanne and read through the initial supplemental reports. "Then when the detectives got the case and realized who Jason was, it went up the chain of command and the chief assigned Captain Emery to supervise instead of Buelow."

I looked at Casey who shrugged. "I've never worked for Emery. I know he takes his car to the carwash every morning, but beyond that I don't know a whole lot."

Ruthanne took back the reports and stood. "I had to borrow these from Gail Redfox. She's the lead detective and apparently Emery isn't too happy about it. He wanted his buddy Michael Jonas to handle it, but the chief wanted the most experienced detective on it, and that's Gail." She shook her head. "Emery was really thrilled when Gail asked the chief to temporarily assign me to work with her since she and I had been partners in sex crimes for four years before I transferred to homicide. I just started this morning, right before Casey called and I can tell you I'm not too thrilled with the idea of working this case."

Casey and I both nodded, not envying her one bit. I'd already had a run-in, or several run-ins with Buelow and I didn't want anything to do with convicting his son of rape. Casey surprised me when she crossed her arms and looked me squarely in the eye. "Did you notice the name of the bar where the rape supposedly occurred?"

I shook my head.

"They were at Fernando's."

I smiled. Fernando and I have been friends for years, ever since I helped him find his eight year old niece who had been stolen by her crazy biological father, but that's another story all together. Casey rolled her eyes and bent toward me. She enunciated as though talking to a slow child. "Fer...nan...do's." There was no doubt I was missing something so I raised my eyebrows silently asking what she was talking about.

"What self respecting gay man would go within a mile of that bar?"

I thought a minute. "I don't know. Megan and I just sometimes go when she wants to dance and I hang out with Fernando. But now that I think about it, it is a machismo kind of bar."

She snorted. "Kind of? Men who even look slightly effeminate there have to prove their manhood by bashing in some guy's face to prove they're not gay. Why would Jason even consider going to a place like that?"

"What does Jason look like? Does he look gay?"

Shrugging, she turned and headed out the door. "What does gay look like? I don't know, but I'm glad Gail and Ruthanne are the one's handling the case. At least the guy'll get a fair shake."

I nodded as I followed her out to the elevators.

CHAPTER 8

When we walked into the office, Kate looked up from a stack of papers she held in her lap. A blonde man was sitting in the chair in front of her desk, and when Kate looked up, he turned and looked over his shoulder as well. He was dressed in an expensive, tailored black business suit, and even seated I could tell he probably stood around six foot four or more. His ruggedly handsome face reminded me of Carl Boyd, a rodeo clown I'd befriended on an earlier case. I smiled and nodded. His eyes lit up in a silent, cheerful greeting before he turned back toward Kate.

Kate nodded at us and resumed her reading. A few minutes later she walked by our desks with the man close on her heels. "Casey, Alex, come on into the lieutenant's office a minute. Alex, grab an extra chair, will you?"

I wheeled Casey's desk chair into the small office and reached for the door to close it. I looked at Kate with raised eyebrows and pointed to the door. She nodded. "Close it please, Alex. I'd like to keep the lid on this as much as possible."

I closed the door, took a seat, and silently studied Kate's visitor. I also watched Casey who was already seated with her hands clasped quietly in her lap, waiting. Her thumbs slowly circled one another, a habit that meant she was curious about what Kate had to say. Casey is the master of the inscrutable poker face. If she knew I'd learned to read her little telltale signs, she'd work religiously to break herself of each and every habit she'd unconsciously acquired throughout the years.

Kate, who sat behind the lieutenant's desk, motioned toward the man who was seated in the chair closest to the window. "Ladies, this is Craig Stafford, an old friend of mine. I contacted him yesterday after my conversation with Mr. Myung at the racetrack. Craig owns Stafford Limited." She gestured toward Casey. "Craig, this is Detective Casey Bowman. She's worked for me for about two years now and there's no one I'd trust more to keep a confidence than her."

Casey's face reddened from the compliment. Her right thumb went from circling to tapping which happened when someone drew attention to her. She liked nothing more than to do her work and blend into the background as much as possible.

Kate pointed at me. "And this is Detective Alex Wolfe."

I waited for her to tell him what my strengths were, but nothing was forthcoming. I stared at her a minute, then slowly reached around Casey to shake Craig's hand. When he returned the handshake, I was surprised to feel thick calluses on his palm. For some reason I took him for a behind the desk type of guy. Strong fingers enveloped mine but instead of barely squeezing my hand like so many men feel is appropriate for a woman, he applied just enough pressure to show he respected my position as an officer instead of treating me as though I was a dainty wallflower. I liked that, and as an added bonus, his hand was dry so I didn't have to wipe off any sweat. Two points in his favor already. No wait, make that three since he had the most disarming smile I've ever seen.

I turned my attention back to Kate who opened the bottom drawer on the desk just enough for her foot to rest on the top rim when she leaned back in her chair. She crossed her leg over her knee and began tapping her thigh with her pencil. "As I said, what I'm about to tell you is confidential. Craig is retired CIA. His specialty is Eastern European organized crime, specifically those involved in human trafficking."

I nodded, trying to put the pieces together as she spoke. "Eastern Europe…I thought Mr. Myung was from the Far East, like one of the Korea's or something."

Kate nodded. "He is, North Korea to be exact. About a year ago, his—"

I sat bolt upright in my chair. "Wait! Eastern Europe…Lithuania. Those idiots who tried to kidnap me were from Lithuania!"

Kate rolled her eyes and smiled at Craig. "She's quick, this one. Mind like a steel trap."

I scowled at her and sat back in my seat.

Craig sent me a sympathetic smile. "You probably hadn't connected Mr. Myung to your scare at the coffee shop, but I'm willing to bet it's all tied together somehow. That's why, when Kate called me, I was anxious to come speak with you." He shook his head. "I can't quite figure in the body at the racetrack, or the Angelino connection. I understand you've managed to penetrate Gianina Angelino's inner circle?"

I glared at him a minute, then crossed my arms and mentally pinched my lips shut. I didn't trust myself not to bite the guy's head off. I figured I'd only just met him so I'd give him the benefit of the doubt. I hoped he wasn't thinking what I thought he was thinking.

Kate spoke up. "Relax, Alex. We're just trying to connect the dots right now. Nobody's accusing anyone of anything."

I turned and glared daggers at Kate until Casey reached over and put her hand on my shoulder. "Hey, relax. You can't listen if you're thinking about tearing somebody's head off. No sense getting pissed off before you actually know what's going on."

Craig's confusion was evident by the way his head swiveled first to me, then to Kate, back to me, to Casey, and back to me again. He reached up and pulled at his right earlobe. "I have no idea what you ladies are talking about." He turned back to Kate. "Didn't you tell me…"

Kate raised a hand, stopping Craig mid-sentence. "Alex hasn't 'infiltrated' anything. Through a strange set of occurrences, she and Ms. Angelino have become good friends." She uncrossed her legs and leaned forward, clasping her hands together and resting her forearms on the desk. "Okay, let's start at the beginning, shall we?"

I took in a deep breath, uncrossed my arms and sat back to listen to Kate's briefing. When I sat back, Casey relaxed as well. I chuckled silently to myself when I realized she'd been ready to grab me if I happened to leap over her chair to grab Craig by the throat. I leaned toward her and whispered, "I'm not that out of control, you know."

She snorted and I realized Kate had stopped talking. When I turned back to her, she raised her eyebrows and lowered her chin. "Is there something you'd like to share with the rest of the class, Alex?"

I shook my head. "Nope."

"May I continue the briefing then?"

"Sorry, Boss. Go ahead."

"As I was saying, let's start with the first occurrence today, finding the body."

I raised my hand. "Actually, the fire was the first thing, the body was the second."

Kate reached up and rubbed her eyes. "I think I need to go even further back than that. Back in the early fifties, Mr. Myung and his family, specifically his grandfather, lived in North Korea. His grandfather believed that communist rule, or really Russia's brand of communism, would strangle his people, their beliefs, and most importantly their unique culture and traditions."

Casey spoke up. "Let's see, my history isn't all that great. I know that was after World War Two, but was that during or after the Korean War?"

Craig nodded. "The Korean War took place between 1950 to '53." He looked at Kate. "I think you're talking about after that war, right?"

My history was as bad as Casey's, but Kate had definitely piqued my interest. I didn't have a clue about what all this had to do with the crispy critter in the barn, or with the Lithuanians, or, to be honest, with me. I watched as Kate scratched her head, obviously trying to keep dates and specifics clear in her own mind.

"Yes, after Korea. The grandfather had assisted the United States and the South during the war and had been able to keep his involvement, or rather, his treason, a secret. Do you remember Mr. Myung telling us that his grandfather was a seventh degree black sash in…" She paused trying to remember what he had said. "In whatever martial art that was."

Casey and I nodded.

"As you can imagine, even though he was only a peasant, he was highly revered in his country. Anyway, after World War Two, North Korea was occupied by Russia under communist rule where organized crime flourished." She motioned to Craig with a flick of her fingers. "Can you take it from here?"

Shrugging, Craig picked up the narrative. "Well, I haven't spoken to Mr. Myung yet, but I did a little research last night on his grandfather whom, from all I can gather, was an incredibly honest, forthright kind of guy. Through a friend of mine who is still in the CIA, I was able to access some of the earliest records from the agency's archives."

My cell phone chose that moment to ring with Megan's signature Tarzan yell. It took me a minute to retrieve it from deep in my back pocket and another few seconds to silence the ring. I sheepishly set it on vibrate and returned it to my pocket. "Sorry."

Craig nodded and Kate's jaw rippled. Craig continued. "The grandfather, Myung Kyung Tai, hated that the communist rulers were systematically stripping his people of their heritage. He was very aware of his government's brutality and of their complicity in the growing strength of the Jug-eum, an organized crime group that started in South Korea but eventually moved into parts of North Korea as well. Literally translated, Jug-eum means death."

I was starting to lose focus. "And all of this pertains to us, how?"

Kate sat back. "We're getting to that, Alex. According to Mr. Myung, his grandfather organized and trained loose bands of patriots who fought against both the communist leadership and the Jug-eum. His disciples were pretty brutal. Apparently they became a covert, elite group of martial arts experts who assassinated corrupt politicians, protected innocent citizens and businesses, and aided U.S. infiltrators who were working to undermine the North Korean government."

Craig chimed in. "By doing so, Myung Kyung Tai made a lot of enemies." He shook his head. "No, actually enemies is too nice a word. Maybe fanatical, rabidly vengeful extremists would be a better way to describe them. Believe it or not, the battle between Kyung Tai's descendants and Korean organized crime is still raging on into the twenty-first century, with your Mr. Myung leading the way."

Casey lifted her hands palms up. "So what does all this have to do with the fire and the body?"

We both looked at Kate for an answer. "Well, apparently, about six months ago, Mr. Myung single-handedly killed the head of the modern day Jug-eum and four of his bodyguards. In retaliation, the new head Mafioso kidnapped Myung's granddaughter. Apparently, selling her into a life of sexual slavery was more of an insult to Myung and his group than simply killing her. Myung managed to track her to a slave ring headquartered in..." She nodded at me. "Lithuania."

"From Lithuania, Myung tracked her to Philadelphia, and then to Tucson." Craig reached into a briefcase that was leaning against the legs of his chair. He retrieved a two-foot long cardboard tube and slipped out a rolled up piece of paper. As he rolled it out onto the desk, Casey and Kate began pinning the corner's down with some of the lieutenant's items. Casey grabbed an antique desk clock and carefully set in on the corner nearest to her chair. Kate slid over a beautiful letter opener that I've always admired. In fact, I asked the lieutenant to leave it to me in his will, but he declined. The handle was an ornately carved giraffe's head and both edges of the blade had been honed to very sharp cutting surfaces. Definitely something that could be used to slice open your enemy, or, more probably any mail the L.T. received.

When they'd finished unrolling and pinning down the paper, it covered about three-quarters of the desk. It was obviously a map of the Western United States. Red, green, yellow and blue lines had been drawn in using various colored markers. Craig began running his finger along one of the yellow lines. "These concentric rings represent the larger organized crime groups here in this part of the United States. For example, this yellow one centered around Phoenix is a fairly small crime family dealing mainly in drugs."

He then traced the next larger, green ring with his finger. It took in all of Arizona, small portions of Southern California and Southern Utah. "This one represents a more powerful family who controls all of the gun smuggling and prostitution rings in the area. They also get a take from the smaller drug family, and in turn pass along some of their profits to the largest controlling organized crime group in the western United States. That would be this one."

Craig traced the largest ring that had been drawn with a red marker. It contained the first two circles, plus the rest of California, all of Utah, Nevada, Colorado, New Mexico, and parts of Texas. "This larger area is controlled by your friend, Alex, and both of the crime bosses running the other rings defer to her, and pay her a percentage of their profits."

I sat back, stunned. "No way."

Craig smiled. "Yup." He waited a minute to let that sink in.

Casey pointed to the lower corner of Nevada. "Does she control Las Vegas?"

He nodded. "Mostly. This blue line represents an up and coming organization that's been trying to take over from the Angelinos. The sex slave trade has been oozing its way into that part of the country for a while now and this rival syndicate is responsible for ninety-nine percent of it. Gianina allows prostitution in the areas under her control but she viciously wipes out any sexual slavery she finds within her borders."

I continued to shake my head. "No way. There's no way Gia controls all that." I looked up from the map and found Kate staring straight at me. Neither of us looked away and I shook my head again. "There's no way, Kate. I know she's powerful, but..." I waved my hand over the map. "No way."

Kate shrugged. "Whether she does or not is a moot point. What I care about, is Mr. Myung had been following a man connected to the blue group whom he thought might be able to lead him to his granddaughter. The man led him to the racetrack. The next thing he knows, the barn is on fire and the rest is history. How all this relates to the Angelinos, other than the barn being theirs during the racing season, is anybody's guess."

I was trying to figure out where my Lithuanian friends fit in as well. "You know, just because he traced his granddaughter from Lithuania to Tucson, doesn't mean that's tied to what happened with me. Are you trying to imply that they were going to kidnap me to sell me into sexual bondage?"

Craig shook his head. "No, you'd be way too high profile a target for that. They usually take runaway kids, prostitutes, young boys with no homes or family. I have no way of knowing what the heck was going on with the group who tried to take you. Unfortunately, the man you arrested was bailed out of jail hours after he was booked, so Kate couldn't get me in to talk to him, if that would even have been possible."

I looked at Kate. "Who bailed him out?"

Kate's gaze slid to the ceiling. She took a deep breath, let it out slowly through her nose, then lowered her gaze onto me. "William Silverton."

Nothing could have floored me more than those two words. Silverton was Gia's private attorney. Kate and I stared at each other, although I can honestly say I wasn't seeing her, or anything else for that matter. The words "William Silverton" kept bouncing around in my head until I had to stand up to try to clear my thoughts. Don't ask me why that helps, but if something completely stumps me, if I can somehow physically change position it kick starts my brain into working again.

Casey shifted around until she was looking directly at Craig. "Why would William Silverton bail out the man who attacked Alex? That makes absolutely no sense, whatsoever."

Craig flicked a glance at Kate, then answered Casey directly. "It does if he's disappeared without a trace. I tried to find him at the address he gave when he was arrested. The hotel clerk said people matching the description of the group who tried to kidnap you were booked into the hotel for a week, paid up in full. Last night, he said some guy came, packed up all their stuff and left with it."

Kate stood as well, grabbed a sheet of paper and wrote something on it. "This is the hotel where they were staying. I want you two to go and talk to that clerk. Get all the information you can about the Lithuanians and about the man who showed up last night. I don't need to tell either of you that I want this whole thing kept quiet for now."

Craig pulled out two business cards, wrote a phone number on the back of each and handed one to both of us. "Here are both my business and cell numbers. If I don't answer one, I'll definitely pick up the other. I'm here to help. I may not know a lot about many things, but I do know a hell of a lot about organized crime."

I absently took the card, not really hearing what was being said. My mind had fixated on Silverton and his involvement with those idiots who'd tried to grab me yesterday. I was still trying to digest that fact as I stepped out of the office and slowly walked to my desk. Casey followed me and grabbed her briefcase. "C'mon, Alex, grab your stuff and let's go."

I started to follow, then stopped and turned. Kate had come out of the lieutenant's office. She'd been talking to Craig and when she stopped and looked my way our eyes met. She nodded slightly, raising her eyebrows just enough to let me know she was wondering what the hell was going on with the whole William Silverton thing herself. I drew in a deep breath, then turned to follow Casey out to the elevator where she was holding the doors open for me. When I stepped inside, she chuckled and let the doors slide closed. "Some weird shit's goin' on."

CHAPTER 9

The hotel was close to the airport and it took us a good twenty minutes to get there from the station. Neither of us said anything, which in and of itself was noteworthy, but the fact that her slow, methodical driving didn't aggravate me spoke volumes.

Tucked back into one of the neighborhoods, the hotel obviously catered to the quickie crowd. Plane lands, three-hour layover, fifteen minute lay, plane takes off. A routine I'm sure happened many, many times over the course of a typical day. The place was less than a dive. Paint was non- existent, windows were cracked and the office had a walk-up window with what looked like bulletproof glass. Go figure. You'd think if they could afford a window like that they could do a little maintenance around the place. I walked up to the window and looked inside.

The office actually looked semi-respectable. The floor was clean... ish, the desk was uncluttered and the preppy guy sitting behind the desk appeared well groomed. A huge smile spread across his face when he looked up from his iPad and saw me standing in front of his window. He jumped up and came bouncing over to the circular talking port in the center of the glass. "Hi there! You two ladies looking for a room?"

I glanced over my shoulder at the wrecked rooms, then turned back and returned his smile. "You have got to be kidding me, right?"

He shrugged. "Hey, it may not look like much, but it's mine."

I didn't think he looked old enough to vote, let alone own a hotel. "What do you mean it's yours?"

His posture stiffened when he noticed our guns and badges. "Oh, hey, sorry. My gaydar must be screwing up or something. I thought you two were together. Here, let me adjust my antennae." He reached under the counter by the window and pulled out a green skullcap with two green antennae poking up. He put on the cap, then began little jerky movements of his head as though recalibrating his brain. His eyes moved left to right several times before his gaze finally came to rest back on me. "Better?"

I realized my jaw had dropped and I quickly shut it. The man burst out laughing and started turning little circles around the office, raising his hands in the air in a kind of victory dance. He spun around and pointed at me. "Got ya!" He reached up, pulled off the cap with one hand and ran his hand through his short-cropped hair with the other. "Hey, huge science fiction fan here. So, now that I got that off my chest, how can I help you?"

I glanced back at Casey who had her head down while she rubbed her eyes with her thumb and index finger, probably trying to get that last sight out of her mind. Smiling, I pulled the paper Kate had given me out of my back pocket. I took a second to smooth out the wrinkles and held the paper up to the window. "Put your skull cap back on and tell me what you know about the people who rented this room. Tell me everything you know."

He read the room number on the paper then shrugged. "Not much to tell really. They came three nights ago. There were six of them. Three men, a woman, and two teenaged boys. They rented one room for all of them for the week, but ended up staying only one night."

"Describe them."

The man straightened, then cocked his head to one side as he considered his response. "Only one of them spoke English. Two of the men were in their twenties, and the third guy was, I'd say, thirty-five to forty. That's about how old the lady was as well. And mind you, I use the term lady very loosely."

Casey stepped forward and rested her hand on the glass. "Why do you say that?"

"Well, she just had a kind of sneer about her. Her lip kinda curled up and she always seemed to be saying something nasty or mean. I mean, I couldn't tell exactly what she was saying, but it wasn't hard to figure out her meaning."

Just then a cab pulled up in front of one of the rooms. A construction worker stepped out of the room and onto the sidewalk. He carefully zipped up his windbreaker and smoothed back his hair. As he was getting into the cab, a hooker Casey and I knew from Miracle Mile followed him out and leaned against the doorpost. Casey hadn't turned from the window, so I tapped her shoulder and motioned with my chin. "Look what the cat coughed up."

When Casey turned, the young woman ducked back into the room and closed the door. "Angel."

I nodded. "Yup. It never ceases to amaze me what some men will put their bratwurst into."

Casey turned back and tapped the window to get the clerk's attention again. He'd picked up his iPad and was scrolling through a bunch of pictures apparently trying to find a photo. When he heard Casey knocking, he raised one finger asking us to wait and continued scrolling. When he'd finished, he stepped back to the window and tapped the iPod screen. "Damn, I thought I'd taken a picture of those people you were asking about, but I can't find it. Whenever I get somebody who's really weird here, I try to get their pic, so I can post it on Facebook. A bunch of us who work in the hotel business have a private page where we post pics of our strangest guests and one of those people you're asking about definitely fit the bill."

I let Casey stay with the clerk and wandered over to the room Angel had disappeared into. Standing to the side of the door, I rapped several times, careful not to pick up a splinter from the delaminated wood. Angel didn't answer, and I didn't expect her to. For the most part, I just wanted to make sure she knew I'd seen her and that I knew exactly what she'd been doing with her john. Reaching over to the window, I gave a quick knock and called out, "Hey Angel, I wondered where you'd gotten to. I haven't seen you on the Mile for a couple weeks."

"Fuck off, Wolfe."

"I'd heard Judge Lawrence put you in rehab. I guess it didn't help, huh?"

The knob turned and the door slowly swung into the room. Angel slithered out and leaned against the doorpost. She crossed her arms and glared at me with red-rimmed eyes set too deep into a blotched face that was covered with scabbed over bloody acne. She looked ten times worse than the last time I'd talked to her and I let out a sigh. "Jesus, Angel, you look like death warmed over. You're gonna die, soon, if you don't get straight." I pointed to her face and body. "I've seen this happening to the girls over, and over, and over, and it's pretty obvious you're that close to hitching a quick, free ride to the morgue." I held my thumb and forefinger together about a half-inch apart, hoping she'd hear what I was saying but knowing she really didn't give a shit whether she lived or died.

She hocked up a wad of spit and I backed up a few steps. "You spit in my face and I'll break yours. That's a promise."

Her head turned to the side and she spat a bloody wad onto the sidewalk. When she spoke, the croaking whisper grated on my nerves. "Tanya's dead. Fucked up real good. Nothin' left of her face when he got done."

"I know. A couple days ago, right? I saw the pictures. Look Angel, I can get you into rehab again. You know the old saying, fifth time's a charm."

She blinked several times trying to focus through a heroin-fogged brain. Her tongue slowly felt around cracked lips, moving in and out to the rhythm of the blood pulsing through the distended artery running from her neck down into the collar of her shirt. "I found her." Her head twitched. "What was left of her anyway."

Watching her a minute, I thought about all the times I'd taken her to jail to sober her up, or the times I'd taken her to the homeless shelter or just bought her a cheap sandwich from a nearby convenience store. Casey and I had even done some research and located her family, but they'd wanted nothing to do with her.

The silence stretched out as we stood staring at each other. I knew it was pointless, but I thought I'd give it one more shot. Sometimes, you help a person ten times, and finally, on the eleventh try, something clicks. "Listen, I'm sorry about Tanya. Nobody should have to see stuff like that. But honestly? I'm afraid you're on track to get fucked up just like her if something doesn't change."

Her eyes seemed to focus on my face for just an instant and a ghost of a smile touched her sad, cracked lips. "Fuck you, Wolfe." She pushed off the door jam and slipped back into the room, shutting the door behind her as she went.

The bloody spit on the sidewalk glistened in the sunlight. Shaking my head, I looked from it, back to the door and whispered, "Goodbye, Angel."

I walked slowly back to where Casey was finishing up with the clerk. She slipped her notepad into her back pocket and gestured for me to meet her at the car. We both got in and buckled up. The curtains on the window to Angel's room were drawn, but I thought I saw her face, just for an instant, as the leading edge of the drapery moved slightly before dropping back into place with a finality that gave me a sick feeling in the pit of my stomach. My guess was she'd be dead the next time I saw her.

After we left the hotel lot, Casey reached over and opened the center console. She pulled out a paper sack, set it in her lap and unrolled the top. "Nothing like a good piece of bubblegum to help me work through a puzzle." She pulled out a round piece of Bazooka and tossed it into my lap before grabbing a piece for herself. Biting down on the end of the paper wrapper allowed her to twirl the wrapper open one handed and pop the gum into her mouth. She spoke while trying to chew the hard gum into submission. "You know that kid really does own that place. He said he was a junior in Engineering at the U until last semester when his uncle died and left him the hotel in his will. He decided to take this semester off to see if he can make a go of running the place. I like him. He seems like a decent enough kid."

I unwrapped my piece of gum and popped it in my mouth. "You

know, the taste of Bazooka always reminds me of one time when Megan and I were kids. I had this nasty neighbor, Mr. Contrell. He had this air gun, and whenever one of my dogs was out in the yard, he'd come out onto his porch and shoot at them."

A bubble came poking out through her lips. When it popped, she asked. "Why would Bazooka remind you of an idiot like that?"

"Because one day when he was gone we slipped into his house with a bag of Bazooka. It took us a while, but we chewed every single piece, and one by one we stuffed every wad down the barrel of the air rifle till the barrel was absolutely full." I smiled at the memory. Mr. Contrell's cold, squinty little eyes flashed through my mind reminding me of all the hateful, verbal epithets he'd thrown at Megan and me during our childhood. We could have been the nicest, most innocent children alive and he still would have stuck his head out of his door every time we passed and called us the Spawn of Beelzebub or some other such nonsense.

"So what happened?"

"Huh? Oh. Well, when he tried to shoot at my dog and couldn't, he looked down the barrel and found the gum. He took the rifle and smashed it to pieces against a rock, spewing threats with spittle flying." I couldn't help but laugh at the memory of that evil old man combusting with the vitriol of seventy years worth of nastiness and hatred. "The only bad thing was he didn't replace it with another air rifle. He bought a .22 pistol. I knew what it was because when he brought it home, he made sure to show it to me tell me all about it."

"Did he kill your dog? He'd of been dead meat if he killed one of my dogs."

I blew a bubble and looked at her out of the corner of my eye. "Well, that's another funny story. Megan had gotten a slingshot for Christmas and we were out playing around with it. My parents were gone, which was the only time Contrell would dare mess with any of my dogs. He stepped out onto his porch and aimed the pistol at my Australian Shepherd, Digidy." Casey had to break hard to avoid hitting the car in front of us who had apparently decided to stop for some ghostly apparition only he could see. I braced myself against the dashboard and then continued with my story. "We'd been practicing off to the side of my house, so he didn't know we were there. The next thing I knew, I heard a whiizzzzz next to my ear and the old man fell like a rock. Megan had gotten a lucky shot and had hit him right square on the side of his temple with a rock from that slingshot."

"Oh my God, did she kill him?" Casey slowed and then stopped for an old woman in a crosswalk. The light for us was green but that didn't seem to matter to the woman who was taking halting steps behind her walker. Traffic was flying by us in the curb lane, so I pushed my door open. "Hold that thought."

When I stepped up and gently laid my hand on the lady's arm, she flashed me a grateful smile. Her voice came out high pitched and shaky. "Thank you so much. I absolutely hate crossing at this light. I start out when the pedestrian light shows green, but I'm only halfway through the intersection when it turns red again." Her faintly British accent was charming.

"No worries. Here, let's see if we can safely get you the rest of the way across." I peeked around our car to see if any traffic was coming. Casey had also gotten out and had moved into the lane behind us. She waited for an opening, then stepped into the curb lane and stopped the next bunch of cars heading our way. "Here we go." The lady's elbow was paper mâché thin and I made sure to grasp it very lightly as I moved her the rest of the way across the lane and onto the sidewalk. We stepped up onto the curb and watched as Casey waved her arm in a circular motion to tell the drivers they could move forward again.

She climbed back into our car and drove to the nearest u-turn bay so she could come back to get me. The woman touched my arm to get my attention. "Don't I know you somehow?"

I took a closer look and now that she mentioned it, she did look a little familiar. "You look kind of familiar. Have you had to call the police for anything in the last few years? Maybe I helped you out with something when I worked down here on patrol."

Shaking her head slowly, the woman gazed into the sky with amber colored eyes trying to recall where she had met me before. "No, I've never had to call the police, at least not since you began your career."

Suddenly her eyebrows rose and she held a bent finger in front of my face. "I've got it! I never forget a face. I was your second grade school teacher!"

I shook my head and laughed. "No, my teacher went to prison when I was in second grade for killing her husband. She was really cool though...she'd written a book about a bear or something. I can't remember the name of it but I still have the autographed copy she gave me before she suddenly disappeared. Well, I say disappeared. She didn't have much choice, they'd arrested her, so no opportunities for goodbyes there." Fond memories surfaced as I thought about that school year. "As a kid, I was really sad that she left. She was really cool and I definitely didn't understand what had happened. I liked her a lot."

The cheerful look on her face intensified as she caught and held my gaze. "Dewey and the Little Red Wagon." She sighed and looked away. "I'm sorry that all happened. It seems like that one second in time when my husband attacked me and I pulled the trigger sent ripples and waves out into the universe that I may never realize or know about. I wanted nothing more than to gather my little chicks around me and pretend nothing had happened. There was no way they were ever going to let me come back to say goodbye." She smiled a bit wistfully. "I wanted to though."

I studied the woman, listening to her speak but not really hearing her words. "I..." Nothing could have floored me more than her knowing the name of my little second grade picture book. "Mrs. Hunbling? Dorothy Hunbling?"

Her eyebrows rose again and the smile re-appeared. Spreading her arms wide she nodded at me. "In the flesh."

I moved her walker out of the way and carefully enfolded her in my arms. The loss I'd felt as a little girl who'd loved her teacher came tumbling back. Casey had pulled into a nearby parking lot and she looked more than a little perplexed as she made her way over to us. Her expression clearly said she thought a hug was going a little above and beyond the call of duty after I'd helped a little old lady across the street. I stepped back and really tried to see the younger woman I'd known through eight-year-old eyes. I saw what I was looking for when one side of her mouth quirked up in the lopsided grin I remembered so well.

Reaching over to steady herself on her walker, she pointed to the gun and badge on my belt. "My, haven't you done well for yourself." She turned to Casey. "This one and another little girl," She glanced over at me. "Do remember the name of that little imp you used to play with."

A big smile creased my face and Casey and I both answered at once. "Megan."

"Megan! That's it! She and you were always getting into some kind of mischief."

Casey rolled her eyes. "Color me so surprised."

I punched her shoulder. "Sarcasm does not become you."

As Mrs. Hunbling pulled her walker in close, she reached over and took my hand. "I have a meeting I'm going to right now, but I'd love to talk to you some more. Can you write down my phone number?"

I pulled my cellphone out of my pocket and typed in the number she gave me. "Oh, um, Casey, this is my second grade teacher, Mrs. Dorothy Hunbling. Mrs. Hunbling, this is my partner, Casey Bowman."

Casey gently took Mrs. Hunbling's outstretched hand. "It's a pleasure to meet you, ma'am. I'd love to hear some of your Alex and Megan stories one of these days."

Mrs. Hunbling lowered her chin and looked at me over the rim of her glasses. "I'm not sure the statute of limitations has expired, but I'd love to sit and reminisce. Please call, Alex. Let's get together soon, shall we?" Pushing the walker in front of her, Mrs. Hunbling started on her way down the sidewalk toward her meeting. I watched her go for a little while, then Casey and I headed back to our car.

"I can't believe we stop to help some lady in a crosswalk and it turns out to be my second grade teacher." We got in the car and Casey pulled out into the street. "She was our teacher for most of the second grade, but believe it or not, she was arrested for murdering her husband."

"Self defense?"

"Heck, I don't know. I was only eight when it happened. One day she was there, the next day we had a new teacher. I'd love to find out what really happened though. Maybe when we go visit she'll open up about it."

"You know what my momma used to say, 'Some secrets are better left as secrets.' I think if she wants to talk about it she will, but I don't think you should be the one doing the asking."

My gum had gotten stale. There's nothing worse than bubble gum that's lost its flavor. I rolled down my window and threw it out, then reached into Casey's paper bag and grabbed another piece. "What did that guy say, by the way? You know, after I went to talk to Angel."

"Not much. The only thing interesting was his description of one of the men. He said he was missing one of his ears and there was a scar running from where his ear should have been down to the bottom of his jaw." We both thought about that a second. "That doesn't sound like any of the people who jumped you, does it?"

"It could have been one of the last two guys in the alley. By the time they showed up I was a little pre-occupied." Glancing around, I realized we had entered the neighborhood in midtown where Gia lived. "Where are you going? I don't need to talk to Gia right now."

As she turned onto Gia's street, she reached up, took the wad of gum out of her mouth and wrapped it in a napkin she found stuffed between the seats. "I just have a few questions for Ms. Angelino. You can wait in the car if you want."

I snorted. "Yeah, like that's gonna happen. Listen, I think the best time for me to talk to Gia is when I'm alone and off duty. I think I'll learn more that way."

Casey pulled into Gia's driveway and shut off the engine. She swiveled in her seat until she was facing me. "I think the best time for you to talk to Gia alone right now is never. Something's going on in one of our investigations that involves her, in fact, her name or her attorney's name seems to crop up at every turn. Whatever's going on, I think this'd be a good time for you to start covering your ass." She opened the door and got out and I met her up in front of the car.

"Casey, Gia's not stupid, and everything that's come up so far is stupid and I intend to find out what's going on. My way."

Casey shrugged and walked through the gate in the adobe wall surrounding the home. The usual flowers colored the inner courtyard and a cumquat tree was heavy with the little orange fruit. I walked over, pulled one off and popped it into my mouth, peel and all. Casey stepped up onto the semi-circular gray marble step that led up to the mahogany front door and pushed the doorbell. I'd never noticed before that the same Angelino family crest that decorated Gia's cigar case had been painstakingly carved into the upper half of the dark wood. I joined her on the stoop, and after a few minutes Gabe opened the door. As usual, he didn't say much and since this was Casey's idea I let her take the lead.

"Is Ms. Angelino in?"

Gabe shrugged, then glanced at me. "She's busy right now."

Casey stepped to the side to try to see past him. I knew all she'd see was a hallway filled with classical art. "Can you ask her if she'll talk to us?"

"No."

When she turned to me for help, I just shrugged and gave her my best "I told you so" look. I knew from experience there was nothing to be done when Gabe decided to deny entrance into the Angelino home. He was an accomplished gatekeeper, someone who would have fit right into Kublai Khan's retinue of bodyguards during the thirteenth century. I tried to picture him standing in front of huge iron doors, arms crossed, holding a scimitar in one hand and a halberd in the other. I smiled up at him. "Have you ever considered wearing a knee length tunic and baggy trousers?"

Both Gabe and Casey looked at me with perplexed expressions. "What? You know, with a belt around the tunic and a huge scimitar dangling down to your ankles?" I elbowed Casey. "Don't you think he'd make a great Mongolian Imperial bodyguard?"

Even though we'd worked together for the better part of a year now, Casey still wasn't quite sure where I was coming from a lot of the time. Without looking him in the eye, she asked Gabe, "Do you have any idea what she's talking about?"

Gabe sighed. "Mostly, I don't try to figure her out. Mostly, I just leave that up to Ms. Angelino."

The three of us stood by the front door for a while. I was waiting for Casey to realize she wasn't going to get in, and she was waiting for Gabe to get uncomfortable enough to let us in. I knew full well that wasn't going to happen. Casey gave it one last stab. "Can you ask Ms. Angelino a question for me? I can wait here, I don't need to come in."

Gabe silently shook his head. I grabbed Casey's elbow. "C'mon. The lady's busy. Let's come back another time."

Casey pulled out a business card and held it out for Gabe to take. Gabe took it, then stepped back into the house. "I'll tell Ms. Angelino you came by." With that, he closed the door in our faces.

I pulled a little harder on Casey's arm. "Well, I wouldn't dream of saying I told you so. That would be really uncouth of me." I detoured one more time to the cumquat tree and grabbed a handful of fruit. I caught up to her just as she was going through the gate and I held one out as a kind of peace offering. I knew she'd never eaten one before, so I was curious to know if she'd like it. Without really thinking, she popped it into her mouth, chewed down and promptly spit it out into the street.

"Yuck! They're nasty, bitter and full of seeds. I can't believe you like those things."

I chewed the one I had in my mouth, separating out the seeds from the meat and spitting them into the dirt. "They're good. The peel is sweet and the meat is sour. It's a great combination."

"And what the heck were you talking about—Mongolian bodyguards?" She beeped the doors open with the key fob and let herself into the car. I finished the cumquats and joined her. "I don't know, he just reminded me of a huge gatekeeper and then I started picturing him standing there half naked and then my mind went to—"

"Never mind, Alex. I'm sorry I asked. Do you need to go anywhere right away?"

I shook my head. "No, why?"

"I want to rundown to Fernando's and take a look around."

She didn't say anything more and I watched her out of the corner of my eye. "So, why are we looking into Jason's case? I'm usually the one who goes haring off after ghosts in the wind."

We drove for a while in silence. It wasn't like Casey to stick her nose into another detective's caseload and I wondered if she knew more than she was telling me. We pulled into Fernando's parking lot, which was relatively empty at this time of day. The few cars there probably belonged to some of his employees or to those early Happy Hour patrons who didn't work and could come in early enough to take advantage of the lower prices and the watered down Margaritas. I saw Fernando out back by the garbage bin and as Casey went to the front entrance I detoured over to talk to him.

"Fernando! How's life treating you?" Over the years I'd become accustomed to his style of greeting and we embraced and pounded each other on the back like the best of friends.

"Detective Wolfe, it's been too long since you've come to see me. I miss you and your smiling face when you no here." Even though he'd been in the United States for over twenty years, he still had a thick Mexican accent and tended to pronounce his y's like J's.

"Fernando, when are you ever going to just call me Alex instead of Detective Wolfe? I feel like I should be calling you Mr. Cabrera or something."

"No, no, no. Respect for the law is something my mother taught me from the time I was a small boy. It's just the way I am and you wouldn't want me to go against my mother's wishes now would you? She's one hundred and two years old and still makes her own tortillas. Can you believe that?"

"No, I find that pretty hard to believe. Does she live here with you?"

"Oh, there's a story all by itself. I have twelve brothers and sisters. Can you believe that? Twelve! Every one of us owns a house, some in Mexico, some in the states. Do you think she will live in any of our homes? No! She has her house by the little river that flows through our village and she refuses to live anywhere else." He smiled proudly. "She is one hundred and two years old! Can you believe it?"

"I wish I could meet her. She sounds like quite an imposing woman."

He picked up the trashcan he'd brought out, lifted it above his head and upended it into the garbage bin. He grimaced as he set it back on the ground. "Ugh, I twisted my back the other day trying to catch my daughter's horse that had gotten out of its corral. He came running by me and when I tried to stop him he swung me around and I felt something ping right here." With great care, he stiffly pivoted on one foot and pointed to his lower back, using his knuckles to dig into the muscles closest to his spine.

Now I felt bad for the traditional pounding we'd exchanged. "Ouch. Aren't you a little old to be catching horses that come racing by you?" Fernando wasn't a tall man, but he was lean and well proportioned. He wore his gray hair pulled back in a ponytail. Having his hair pulled up off of his face emphasized the high cheekbones he'd inherited from his Tarahumara ancestors.

He shrugged, continuing to rub his lower back with his fist. "My people believe to slow down is to die, so, I'd rather die than slow down."

I had to admit that philosophy had seemed to work wonders for his mother. Picking up the can once again, he winced and started for the back door of his bar. "So, what brings you here my friend? I know you didn't come to talk about my tiny little mother."

I fell into step beside him and reached ahead to pull open the screen door. "Well, even though I've missed coming in for the shredded pork gorditas you serve for happy hour, there is something I wanted to ask you about."

"Did you know the recipe for those gorditas came from mi abuela..." He hesitated, "...my grandmother, who lived down in the canyons? And she learned it from her grandmother, too? Can you believe that?" Fernando had often told Megan and me stories of his family who'd lived in the Copper Canyons of Chihuahua, Mexico for hundreds of years. When I smiled and nodded, he continued proudly. "We are the Tarahumara." He returned my smile and clapped me on the shoulder. "There are no greater runners on the face of this earth."

Ever since I'd started listening to Fernando's stories, I'd read quite a lot about the Tarahumara Indians, or "those who run fast" as they call themselves. They absolutely fascinate me, but today, I needed to talk to him about Jason. "Nando," I used the nickname he'd asked me to use shortly after we'd met. "I was wondering if you had any more information on that woman who was raped in the bathroom the other day. You know, anything you might not have told the investigating officer."

He stopped in front of the door without going inside. I watched him look into the gloomy interior of the kitchen before reaching out and gently pulling the door out of my hands. He deliberately pushed the screen shut, taking his time to gather his thoughts. A lot of people misjudged this genial, easy going bar owner, but I'd known him long enough to have recognized the shrewd mind behind the friendly mask.

Many of his employees were from Mexico but he had assured me on several occasions that each and every one of them had a valid green card. He was very proud of that fact and of his people, but he'd told me once that while they were his fellow countrymen, he didn't completely trust any of them, no matter how honorable or honest they seemed. "But then again I don't trust your countryman either." He'd affably told me one rainy day when Megan and I were sampling various flavors of his signature Margaritas.

Steering me away from the door with his hand on my arm, he lowered his voice to make absolutely sure no one was listening. "I have a man who works for me here, Justíno." As he leaned closer, I could smell the garlic he used everyday in his cooking. "I think it is important for you to talk to Justíno."

"Why?"

Just then the back door opened and Fernando's daughter, Celia poked her head out. When she saw me her face lit into a smile. Wiping her hands on the dishtowel she was carrying, she quickly stepped over to us and shook my hand. "Detective Alex, I should have known you would be here since your partner is asking questions inside." The quick glimpse of fear I saw in her eyes startled me.

I turned my attention to Fernando who had once again picked up the garbage can. He'd been wool gathering, but when I looked at him, he shook his head and smiled. "Dios Mío. Come, let's go inside and see our good friend Detective Bowman." The quiet worry in his voice along with Celia's apprehension gave me a lot to think about as we made our way through the kitchen and out into the bar and restaurant area.

Casey had never felt comfortable with the gregarious welcome we always received from Fernando, and before he could envelope her in a huge embrace she stuck out her hand in a friendly greeting. "Mr. Cabrera, it's good to see you again."

"It's always good to see you, Detective. Please, can I get you something to eat or drink? On the house, what do you say?" The man he signaled to nodded and disappeared into the kitchen.

As he led us to a chair, Casey politely demurred. "No thank you, sir. We just came to ask a few questions, in fact, would you mind if I asked you about the other night?"

Fernando blinked, feigning ignorance and doing a poor job of it. What he seemed to be doing a good job of was either stalling, or changing the subject. "The other night? I'm not sure what night you wish to know about, but I know if you just give me a minute I can find something you would like to eat or drink." As he spoke, he was backing toward the kitchen and when he reached the swinging door he pushed it open and disappeared inside. Celia hadn't followed us into the bar area so Casey and I were left to ourselves.

I was staring after Fernando and hadn't realized Casey had spoken until she reached over and waved her hand in front of my face. "Hello, anybody home?"

I'd been so lost in thought that the movement in front of my face startled me. I jumped back and batted her hand away. It took me a second to re-orient myself to where I was and to the fact that she'd said something. "What?"

We both pulled out a chair and sat at one of the square topped tables. "I said I didn't find out anything particularly helpful, did you?"

"I'm not sure. Who'd you talk to?"

The little notebook she always carried in her back pocket was already out and sitting on the ceramic tabletop. She wet her finger and pushed back through the pages until she came to the one she was looking for. "Let's see, the waitress, Carmen, wasn't on duty that night and hasn't spoken to anyone about what happened." She looked up from her notebook. "Which I find peculiar. If a rape happened in a place where I worked, I think I'd at least be curious enough to ask about it, wouldn't you?"

I shrugged. "I guess so. Did she know the lady who was raped?"

"No. She said she's seen her in here once or twice, but that's about it." Flipping forward a page, she tapped the little paper. "The bartender says he was working that night, but that he didn't know something had happened until the police showed up." She got up and walked to the short hallway where the restrooms were located. "Stand over at the bar, would ya?"

I stood and stepped to the bar where I greeted Jesus, or Chuey as everybody called him. He was standing behind the bar rubbing the countertop down with a towel. "Hey, Chuey, how's the little one? She must be almost six months now, huh?"

A sparkle lit up his dark eyes when I mentioned his new daughter. "Five months yesterday, Detective Wolfe. She can already roll over from her back to her stomach and she kicks like she wants to crawl. She don't come near to crawling, but she's trying." Jesus wasn't exactly a handsome man. I'd decided a while back that he reminded me of a particularly tough alley cat. Someone who's not afraid of a fight, and who even goes looking for a good brawl every now and then. I was pretty sure Fernando kept him around to intimidate some of the toughs who hung around every night drinking and playing pool. He ran his hand through his thick, black hair. He kept it cut short on the sides, not high and tight like a marine, but still trimmed neatly above his ears.

Casey called over from the bathrooms. "Hey, Alex, turn around."

I looked behind me but didn't see her. "Where'd you go?" At this angle, all I could see was half of the door to the ladies room. The rest was blocked by the arch that spanned the entrance to the bathroom hallway. Casey stepped out from behind the left side of the arch.

"Could you see any part of me?"

I shook my head, wondering where she was going with all this. "Nope."

She took two steps back. "Now?"

"I can see most of you." After two more steps she'd disappeared behind the wall again. "Right there, you're gone completely from sight." Fernando hurried out of the kitchen carrying a plate full of little pork gorditas, guacamole, and a bowl of chips and salsa with large chunks of tomatoes, chili peppers and onions chopped up throughout. "Here you go, Detectives, straight out of the oven." He set the dishes down and looked around. "Where did Detective Bowman go?"

"Right here." Casey walked to the table and pulled out a chair, taking in a deep breath and letting it out with a sigh. "That smells like heaven." She glanced over at me. "I guess it wouldn't hurt to take just a little bit of extra time here, would it?"

Fernando beamed. "I knew the smell of fresh gorditas would change your mind! Sienta te! Sit, please, and enjoy."

Casey began to sit in the chair she'd vacated earlier, then changed her mind and sat in one facing Jesus. I looked over at the bartender who had his head down as he scrubbed the counter top. I could swear he was watching us from under hooded eyes. When Casey changed seats so that she faced him he subconsciously began wiping faster and harder than before.

I purposely chose the chair that put my back to the bar. I leaned forward and plucked a couple of the little pork filled tortillas from the serving plate and put them on the small appetizer plate Fernando had set before me. As I scooped some guacamole onto each one, I spoke softly so only Casey would hear. "What's wrong, Case?"

She smiled around a mouthful of chips and salsa. "Nothing's wrong. Well, nothing I can put my finger on anyway. I just got the feeling that Chuey's hiding something and I want him to know I know."

The spices mixed into the pulled pork made my taste buds spring to life. I savored the sensation while I thought about what might be going on. Truthfully, I had no idea, so I hoped maybe my partner would come up with something brilliant and we could move on. We ate in silence for a while, watching the occasional patron come in or the occasional drunk go out. Nobody was really falling down drunk and I guessed that was probably because Casey and I were sitting in the middle of the room with our guns and badges attached to our belts. While we ate, two very mean looking Mexicans came in and sat at the bar. I had to swivel around in my chair to get a good look at them.

The first man had a full head of dark, wavy hair and close-set eyes above a nose that had been broken and badly set. There were some muscles there under the layers of fat and I wouldn't underestimate him in a fight. If the first guy reminded me of a gutter rat, the second one put me in mind of a venomous cobra ready to strike. He had deep slate gray eyes that were hooded by heavy eyebrows and a sharp straight nose above tight, thin lips. Him I would definitely take out first in any kind of bar fight.

They must have been regulars because Jesus set two beers in front of them without them saying a word. The rat man practically downed his bottle in one long swallow while the other picked up his beer and sauntered into the kitchen with obvious familiarity. Jesus watched him walk into the back, then folded the towel he'd been using and laid it on the counter. He started to follow, but Rat Face said something to him that made him stop and return to the bar. His face flushed a deep shade of red and he pierced the rat with a severely hate-filled glare. Rat snapped his fingers and Jesus grabbed another bottle, angrily popped off the top with a nasty looking bottle opener attached to his belt and practically slammed the beer down in front of the man.

Jesus darted a glance in our direction, which caused Rat Man to turn and look our way. I guess he hadn't noticed us when he walked in because when he saw us, his eyes narrowed into little slits. The beer must have been calling to him because he reached around, grabbed the bottle and took a huge swig before pushing up and following the other man into the kitchen. Less than a minute later, the two men returned and immediately walked out the front door. Fernando had also stepped out of the kitchen and I expected either him or Jesus to say something about the two men skipping out on their tab. Neither man looked at us. If I was reading them correctly, I'd say both of them looked a little ashamed or embarrassed at what had just taken place.

I turned back to Casey who was dipping a gordita into the guacamole without taking her eyes off the action at the bar. I leaned close to her and said quietly, "Do you have any idea what that was all about?"

"I don't, but I recognized the man who first went into the kitchen. Do you remember when we were looking for Rafael Rodriguez, the guy who shot Jack Dougherty and stabbed all those hookers a few months ago?"

"Yeah, of course I do."

"Well when I was trying to find him, I went to his grandmother's house to see if any of them would help locate him. That guy was there."

"The cobra guy? The one who looks like a snake?"

Casey knew I had a tendency to classify people in my mind based on the type of animal, or in this case, reptile, they resembled. She thought about my description for a second, then smiled slightly and nodded. "I guess he does look as mean as a snake. Anyway, I'll have to dig out my notebooks from that case, but I have his name in there somewhere. You couldn't see them today because of the long sleeved shirt, but he has Mara 18 tattoos on both arms and on his neck."

I whistled softly. Mara 18 was one of the most violent gangs ever to come out of the gangster breeding grounds of Las Angeles. "So he's from L.A.?"

"No, I don't think so. Not originally anyway. I think he was one of the more brutal ones who were deported to El Salvador when L.A. was trying to clean up their violent street gangs. They deported the craziest ones who had never bothered to obtain legal citizenship. I spoke to Chuck about it at the time, and I think he managed to get him deported again."

Chuck was a good friend of ours who had worked in the department's Organized Crime division for the last fifteen or sixteen years. I pulled out my cell phone and called him. When he answered, I got right to the point.

"Hi, Chuck, it's Alex. I have a question for you."

"Shoot."

"Do you remember a man Casey told you about a few months back who was in Mara 18?"

"Yeah, Andy Spellman from Border Patrol and I rounded him up and got him deported back to El Salvador. He's a sociopathic killer, no remorse, no nothing when he kills. Why?"

"Casey and I just saw him at Fernando's Bar and Grill. Do you know his name off the top of your head?"

"Rodolfo Aguilar. Hold on a second while I run a record's check." The line was quiet for about a minute before he came back on the line. "Can you still see him?"

"No, he left with some guy who reminded me of a rat. Beady little eyes, chubby."

"Yeah, that sounds like his little brother, Enrique. We tossed him too, but you see how well that works to keep them out of our fair city." He lowered his voice and I could tell he was talking to himself instead of to me. "Now that's interesting...hold on a second."

While I waited for him to come back on the line, I piled some guacamole and salsa on a chip and poured salt on top of the whole thing. "Hey, Alex, do you know what he was doing at Fernando's? Both our records and the feds show him still in El Salvador. He shouldn't have been able to get back in without at least one of the intelligence agencies knowing about it."

I shrugged, "I don't know, but I'll try to find out and let you know."

There was a long spate of coughing at the other end. I waited patiently for him to catch his breath. "Hey, Chuck, you gonna live?"

"Yeah, I just picked up a nasty cold from one of the players on my daughter's high school softball team. We're going into the semi-finals and practically the whole team's come down with it."

"Well good luck with that. Is your daughter still the star pitcher?"

"Yeah, I've had her working with one of the U of A pitchers for the last year. We've had scouts from some college teams come watch her. Can you say full ride? Anyway, I've gotta run, Alex. Thanks for the tip on Rodolfo and Enrique. We'll follow up on it and see if we can't get rid of them for good."

We hung up just as Casey and I both reached for the last gordita. Casey laughed and let me take it, but Fernando had seen that we'd finished the entire plate full of the little rolls. He slowly walked over to our table, the earlier joviality gone. "Detectives, can I get you some more?"

We both declined, but I jerked my thumb over my shoulder toward the door. "Nando, why is Rodolfo coming around here?" I glanced over my shoulder at the bar where Jesus stood polishing a glass and watching us. Fernando looked that way as well, then picked up one of the unused napkins from our table and wiped his damp forehead.

"It's nothing, Detective." He shook his head as though trying to convince himself of the truth of what he was saying.

Both Casey and I stood and we each took out some money to pay for our meal. "No, no, no, I told you, I pay for your meal today."

Casey reached over and put her hand on his shoulder. "We appreciate the thought, Mr. Cordoba, but with the investigation into the rape still going on, it wouldn't be such a good idea for us to take advantage of your very generous offer."

As I said before, Fernando is a very savvy businessman, and when he realized what Casey was saying, he smiled and backed up with his hands in the air. "I didn't mean it as a bribe, Detective. I was just…"

I laid a ten-dollar bill on the table. "Don't worry about it, Nando. We know you were just being a good host." I stepped up to him, turned my back on the bar and spoke in a low voice, "When does Justíno come in next?"

Once more he glanced over his shoulder, then answered quietly, "He was supposed to come in two days ago. Nobody's been able to find him."

"So how am I supposed to find him then?"

He shrugged and held my gaze for longer than necessary. "I think it's very important that you talk to him, Detective Wolfe." With that he turned to head back into the kitchen.

I grabbed his arm and stopped him. "How can I find him?"

He pulled a piece of paper out of his shirt pocket and handed it to me, then turned once again and walked into the kitchen.

As Casey and I walked out into the bright sunlit day, she pulled out her sunglasses and put them on. "Justíno?"

We climbed back into the car and headed back to the station. "I don't know much about him, really, or why we need to talk to him. Celia interrupted us when Fernando was telling me about him. All I know is when I asked him if he had any more information about the rape, he said I should talk to Justíno." I took the piece of paper out of my pocket, read the number and then took out my phone and called dispatch. When my friend Shirley answered I asked her to see if she could find Justíno's address from the phone number Fernando had given me.

When she gave me the information, I relayed the address to Casey who made a u-turn and drove to the far west side of town. The little house we pulled up to had seen better days. Nothing but weeds were growing in the flowerbeds, and the two mesquite trees standing sentinel in the front yard were sorely in need of a good soaking. A sad looking pit bull sat inside the chain link fence surrounding the back yard. He was leaning against the wire looking like he'd lost his best friend. I walked over to him and squatted down on my haunches, not really sure of the reception I'd get when I approached. Big yellow eyes stared out at me from a broad, scar lined face and when he leaned his head against the fence and whined, I reached a tentative finger through the chain link to scratch his ear.

He leaned hard into my finger while his tail thumped a sad couple of times in the dirt. Before I knew what was happening, Casey had opened the gate and was heading for the empty water bowl that sat under a spigot by the side of the house. "Um, Case, don't you think you might ask whoever owns the house before you charge into their backyard?"

"Whatever asshole owns the house should probably make sure their dog has plenty of water to drink." As soon as the water hit the bowl, the pit bull trotted over and started lapping it up. Casey turned angry eyes on me. I knew that look, and heaven help the dog's owner when she lit into them for not taking care of such a sweet pup. She came back outside the fence and pulled the gate closed. "C'mon. Let's go find Justíno and see who owns this dog."

We made our way through the weeds to the cement walkway that stretched from the sidewalk to the front door. We both stood on either side of the door and Casey rang the bell. I didn't hear anything so I pointed to the ringer. "I don't think it works." She knocked on the door several times while I walked to the windows to see if I could get a look inside. "Uh oh."

Casey came over to the window and cupped her hand to the glass to block the glare. "Damn." Blood spattered the walls in several places around the room. Two recliner chairs lay on their sides, one with the footstool still in the extended position and there was a gaping hole in the back wall that looked like a shotgun blast had been fired through it. "I guess we know why that pup doesn't have any water. I'm willing to bet he hasn't eaten in a while either." Leave it to Casey to find a possible homicide scene and be more worried about the animal at the home than the likely victim.

I walked back to the door and ripped a piece of paper out of the notebook I kept in my pocket. Carefully folding the paper around the doorknob, I gently turned it to see if it was unlocked. It wasn't. It's usually not like in the movies where the cops come to a door that's been left partially opened or unlocked. "I'm going around to check the back door. Do you want to call Kate and tell her what we have?"

Casey pulled her phone out of her back pants pocket. "Sure. Let me know what you find, and if it's open, wait for me."

I rolled my eyes. "Yes, mother." When I reached the back gate I rattled it to make sure the pit bull knew I was coming. He was sitting next to his water bowl and when he heard the gate, he walked over and wagged his tail. I slipped through the opening and was careful not to let him out. I'd never hear the end of it from Casey if I did. "Hey, Buddy. I just need to go to the back door, okay? There's a good pup." He trotted along beside me as I made my way around the corner of the house and located the rear door. Just for good measure I knocked hard and yelled. "Tucson Police. Anybody home?"

When no one responded, I used the same piece of paper I'd used earlier and tried the back door. It was locked was well. When I looked through the window in the door, I noticed a slight breeze blowing out a curtain over the sink. Most of these older homes use swamp coolers to keep the temperatures down and it's a common practice to open a window a tiny amount to pull the air from the air handler and circulate it throughout the house. Luck was finally on my side. The window gave a little when I pushed up on the sash, so I pulled out my radio and called Casey.

"9david72 to 73."

"9david73 go ahead."

"I have a window open in the back yard. I'll wait for you here."

"10-4."

While I waited, I knelt down, which caused the dog to slide to the ground and roll over onto his back, exposing his belly. I scratched it while he wiggled under my hand asking for more. Casey appeared around the side of the house carrying half of yesterday's sandwich she'd never gotten around to eating. She knelt beside us and offered the dog her baloney and cheese on sourdough. He very gently took the sandwich from her hand and then wolfed it down in two bites. Casey petted him on his head. "I'll make sure you get more food a little later, okay?"

I stood but before we went inside I wanted to know what the boss had to say. "What'd Kate say she wanted us to do?"

Casey pushed to a standing position and wiped some dirt off her knees. "She said to go in and do a welfare check to make sure there was no one still inside who might need the paramedics. I told her from the way things looked that's not very likely. She said to go in anyway, so, you ready?"

"Yup." I notified dispatch that we were going to do a welfare check inside the house, then slipped my fingers under the window sash and pushed up until I could crawl inside. The dishes in the sink had been there a while. I reached in and moved them from the sink to the countertop and then bent my leg at the knee so Casey could give me a boost in. As I came through the window, I hoisted myself up onto the front of the sink and went in belly first. When I pulled my leg in and tried to move forward, my belt loop caught on the faucet handle and water began pouring into the sink and splashing up onto my clothes. "Shit!"

I less than gracefully pulled myself the rest of the way into the kitchen and rolled off the countertop, luckily landing on my feet instead of on my face. I could hear Casey chuckling outside and angrily grabbed the handle to shut off the flow of water cascading into the sink. "I should make you come in through the damn window. In fact..." I shut up when I heard a noise deeper in the house.

The kitchen door was across the room, and I quickly drew my Glock and started in its direction. Before I got two steps, I heard the sound again and froze in place. There was an opening on the left side of the kitchen that appeared to open up into the living room. Moving to unlock the back door to let Casey in would put me right in the line of fire of whoever was still in the house and I wasn't eager for that to happen.

When Casey saw me draw my weapon, she wasted no time in diving through the window and propelling herself across the sink. Rolling into a perfect somersault, she landed sprawled on the floor at my feet. I stepped in front of her to make it impossible for anyone shooting from the living room to hit her while she quickly gained her feet and drew her own sidearm.

We both moved to the side of the entry and I hugged the wall to the right where I could see into the left side of the room. Casey took up a position behind me. It looked clear so I took the lead. "Moving."

Casey answered. "Moving."

I moved into the room and cleared right, Casey followed and covered left. I immediately said, "Clear." The first thing I saw was a hallway and I let her know what I had. "Hallway." There is no safe way to clear a hallway, which is tactically known as a funnel of death. If one person comes out of a room down a hallway armed with an automatic weapon, there's no cover for the officers. We both took up a position on either side of the opening and I moved around my corner using a technique called slicing the pie. I slowly stepped further and further around the corner until I could see that there was no one actually standing in the hallway.

"Clear." We both started making our way down the narrow passage. When we came to the first open door, I went in and cleared the room while Casey remained at the door guarding the rest of the hall. We did this to two other rooms, constantly talking to each other as we moved deeper into the home. There was blood everywhere, smeared against walls and puddled in various places around the rooms. There was however, no body.

Unlike with the rest of the rooms, the door at the end of the hall was closed. I heard movement inside and once again announced our presence. "Tucson Police. Come out slowly with your hands empty and where we can see them." When no one responded, I moved to the side with the doorknob and Casey took the side with the hinges. I looked at her and when she signaled she was ready, I turned the knob and threw open the door. She immediately moved inside and cleared right and I followed and covered left.

Both of us very nearly shot the big tabby cat that stood arched in the corner of the room hissing. I knelt and checked under the bed, then nodded toward the closet. I stood in front and when Casey opened the door I quickly discovered it was empty. "Clear." I looked back where we had just come, then holstered my weapon. "Did you see a body in any of the rooms?"

Shaking her head, she retreated back through the house to see if we had missed anything on our way through. I got on the radio. "9D72, the house is clear."

Kate came on the radio. "9D70 to 72. What do you have?"

I didn't want to announce to the world what we had, so I told her I'd call her. "I'll 21 you." When she answered the phone, I filled her in on what we'd found.

After she'd heard everything I had to say, she had a few questions of her own. "Casey told me that the bar owner, Fernando Cabrera, said he thought you should talk to this Justíno. Why didn't Mr. Cabrera mention anything about him to the detectives who interviewed him the night of the rape?"

"I don't know. I think he wanted to tell me, but he seemed really nervous. He didn't even want his daughter to know that he was telling me anything. I'm going to have to try to talk to him when there's no one else around. I don't think we'll get anything if we confront him at his bar."

"Casey also told me that a man named Rodolfo Aguilar and his brother Enrique came in. What do you know about them?"

I thought back to my conversation with Chuck. "Not much really. I talked to Chuck who confirmed what Casey had said about the guy being in the Mara 18 gang from L.A. and El Salvador. He's a real bad ass. I don't know why he was in the bar, but I'm gonna find out."

"No, actually, you're not. Gail Redfox and Ruthanne are on their way to relieve you two right now. They should be there shortly. Once you give them all your info, I want you to head back to the station. This is their case, Alex, not ours."

She hung up before I could argue with her. I knew it was their case, and I hadn't intended to get involved until Casey had dragged me along to the bar. But now it was personal. I hadn't known Jason, and I trusted Ruthanne to sort everything out. However, I'd known Fernando for a lot of years and I didn't intend to just leave him hanging in the breeze. If this Mara 18 asshole was threatening him or his family in any way, I intended to find out and put a stop to it one way or another.

CHAPTER 10

When Casey and I got back to the office, Craig was at my desk waiting for me. I shot a puzzled glance at Kate as I passed her cubicle, then walked the rest of the way to where he was sitting in my chair talking on my phone. He saw me approaching and held up a finger telling me to wait a second. I didn't have much choice since he occupied the only chair in the immediate vicinity. I set my briefcase down and returned to the front of the office to pick up any mail that had been left for me in the cubbyholes hanging from the wall next to the secretaries' desks.

I glanced through several supplements, then grabbed some candy out of the plastic M&M man's tray and returned to my desk. Craig was just getting off the phone. He jumped up and motioned to my chair. "Here you go, Alex. Kate was nice enough to let me borrow your phone while you were away."

"That's fine. Have you found out any more about, well, you know?"

He reached up and ran a hand through his hair. "Not much. How about you, did you learn any more about the Lithuanians than I did from the hotel clerk?"

I looked back at Kate who was busy with another detective. I didn't want to brief Craig without her being there, not because I didn't trust him, I just didn't want to have to go through the whole story twice, plus, Kate had said she wanted this kept quiet, and talking about it in the middle of a bullpen full of detectives was definitely not how to keep things on the low down. He must have realized his mistake because he began glancing around the room to see if anyone had overheard him. The only one who appeared to be listening was Nate. He raised his eyebrows, not sure why I was glaring at him so pointedly. I stepped over to his desk and spoke quietly so no one else would notice. "Is there something you need?"

His flush told me he knew he shouldn't have been eavesdropping. "No, I'm waiting for Hank to get back from lunch and was wondering what some strange guy was doing sitting at your desk. I was just kind of curious when you came back and didn't take his head off for using your phone and chair." He leaned forward and spoke into his hand so no one could see what he was saying. "He was kinda poking through some of your stuff. File folders mostly. I don't know what he was looking for, but it seemed a little strange. I didn't stop him because Kate didn't seem upset that he was sitting there, but it just didn't seem like he should be doing that, ya know?"

I clenched my jaw, trying but not succeeding to control my temper. What the hell was Craig doing going through the stuff on my desk? I nodded at Nate. "Thanks, I owe you one."

He nodded. "Always got your back, Alex. You know that."

When I looked back at Kate's cubicle, the other detective was gone. There are times when I have a quick temper, and this just happened to be one of those times. I headed into her cubicle and leaned over her desk. I spoke quietly so only she could hear me. "What the fuck is he doing going through the shit on my desk?"

Kate stood and leaned towards me. "I don't think that's exactly how you meant to say that." If she'd been a dog her hackles would have been standing on end. "Sit down."

I glared at her a second, then reined in my growing temper and sat. That didn't last long. I stood up again and she canted her head sideways. Sparks flew from her eyes when she ground out one word. "Sit."

I took a deep breath, let it out slowly and sat. I knew closing my eyes and breathing would help clear my mind, so I did. When I opened them again, Kate was sitting down as well, and Craig stood leaning against the opening to her cubicle. He looked down at me. "Something wrong? I didn't think you'd mind if I used your phone."

I opened my mouth to spit some venomous words in his direction but Kate stopped me with an upraised hand. "Alex seems to think you were going through some of the papers on her desk, but I'm sure she's mistaken. I can't imagine you'd break my trust like that."

"Going through her stuff? Where does that come from? I was using her phone and may have been absentmindedly pushing some papers around, but that's it. I wasn't going through anything." Craig had worked enough undercover to be able to do a quick song and dance without seeming the least bit worried. Luckily, Kate had been playing in that same arena for a very long time as well. "There are no files on the Angelino family on or in her desk. She is not now, and never has investigated them for any criminal activity."

I enjoyed when Kate made people splutter, and I thoroughly enjoyed watching Craig do it now. His eyebrows rose into his hairline and his mouth was working but nothing intelligible came out. When he barked out a quick laugh, I knew that what Nate had seen wasn't just someone absentmindedly pushing some papers around on a desk. I stood up and faced him. "Why are you really helping us anyway?" I looked back at Kate. "And what's this about the Angelinos?"

By this time Casey had walked over with Nate not far behind. Craig turned to look at them, then held his hands out to his sides. "C'mon, Kate. You know me better than that. I came to help you out. I'm not CIA anymore and getting the goods on Gia Angelino is the farthest thing from my mind. The only thing I'm interested in is helping to gather information on the people who attacked Alex. Period."

The room was silent for a minute. No one said anything until the lieutenant walked in and saw all of us standing around Kate's desk. He turned to Kate and indicated the rest of us with a flick of his hand. "You guys come up with anything new on the people who tried to grab Alex?"

Kate shook her head. "No, but this is an old friend of mine," She put the emphasis on the word friend, "Craig Stafford, who is retired

CIA. His specialty is Eastern European organized crime. I called him to see if he could shed any light on what's been going on in Tucson that might account for them trying to grab her. Craig, this is Lieutenant Lake."

The lieutenant and Craig shook hands. "Any help you can give us would be great. Kate, would you and Craig come to my office and fill me in on the latest? I have a briefing with the Captain in about an hour and I need to know everything you've got so far."

Kate nodded. "I'll be there in a second." The lieutenant and Craig disappeared into his office while Casey and I sat in the two chairs in Kate's cubicle. She took her seat behind her desk and steepled her fingers in front of her chin. "If I had known he'd be rifling through your stuff, I never would have let him sit there. I'm sorry about that."

I shrugged. "I don't have any secrets so it's not that I'm worried about what he might have seen. I'm just pissed that he actually had the audacity to go through my stuff."

Kate smiled. "I think audacity is one of the prerequisites for joining the CIA. If you don't have it, don't apply." She sat back. "Now, did you two find out anything I should know before I brief the L.T?"

Casey let out a big sigh. "Well, other than what we found at Justino's house, the only new information we have is something you probably already know. The clerk said he'd given the info to Craig so I assume Craig passed it along to you."

I hadn't been with Casey for a lot of the time she'd been talking to the clerk, and we hadn't had a lot of time afterwards to discuss what she'd learned. Kate tapped her chin with her steepled fingers and nodded. "He probably did but why don't you tell me just in case."

Details are the butter to Casey's bread. She listens to every word said and follows up on every small bit of information someone gives her. "Remember Craig told us that a man went to the hotel last night and gathered up all of the belongings that had been left in the room?"

Kate nodded and Casey continued. "The clerk said that about two hours later, two people drove up to the room in a black, older model SUV. He said it was the same SUV the people in the room had been driving when they first checked in." She flipped through her notebook.

"He gave me the license plate. I ran it and it came back to a local rental agency. I haven't had a chance to follow up on who rented the car, but my guess is the guy's name will end up being Walt Whitman or Clark Kent."

Both Kate and I nodded in agreement. Casey gathered her thoughts a second. "What was strange was that when the two men in the vehicle got out and went into the room, they were joking and patting each other on the back. One of the men was that guy who only has one ear. You know about him, right?"

I looked over to Kate who slowly shook her head. "No, I don't believe I do. Where does he come into the picture?" Surprisingly, Kate looked to me for the answer.

I raised my eyebrows. "What?"

Kate shrugged and leaned forward, resting her forearms on her desk. "You never mentioned that one of the people in the alley only had one ear. That's a piece of information I wouldn't expect you to leave out of your report."

Obviously, since I hadn't seen anyone with one ear, I couldn't have reported on it, but I decided maybe I shouldn't put it to her in quite that way. "The clerk at the hotel said one of the six people who checked in that night only had one ear. He also said the guy had a scar running from where his ear should have been down to the bottom of his jaw. That could have been one of the guys who jumped over the fence at the end of the alley, but I didn't get a good look at either one of them. Maybe Ruthanne or Nate saw something like that when they were chasing them."

The familiar tapping started and I glanced down at the pen Kate was bouncing on her desk. After a few seconds she pulled a small square of paper from a stack she kept on the corner of her desk and wrote something on it. She picked up the note and handed it to me. "See if you can find a mug shot of this man." She tapped the paper in my hands. "He's someone I arrested several years ago for raping a six year old child. The little girl's father got to him a few minutes before I got there and had already started carving the guy up. The father had already flushed the ear down the toilet, so there was no way to reattach it. Take the mug shot back to the hotel and see if the clerk identifies him as the man who checked in with the other five people." She turned her attention back to Casey. "Go on."

Casey sat forward and rested her forearms on her knees. "The guy said the two men were laughing on the way in, but a few seconds later they rushed out of the room. He described the guy with the one ear as extremely pissed off, and the other man as scared. He said the second guy kept looking all around the parking lot as he ran to the passenger side of the SUV and jumped in. The SUV then fishtailed out of the lot at a high rate of speed."

It occurred to me that if Craig was any kind of detective, he would have remembered the clerk giving him that kind of information. I stared over my shoulder at the lieutenant's closed office door wondering why he hadn't mentioned that little detail to Kate when he'd briefed her. I heard Kate tapping again and swiveled back around to face her. She was staring at the closed door too. When I turned, her gaze slid over to me. There was very little doubt in my mind that she was thinking exactly what I was thinking, but instead of saying anything about it, she rose from her chair and came around her desk on her way to her meeting with Craig and the Lieutenant. She motioned to the paper I was holding. "It's late and that can wait until the morning. Let me know what you find." With that she turned and strode down the aisle towards the lieutenant's office.

Casey shifted in her chair so she could face me straight on. "Alex, what the hell is going on here?"

"I wish I knew." Both Casey and I returned to our desks to gather up our belongings before heading for home. I stole another M&M on the way out and popped it into my mouth, savoring the chocolate candy while my mind worked overtime trying to sort through everything we had learned in the last few days.

CHAPTER 11

My two dogs joyously met me at my front door with slobber from Tessa and straight up jumps in the air from Jynx. I quickly found Tessa's Kong, hurried into the kitchen and pulled out my family sized jar of peanut butter. I grabbed a knife and pulled out a huge gob of the sticky stuff, which I unceremoniously stuffed into the hard rubber opening. Unfortunately, the routine caused Tessa's incessant licking to become ten times more disgusting as her salivary glands kicked into overtime. I tossed the Kong into the corner where she happily retrieved it and holed up in the corner of my living room where I'd placed a bunch of old, worn out towels for her to lie on.

With that nightly task complete, I picked up Jynx, my Papillion Chihuahua mix and carried him with me into the bedroom where I knew he hid his favorite squeaky toy from Tessa who had the annoying habit of tearing the squeaker out of every one of Jynx's stuffed animals. I got down on my hands and knees and retrieved his blue bunny, squeezing it a few times to make sure its squeaker was still intact. Jynx grabbed the bunny out of my hand and leapt from my arms onto my bed where he happily began chomping down on bunny's tummy to listen to his most favorite sound in the whole wide world.

With those two chores done I was finally able to strip my holster and badge off my belt and pull my TPD polo shirt over my head. I stepped out of my Dockers, gathered up the rest of my clothes littering the floor and headed for the washing machine in nothing but my bra and panties. I shoved the clothes in, slammed the door, added detergent and just as I pushed the start button the doorbell rang. Megan was supposed to stop by for dinner so I walked into the living room and called out, "Come on in, the door's not locked."

When the door swung open, I'm sure the shocked look on Gia's face mirrored my own. Gabe, who was standing behind Gia looking over her shoulder, smiled appreciatively, the dimple he kept reserved for special occasions appearing impishly as he slowly turned and headed back down the walkway to go sit in the Jag. Gia turned and watched him go and I took the opportunity to run into my bedroom and grab a pair of sweat pants and an old green pullover sweater I keep stashed under my pillow in case I get cold in the middle of the night.

Returning to the living room I glanced around expecting to find Gia waiting for me on the sofa. What I didn't expect was to see her running her perfectly manicured finger over the bottles of alcohol I had stashed in a baker's table my mom had given me several Christmases ago. My mother may drive me crazy a lot of the time, but one attribute I love about her is the ability to recognize and buy quality items, whether they be jewelry, furniture, clothing or anything else for that matter. She had bought this particular piece in Provence, France. Since I didn't remember what types of alcohol I had, I walked over to take a look. "I don't have any expensive stuff, but you're welcome to anything I do have."

Stepping back a couple paces, she was able to see the entire table. "This is a wonderful old piece of furniture. I don't remember seeing it the last time I was here."

I loved the old baker's table and I was inordinately pleased that she did as well. "It was at my mom's house until last August. She had it shipped over from France about two years ago. I didn't want to ruin it by bringing it here and maybe, I don't know, maybe breaking it or something." I glanced around the room at my other rather old and shabby furnishings.

She turned amused eyes on me. "So what made you finally bring it here?"

I shrugged, a little embarrassed at what my decorating looked like compared to hers. "Honestly? I read something that Erma Bombeck wrote before she died. She said, 'If I had my life to live over again, I would have burned the pink candle sculpted like a rose before it melted in storage.'" Okay, I'd just embarrassed myself for the second time in five minutes. I could feel the blood rushing into my cheeks so I walked up to the baker's table, knelt down in front of the cubbyholes under the tabletop and pretended to study the bottles.

Gia stepped up beside me and ran her hand across the aged wooden panel of one of the drawers above the wine rack. "Do you see how old the patina is on all the wood? That gray coloring is what many designers try for on a lot of custom built cabinetry these days."

Since I didn't see much custom built cabinetry in the types of houses I visited while breaking up family fights or arresting the local neighborhood scumbag, I decided to nod as though I knew what she was talking about. She knelt down beside me, pointing to various places on the wood. "Look here." Her gaze traveled over the finish until she found what she was looking for. "And here. Do you see those holes? Do you know what they're from?"

I'd never noticed the holes before and wondered if they were a flaw in the design. "I don't know, do you think whoever owned this piece over in France messed it up or something? You know, knocked into it with something sharp." I reached over and felt the hole. "Damn, I never saw those before. I wonder if my mom noticed them before she bought the dang thing and had it shipped half way around the world."

Gia laughed and swiveled toward me. She put her hand on my shoulder and held my gaze for a second. "Alex, you are so unpretentious. It's such a breath of fresh air for me to be able to talk to someone who's not trying to impress me with their knowledge or," She pinched the shoulder of my sweater, "who can surprise me by asking me to open her front door while she's standing there in her orange and green geodesic underwear and bra."

Now I definitely felt the blood rushing up into my face and knew from previous experience my chin, cheeks and forehead were in the process of turning a bright, exotic shade of crimson. To save myself further embarrassment, I pulled a bottle out of the wine rack and read the hand printed label. "Pitorro. Here's a homemade flavored Rum Megan smuggled in from Puerto Rico. I guess it's their equivalent of moonshine. You want to try it?" I stood up and headed into the kitchen without waiting for an answer. I really just wanted a few minutes to get my glowing face under control.

Gia followed me in and took a seat at the table. I pulled two plastic glasses out of the dishwasher and grabbed a can of coke from the fridge. While I was mixing the rum and coke, Gia quietly watched me. After a few minutes, she continued her lesson about the baker's table. "About those two holes I pointed out? They aren't flaws. In fact, I'm sure those particular pieces of wood were chosen specifically because of the holes. You see, I don't think the baker's table itself is all that old, but it was made from extremely old barn wood, possibly from wood that was milled two or three hundred years ago. Those are the old nail holes. Did you notice they were square instead of round?"

I turned to look at her. "Huh uh. Am I supposed to put ice cubes in rum and coke?"

"I'll just have two cubes, please.

I poured two fingers of Rum into both of our glasses, then decided I could really use some help relaxing and added a little extra to mine. I added the ice and coke, then set her glass on the table in front of her and put mine down as well. "Let's see. We need some snacks or I'll be on the floor under the table after about two sips." I rummaged around in my mostly empty cupboard looking for something edible.

I'd completely forgotten about Megan until I heard the front door swing open and watched as Sugar bounded into the kitchen. Megan called out from the living room. "Alex! Did you know Gabe's sitting in front of your house scowling at anybody who drives up or walks past your house? He's such a hotty, he can plow my field any day of the..." As she walked into the kitchen she caught sight of Gia and lost every bit of color in her face. "Uh, hi Gia..." She quickly walked over to the bottle of rum, grabbed a glass out of the dishwasher and poured herself a generous amount. She added what looked to me like about four fingers of rum and very little coke. She raised the glass to us in a toast and took a big swig.

The color and smile immediately returned to her face until she heard something out in the living room. "Shit! The pizza! Tessa don't you dare!!!" She ran back out into the living room and returned carrying a large flat box. "Thank God. I thought it was a goner." She plopped the box down, grabbed some paper plates and tossed them onto the table next to the pizza.

Gia watched the whole scenario while resting her forehead on the tips of her fingers. She looked a little tired as she pulled a paper plate close, opened the pizza box and selected a slice. I took another sip of rum then did the same. Megan had ordered ham and pineapple, which was her favorite combo. I liked it all right, but it was an acquired taste and I wasn't sure Gia had acquired it yet. "Is ham and pineapple okay for you?"

Picking up her slice, Gia examined it before taking a tentative bite. As she chewed, a surprised expression flitted across her face. "Not bad. I've never tasted it before. In fact, I rarely eat pizza. My chef is more of an epicurean elitist and if he knew I was sitting here with a paper plate eating a slice of pizza without the benefit of a fork and knife I think he might return to his post as a master instructor at Le Cordon Bleu." She thought about that a moment. "Until he received his first paycheck I would imagine. Then I think he'd be back at my door, toque in hand."

I'd never heard that word before. "Toque?"

Megan, who was still standing next to the counter, picked up my roll of paper towels and placed it on her head. "You know, those huge white hats chefs wear."

I smiled at her antics. "Ah, got ya."

She put the towels back onto the neck of my bronze paper towel holding giraffe, picked up her cup and joined us at the table. Since I hadn't invited Gia and she hadn't called to let me know she was coming, I was curious as to what had brought her here. Even though I was glad Megan had shown up with food since I didn't have much on hand, I kind of wished she had waited another fifteen minutes to arrive so I could have had the time to find out from Gia what had brought her out on a chilly Thursday night.

Gia took a tentative sip of her rum and coke, raised her eyebrows slightly, then gingerly set the cup back on the table. Megan piped up. "Whaddya think? My cowboy and I took a cruise from Puerto Rico. We sailed around the islands and then back to the Isle of Enchantment as they call it. We met a guy who lived there, and he took us on a hike to the El Yunque National Rain Forrest. We went swimming underneath a recessed waterfall, and then he took us to this old man's hut. Boy was that place a dive."

She took another sip, then stared into the clear plastic cup. Reaching back, she grabbed the bottle off the counter and set it on the table. "Do you see how clear it is? This old man made his own rum. He took me out and showed me his sugar cane field. He grew it and crushed it, cooked it. I mean, he did everything." She looked over at me and I knew she was wondering if she was babbling too much. I was interested in her story and motioned for her to continue. She pushed the bottle toward Gia. "You see the label? See that x there? I think that was the only letter he knew how to write because when I asked him to sign the bottle, that's all he did. The old guy had a great set of teeth, but when I started choking on a mouthful of his rum, he laughed so hard both the uppers and lowers flew out of his mouth!"

We all had a good laugh at the old man's expense, and then Megan took a last bite of her pizza, broke the crust into three pieces and tossed one to each of the dogs. Sugar caught hers mid air and daintily chewed her piece, Jynx let it fall to the ground before grabbing it and running under the table to protect it from the other two, and Tessa, well, the piece conked her on the head and fell to the floor. She glanced around with a puzzled expression until she saw the crust lying on the ground at her feet. She pounced on it, which sent it skittering across the floor straight into Sugar's sphere of influence. When Tessa bounced over to claim her prize, Sugar simply covered it with her paw, then lay down to wait until Tessa got bored or forgot what she'd come for.

Gia chuckled and called Tessa over to her. "Here you go. You can have mine." When she held her crust out, Tessa smelled it, took it from Gia's fingers and disappeared into the living room. I knew exactly where she was going with it. "You know that's gonna end up under my pillow, right?"

Megan picked up a paper plate. "I'll take some pizza to Gabe. He's probably hungry sitting out there. Why doesn't he ever come in with you anyway?"

Gia simply nodded. "I'm sure Gabe would appreciate a slice. Thank you, Megan." Once Megan had gone, I sat and waited, hoping Gia would tell me why she'd come. She took another sip, then glanced up at me with a serious glint in her eyes. "I understand you're working with Craig Stafford."

"What? How did you know that?" I shook my head. "Never mind. Stupid question. So what if I am?" I stared at her, wondering where she was going with this.

"I also understand he and Kate are old friends."

Not wanting to discuss anything about Kate or work, I sat quietly waiting for her to get to the point. She reached into a pocket, pulled out her cigar case and studied it for a minute. Without looking at me, she said, "My father and Craig's father were friends." She raised her gaze until her eyes met mine. "Ask him about his father sometime."

Not being able to put together all the puzzle pieces had had me on edge all day and I spoke with a little more venom than I intended. "Why don't you just tell me about him instead of being so cryptic? I swear, the last few days have been full of nothing but riddles and confusing incidents that may or may not be connected, and honestly? You figure into just about every incident in one way or another. What's going on, Gia?" I suddenly remembered a question I needed to ask. "And by the way, why did William Silverton bond out that Lithuanians who tried to grab me?"

"Did he?"

I angrily pushed back from the table. "Damn it, Gia! Don't play games with me. What's going on?"

I should know better than to get angry with Gia because she always responds in kind. The only difference was, her angry was usually quiet and cold. "All right, Alex. You want to know why William bonded him out? Because there's a lot going on right now that you know nothing about. Do you really think them trying to kidnap you was random? I sent a message to some people with that man, or with part of him anyway. That message said no one touches anyone I deal with. Do you want to know more or does that give you an idea of why you should probably mind your own business?"

I jumped out of my chair. "Gia! What the hell?" I hoped she wasn't saying what I thought she was saying. "And those kids? The teens and their mother, or their so-called mother? What about them? What did you do to them?"

Megan chose that minute to walk into the kitchen. "Alex! Don't talk to her like that." She reached over and picked up my cup. "Here, have another drink and relax."

I pushed the drink away and glared at Gia whose hackles were definitely raised. "We put the three of them on a plane back to Lithuania."

Megan watched both of us a second, then gave a valiant try at changing the subject. "How's Shelley doing? I haven't seen her lately."

Gia's gray eyes flashed a cold message to me before she turned to answer Megan. "My niece is fine, thank you. I've sent her away for a while."

"Where?"

Megan's innocent smile stole a little of Gia's thunder and her demeanor softened somewhat. "Somewhere safe."

There was something not quite right with the way she'd said that. "Why safe? What's wrong?"

She let out a long sigh. "Nothing I can't handle, Alex. You just make sure you think before you do or say anything, and right now, you need to listen to everything Kate says, does, or doesn't do. There have been very few cops I trust and fewer who have the instinct to know when to back off and when to go for the jugular." She lowered her chin and continued to glare through upturned eyes. "Unlike me on the other hand. I always go for the jugular."

Megan giggled nervously. It was a habit of hers that could get out of hand depending on her level of fear or on her level of inebriation. I knew Gia scared her, so in deference to our friendship I made myself relax. I motioned to her chair before taking a slice of pizza and placing it on her plate. "C'mon. I don't know why things got so serious all of a sudden. How can that happen when we're eating pizza and drinking smuggled in homemade rum?"

Gia nodded and smiled at Megan. "Please sit back down and eat, Megan. I have a meeting I have to attend in about a half an hour so I really must be going. Thank you for the pineapple and ham." She slipped her cigar case back into her pocket, then stood and pushed her chair in under the table. "Walk me to the door, Alex." When I didn't move, she softened her tone. "Please."

I got up and followed her through the kitchen door and into my living room. I stepped ahead of her and pulled open the front door. When I looked out I saw Gabe immediately get out of the driver's seat and walk towards us, buttoning his suit coat on the way. Since I hadn't been outside when Gia arrived, I hadn't noticed the two black cars parked at either end of my street. I quickly turned to Gia. "Are those cars with you or..."

She put her hand on my arm. "Yes, they're with me. Alex, listen to me when I say you need to pay attention to Kate. There's a lot of experience there, and..." She hesitated. "And just keep very aware of your surroundings for a while, okay?"

I nodded. For once, when I shot Gabe a half smile, he didn't respond. He seemed too preoccupied with his surroundings and I wasn't even sure he'd seen me. When Gia stepped outside and began walking to the Jag, he stayed slightly in front of her, which was curious because I'd only ever known him to walk slightly behind. Was he shielding her, and if he was, what had changed so drastically that she needed him plus, two other bodyguards to keep her safe?

I shut and locked the door, then did something I've never done before within the confines of my own home. I walked into my bedroom, picked up my Glock and shoved it into the back of my pants. I wasn't sure what was going on, but if Gabe was nervous, and I'd never known the man to break a sweat, then so was I.

Megan was standing at the sink when I walked in. I thought she was rinsing some dishes, but when I approached, I saw she was staring at something out the window. I scanned the part of the backyard that was illuminated by my exterior lights. There was nothing unusual that I could see. "What are you looking at?"

Meg reached up and pulled down the blinds. "There was someone out there. He had on a suit like Gabe, so I guess he was with Gia?"

I stepped over and shut off the both the kitchen and the backyard light. When my eyes had adjusted, I lifted the blind slightly and once more studied the yard. There was enough of a moon to let me see the areas that had been in darkness beyond the illumination of my porch light. No one was in my yard and I assumed they had left when Gabe had driven away with Gia. "It looks like whoever was there is gone now, and I, for one, would just like to take the pizza and rum, pop in a movie and relax for the rest of the night."

CHAPTER 12

Megan had gone home around ten and since I was already wearing my pajamas—maroon sweat pants and green sweater—I climbed into bed and quickly felt myself drifting off to sleep. I'm not sure exactly what awakened me, but as I came out of the fog of a deep sleep, I had the unshakable feeling that something was wrong. I reached over and felt the pillow where Tessa usually slept but she was gone. Still not too alarmed, I searched under my covers with my feet trying to find Jynx. Normally, that would be a no brainer since Jynx slept curled in the concave warmth directly behind my bent knees. He wasn't there either.

"Tessa? Jynx?" I heard the fwap, fwap, fwap of Tessa's tail, however that was apparently as far as she was willing to go to acknowledge me. "Tessa come here." The tail thumped on the floor again, but she definitely wasn't coming. Now I was getting pissed. Not only had something unknown awakened me but add to that the fact that my dogs were being weird was enough for me to reach over to the lamp on my nightstand and flip it on. "Shit!" I jumped straight up and landed flat-footed on top of my pillows looking around frantically for my Glock.

Mr. Myung spoke quietly. "Your weapon is where you left it, there on the table next to your lamp." He was slowly rocking in my rocking chair with Jynx in his lap and Tessa at his feet.

I looked down. He was right, the gun was exactly where I kept it every night, sitting within easy reach if I ever needed to grab it in the dark. The only problem was, Mr. Myung had startled me so badly I was now standing on top of my pillows and the gun was no longer within comfortable reach. Usually with me, anger comes after a fright, and now was no exception. "What the hell are you doing in my house? In my bedroom for Christ's sake!"

He calmly stroked Jynx between his bat-sized ears. "My apologies if I frightened you. I find that recently, I must move within the shadows or, most certainly, become consumed by them." He stopped rocking and Tessa, the little turncoat, laid her head adoringly in his lap. "Much has happened since we last met. I have discovered a string stretching from you to Yeomra, and with him in control of the strands of your life, you must be prepared for the evil that always follows. I believe it is time for you to learn a small portion of my grandfather's skills."

It was hard enough waking out of a sound sleep to find a man sitting in my chair, let alone try to decipher what he'd just said. I climbed off my mattress and sat on the side of my bed. "Okay." I rubbed my head while I tried to clear my thoughts. "Who's Yeomra?" I thought maybe he was one of the leaders of the Korean mafia he was chasing.

"Yeomra is the king of the underworld."

"Uh huh." I glanced over at my Glock, wondering if Mr. Myung was a few shrimp short of a wanton.

"I have come to teach you two strikes and two defensive moves, if you would learn. There is no time for more." He sighed. "There is no time for two strikes, but...." With that, he set Jynx on the floor, stood and walked out the door into my living room. I stared at the doorway considering my options. I could follow him. I could call Kate. I could kick him out, or I could grab my Glock and hold him until patrol arrived.

"Come here."

Warily, I stepped up to the door and peered through. Mr. Myung had moved all of my furniture to the sides of the room, leaving an empty circle in the middle. He stood there now, relaxed and patiently waiting. I stepped into the room and joined him. He bowed, and held the position until it dawned on me that I was supposed to do the same. Slightly embarrassed, I sketched a quick bow. The amused look on his face when he straightened helped relax me a little. "We begin."

Taking my right hand, he shaped it into a thumb over fingers fist and tapped the first two knuckles. "This is the striking surface you will use for now." He stood to my side and bent my arm at the elbow, then positioned my fist palm up at my waist. "You will strike just so." He held his fist at his waist, palm up, then slowly extended his arm forward, twisting it as he moved so that when he finished his arm was held straight out with his hand in a palm down position.

"Now you." He motioned for me to try the punch, which I did. "Again." I pulled my arm back to my waist and punched again. He adjusted my hand position and kicked my back leg so that I was standing on a more stable platform. "Again." He had me repeat the move over and over until the muscles of my arm were on fire. Then he had me start all over again with my other hand. The entire time, he walked around me correcting my shoulders, my stance, sometimes making no more than a tiny correction before motioning for me to continue the strike. "Your target is not on your opponent's body. It is past." He stopped a moment, trying to come up with the correct word. "It is beyond his body. You strike through what your target would normally be. Let the energy of your motion carry out into the universe without stopping. Strike here." He punched my stomach with straight fingers, right below my ribcage.

"Ooof." He'd knocked the wind out of me with just two fingers.

When I straightened, he stepped to the side. "If you are to his side, strike here." Thankfully he just tapped the side of my neck. "Hit here, and your opponent will fall." I nodded. Exhaustion was creeping in, and I hoped we were nearly done with the lesson. He slipped off his shoes. "Now, the second strike." When I moaned he tapped my temple. "Control your mind. Your body is not tired unless your mind tells your body that it is so." He knelt and ran his finger along the outer edge of my foot. "Your second striking surface." He stood, then brought his foot up level with his hips. He kicked straight out, turning his foot so that it was parallel to the ground at the end of the strike.

All the while we were working on my strikes and kicks, I couldn't help but wonder what the heck I was doing with Mr. Myung in my living room at four in the morning. Actually, we'd started at two, and now it was five and almost time for me to get up and get ready for work. It was still dark by the time he called it quits. "You must constantly practice your strikes. As you pass a wall, strike. A tree, strike. You must harden your knuckles." He showed me his hands, which seemed to be one big knuckle callous.

I absently rubbed the back of my head. "Punch a wall? How do I do that without breaking my knuckles?

Walking to where he was within striking distance of my wall, he motioned for me to join him. "Begin slowly, just so." His fist struck out and barely grazed the wall. "As you become more proficient, strike harder. Your hand will harden as you practice."

As I punched the wall a few times to get the hang of it, Mr. Myung again adjusted my stance. When I had finished I turned to study his face. "Why are we doing this? There's no way I'll learn in a few days what took you sixty years to perfect."

There was a glint in his eye as he answered my question. "I believe even a kernel of knowledge is more powerful than complete ignorance."

"Ignorance? We have defensive training every year. They teach punching and pressure point manipulation, that kind of stuff."

"Do you practice daily?"

I shook my head.

"Do you hit your opponent like this?" He lifted his fist to shoulder height and punched like a boxer. When I nodded, he asked. "And how many of your officers who punch in this way have come away with fractures in the hand?"

I thought back to several of my friends who'd been in fistfights and who'd had to have surgery to repair the metacarpal bones in their hand. "I think they call it a boxer's fracture. Well, actually, I went with an officer to the emergency room once and the E.R. doc called it a brawler's fracture. He said the term boxer's fracture was a misnomer because boxer's don't usually break those bones, but brawlers do." I hesitated before asking the million-dollar question. "So, what do you know that I don't? I'd like to know where you see the danger coming from."

"I only see shadows and dark mist. A word here, a person where they shouldn't be or a glance that lingers a moment too long."

I stepped back a pace. "Have you been following me?"

He shook his head. "I know only when our paths cross. Unfortunately, they cross with greater regularity than I would like. So I will come to you in the shadows each morning and provide you with a small kernel that may someday give you the balance needed to remain on this side of the veil."

There was more behind those dark, intense eyes than what he was saying but I decided to let it go. Worrying about trouble never stopped the trouble from happening so I put it out of my mind. "Have you located your granddaughter yet?"

His expression darkened. "I have not, but there are signs that she is not far away. I will find her and bring her home with the help of my ancestral gods."

I smiled. "I'll be glad to help too. You call me if the gods need a hand, okay?"

He didn't return my smile. Instead, he bowed politely and let himself out through my kitchen door.

CHAPTER 13

Just as I stepped out of the shower, my phone rang with Ruthanne's ringtone—Toby Keith and Willie Nelson singing *Whiskey For My Men And Beer For My Horses*. I grabbed a towel and dripped my way into the bedroom to retrieve my cell. "Good Mornin', Darlin."

"Aw Alex, you are such a tease. Hey, I just called Casey who said she's good with meeting Gail and I at Fernando's bar. How 'bout you?"

"Sure, when?"

"Now, if you can."

"I need to get dressed and then I'll meet you guys there. Order coffee for me, will ya?" I yawned as she promised she would and hung up. I pulled into the lot just as Casey was getting out of her car and the two of us walked in together. Ruthanne and Gail were already seated at a table. Ruthanne had a plate full of machaca and eggs in front of her and Gail was using a tortilla to scoop up some refried beans.

Celia came to heat up their coffee and take our order. "Good morning, Detectives. Do you already know what you want to order? The special this morning is machaca and eggs."

Casey loved machaca, which is beef that's been marinated, cooked, shredded and dried. Once the meat is cooked, the chef adds onions, garlic, jalapeños, bell peppers, tomatoes and various spices to create an exceptionally mouth-watering treat. Casey ordered a breakfast burro full of machaca, potatoes and refried beans. Today, the simple idea of rice and refried beans with a flour tortilla appealed to me so I ordered that and thanked Ruthanne for ordering me a cup of coffee with extra caffeine. Celia chuckled at the order. "And just how much extra caffeine do you need this morning, Detective Alex? Were you out late partying last night?"

I shook my head, smiling back at her with what I hoped would be a rueful expression. "I wish. No, a friend and I stayed home, ate pizza and watched The Maltese Falcon. We've seen it so many times we can quote the dialogue before the character even thinks about saying it."

Celia's face lit up. "I love Humphrey Bogart. Every Saturday night my Tata and I used to rent a movie starring one of the old movie legends, either Humphrey Bogart or Katherine Hepburn, or someone like that. He and I would also go to the library and check out biographies, you know, like *Mommy Dearest*, or, um, Veronica Lake's autobiography, stuff like that."

Ruthanne pointed at Celia with her fork. "Wasn't *Mommy Dearest* about Joan Crawford?"

Celia nodded. "Oh, sí. Somebody like that makes most people's moms look like saints." She hesitated, obviously realizing who she was talking to. "Well, most regular moms, probably not the ones you guys have to deal with all the time."

We all nodded. I'm sure each of us was thinking about some of the more brutal child abuse or child homicide cases we'd had over the years. Celia tucked her note pad into the front pocket of her smock. "Anyway, Detective Alex, do you know this line… 'We didn't exactly believe your story, Miss O'Shaunessy.'"

I'd never heard Bogart quoted with a Mexican accent before, but I tried for my best Bogy lisp and finished what she'd started. "'We believed your two hundred dollars…I mean, you paid us more than if you'd been telling us the truth, and enough more to make it all right.'"

Everybody laughed at my exaggerated accent and Celia took off to put in our order. Once she'd left, Casey got right down to business.

"Why are we eating here? I'd think if we wanted to discuss Jason's case we'd want a more private location."

Gail pinched some beans into her tortilla. "I know. But so far, nobody's talking to us. The only even tiny bit of information we got out of here came from you guys asking around, so we thought we'd see if we could give you some of our questions and you two could see if you can get anyone to answer them."

Casey motioned to me with a flick of her fingers. "Alex got all the info about Justíno when she spoke to Fernando. I got zip." She made a circle with her thumb and forefinger.

My nerves were already on edge after Gia's visit the night before and Mr. Myung's lessons this morning. The thought of trying to squeeze some more information out of Fernando didn't help. I rubbed my forehead, pushing my thumb into my temple to try to loosen the muscles. Celia returned with two coffee cups and the carafe. She heated up Ruthanne and Gail's cups after filling the two empty ones.

I grabbed some packets of sweetener and poured a liberal amount of creamer into the steaming cup. After Celia went back into the kitchen, I asked, "What did you find out about Justíno? Are we looking for a corpse or just somebody who got the shit beat out of him?"

Gail shrugged. "We're not sure. We've checked all the call records. No one has been dispatched to that address for about a year. Last year, Justíno was the victim of a domestic. His then girlfriend beat the crap out of him with one of those cast iron skillets. We located her and she hasn't seen him or heard from him since she got out of jail six months ago."

Ruthanne picked up the story while Gail ate. "We checked all the hospitals and the morgue. He hasn't been to any of them, and honestly, we don't even really know how he fits into all this. Do you have any idea why Fernando said you should talk to him?"

I shook my head. "No, and I don't think he'll tell me while we're anywhere near this place. He was pretty nervous yesterday when I was talking to him." I glanced around the bar. Fernando's was a popular breakfast place on the south side because he served traditional Mexican food, but he didn't charge as much as most of the other places. He once told me he'd rather have his neighbors and friends come to a place they can afford than have a bunch of rich people he didn't know coming in. "Is he even here today?"

Ruthanne nodded. "Yeah, he came out of the kitchen when we first got here. He didn't seem particularly worried to me, but then again, what do I know?"

"So other than the obvious questions about Justíno and why we need to talk to him, what else do you want me to find out?"

Gail popped the bit of tortilla she was holding into her mouth and pulled a notepad from the briefcase at her feet. She flipped a few pages before finding what she was looking for. "For starters, I need to know who this lady named Gloria is who placed the original 911 call. She didn't give the 911 operator her last name and was gone when Arnold arrived to take the original report."

I nodded and filed the name Gloria in the back of my mind for future reference. Gail continued, "Second, I know the victim isn't a regular here, but the bartender said he'd seen her around on occasion. He couldn't remember who she'd come in with in the past, but I got the feeling he was holding back. We asked Carmen, but when I showed her a picture of the lady, she said she'd never seen her before. And third, what the hell was Jason doing here? Granted, he's a body builder who, from everything I've been able to gather, doesn't," She held up her fingers in little quotes. "look gay. But still, no self respecting gay man would ever come here." She took another bite, then spoke around the food in her mouth. "Especially at night."

Both Casey and Ruthanne nodded at that. Personally, I'd never paid much attention to whether there'd been gay men or lesbians in the bar whenever Megan and I had come in, but I don't usually make those kinds of distinctions anyway so I wouldn't be looking in the first place. "Have you asked Marcos why Jason was here?"

Ruthanne nodded. "He insists Jason was with him the night of the rape, and since he is Jason's alibi, I don't think he'll ever change that story."

I looked over at the bar. It hadn't opened yet so Jesus wasn't anywhere to be found. When Celia returned with the plates of food for me and Casey, I caught her attention. "Hey, Celia. What time does Chuey come in today?"

She blew out a long breath as she looked into the distance, apparently trying to see the employee schedules with her minds eye. "Let's see, this is Friday so I'm pretty sure he comes in a little early to make sure the weekend delivery has arrived and he has all the stuff he needs. I'm thinking he gets here around eleven." She nodded to herself. "Yeah, I think around eleven. Why? Do you need to talk to him?"

I shrugged. "Maybe."

Gail flipped through her notebook, then stared up at Celia with a puzzled look on her face. "Has anybody talked to you yet about the night of the rape?" Celia slowly shook her head and Gail continued. "Is there somewhere we could go where I could ask you a few questions?"

Celia turned to me with a beseeching look. I could tell she didn't want to talk to Gail, but I also saw that she knew something about that night. I moved my foot under the table until it rested on top of Gail's shoe. She glanced up at me but knew enough not to say anything. I reached over and tapped her empty tortilla plate. "Dang, Gail, you've still got beans but nothing to scoop 'em with. How tragic is that?"

Gail laughed and Celia hurried off to get her some more tortillas. When she was gone, Gail motioned towards me with her chin. "You think she'll be more willing to talk if it's just the two of you?"

I shrugged. "Maybe, but I think you and I should pay her a visit someplace other than here. Not her home, but someplace neutral and safe. Let me think about it for a minute, okay?"

When Celia returned with the hot plate full of warm, buttered tortillas, Gail thanked her profusely and dug into her beans with a relish. Celia took the opportunity to quickly head over to another table to serve some other guests.

When I'd finished my meal, I pushed my chair back and stood. "I'm gonna to go say hello to Fernando. I'll be right back." On the way to the kitchen, I glanced around the room to see if I recognized any of the patrons seated at the other tables. No one looked familiar, but one woman caught my eye and quickly glanced away. I wasn't sure what that was all about. I filed it away for future reference and stepped through the swinging door that led into the kitchen. Fernando stood at a chopping block mincing what looked to me to be an enormous amount of garlic. He already had a large bowl three quarters of the way filled and there was still a large pile of freshly peeled cloves waiting to be minced.

"Ah, Detective Wolfe, Celia told me you'd returned this morning to enjoy our hospitality. Please forgive me for not welcoming you properly, but without Justíno here to help with the food preparation all of the work falls to me and Carmen or Celia." He lifted an elbow to indicate Carmen who was stirring a heavy pot on the stove. "If Carmen is out serving, Celia cooks, if Celia is out, well, as you can see, Carmen stirs the pots."

"Wait a minute. Justíno's your chef? For some reason I thought he helped out with the bar."

Silence filled the little kitchen except for Fernando's chopping. I tried to catch Carmen's attention, but she studiously stirred her pot and refused to look at me. "Carmen, I understand you didn't work the night of the rape, is that right?" I almost missed the small headshake she gave me for an answer. "So do you know who was here that night? Who worked?" She shook her head again.

Fernando continued chopping steadily with his knife. "I've already given Detective Redfox the schedule of who worked that night. You can ask her if you need that information."

I picked a tortilla chip out of a bowl on the counter and took a small bite. "Hey Nando. I have a question for you. What happens if a gay guy comes in here? Does that happen very often?"

Carmen snorted and Fernando shushed her with a scowl. "You have to understand, Detective Wolfe, in my culture, the men are macho." He beat his chest with the fist that was holding the knife. "Many of the Mexicans who come in here are hard men." He resumed his garlic chopping. "Me? I have a little brother who lives with another man." He looked up at me and smiled. "And honestly? I like his boyfriend better than I like my own flesh and blood, can you believe that? But here, at the bar, my customers are macho men who treat gay men very badly. If I see or hear it, I stop it, but mostly I'm here in the kitchen and don't see it, so, gay people, they mostly don't come."

I heard the back door open behind me, and when Carmen muttered, "Dios mío." I turned and came face to face with Rodolfo Aguilar. We stared at each other, both of us sizing the other one up, me wondering if I could take him in a fight, him probably wondering if he could kill me and get away with it. Fernando had stopped chopping and was standing in a way that made me wonder if he thought he could protect Carmen from the viper who'd just slithered his way into the kitchen.

Little brother Enrique came through the door next with a toothpick hanging out of his mouth. He rolled it back and forth across his bottom lip using only his tongue, his little rat eyes flicking from person to person as he gazed at each one of us in turn.

Carmen began backing toward the large freezer directly behind her. Her movement seemed to break the spell holding all of us in its grip. In an instant, the viper reached behind his back and the rat lunged toward Fernando who instinctively brought his chef's knife up into a defensive position. As soon as I saw the viper reach behind his back, I drew my Glock—luckily I was quicker than he was—and yelled, "Freeze, Rodolfo or you're a dead man!"

He froze, not moving a muscle except for a slight movement of his upper lip. It seemed to curl upwards, not into any type of smile but more like a slow motion tic that drew the flesh away from his teeth one tiny bit at a time. Fernando had backed up enough that Enrique hadn't been able to grab him. The rat stood between Rodolfo and Fernando clenching and unclenching his fists.

A half a second later the door to the dining area slammed open and Casey, Ruthanne, and Gail all poured in with weapons drawn. Even with the three women surging in and moving into position, Rodolfo's eyes never moved away from mine. He'd turned to stone, his malevolence searing into my soul with a malignancy unlike anything I'd ever experienced before. I can't explain it, but I felt as if the personification of evil was standing in front of me dragging me down into the pits of hell.

Casey spoke from somewhere off to my left. "If there's a gun in that hand behind your back, drop it now." When Rodolfo didn't move, Ruthanne stepped around the chopping table, grabbed Fernando by the back of his shirt and tried to pull him and Carmen out into the bar.

Fernando lowered his knife. His voice shook slightly when he spoke to her. "No, no, it's okay. It's all a misunderstanding, Detectives. These..." He fumbled around for the right word, "...friends stop by many times." He took a step forward. "Rodolfo, por favor, No hay ningún daño."

Gail spoke up then. "That's right, there's no harm done. Just turn around so we can see what's behind your back. Then we'll talk." Slowly, the viper uncoiled. He brought his arm down to his side and we could see that he wasn't holding a weapon. "Okay, now, lift your shirt and turn around." When he turned we saw he had a semi-automatic handgun tucked into his the waistband of his pants. Since the rest of us all had our guns pointed at his back, Casey holstered her weapon, moved forward and took control of the gun. She then put him into handcuffs while Gail patted down Enrique.

When she found a small handgun tucked into the upper part of one of his boots, she handcuffed him as well. I holstered my weapon and listened while Ruthanne got on the radio and called for a patrol officer to come transport them down to the main station. Both of them were not only convicted felons illegally carrying firearms, but they'd snuck back into the country illegally and I was sure Chuck would be more than happy to send them packing again. Heaven forbid the court system hold them accountable for any of the above-mentioned crimes they'd committed.

Casey and Gail took the two men outside to wait while Ruthanne and I tried to talk to Fernando and Carmen. Neither of them wanted to talk and honestly, with a bar full of people wanting their breakfast, this wasn't exactly the most opportune time to get any information out of them. I signaled to Ruthanne to go wait outside and when she left I pulled up a stool and sat next to the chopping table where Fernando had resumed his decimation of the garlic cloves.

Neither of us spoke for a while. I thought I'd just wait a little to see if Fernando would offer up something on his own. Carmen had also returned to her pots. Out of the corner of my eye I saw her reach up and brush a tear off her cheek. When she realized I had seen what she'd done, her face crumpled and she covered her mouth with her other hand. "Tell her, Fernando. You have to tell her."

He stopped chopping and carefully set the knife on the chopping block. After a big sigh, he said, "I have worked hard my whole life, Detective Wolfe. Never did I believe..." He shook his head sadly.

While I waited for him to tell what Carmen thought I should know, Celia came hurrying into the kitchen carrying a tray full of dirty dishes. She set the tray on the counter and unloaded everything into the sink, then turned to face us. "When all the commotion happened in here, everybody asked for their checks and left."

My patience was wearing pretty thin and I thought it was time to take the plunge. "Okay, you guys. There's something going on here and I can't help you if you don't tell me what you know. So... here's a list of questions. You can pipe in with the answers anytime. One." I held up one finger. "Why are Rodolfo and his brother hanging around here? Two." My second finger joined the first. "Who the hell's Gloria? Three." I put up a third finger and then held my hands out to my side. "What the hell happened to Justíno?"

Celia angrily walked up to me and rested her hands on her hips. "You think we don't talk to you because we don't want to? Those two men you just took are killers. And they come from una familia de killers, so don't think just because you take them away that we are now safe to talk to you." She motioned toward the Glock on my hip. "We don't have guns we carry around, even though sometimes I think we should."

Fernando walked over and put his arm around Celia's shoulders. "My daughter is frightened, Detective Wolfe, or she wouldn't speak to you in this way. We know what you found when you went to talk to Justíno yesterday. We don't know where he is. He's my nephew, and we have many, many people out looking for him."

I pointed out the back door. "Do you think Rudolfo and his brother had something to do with his disappearance?" All three immediately shook their head.

Fernando dismissed the idea with a wave of his hand. "Rudolfo is un demonio encarnado pero he's one we know how to live with. Please, stop asking us questions about the rape. It happened, it's over."

"What does that mean, he's un....whatever it was you called him."

"Demonio encarnado." He tried several times to translate the words into English before giving up and looking to Celia for help.

Celia shook her head. "I don't know the words. It means...a demon walking the earth...?" She seemed to be asking me if that's what it meant and I had no idea. Once again I held my hands out to my sides to show I really didn't understand

"It means evil incarnate." Gail strode into the kitchen from the back alley where she'd been waiting for a patrol car to arrive. "And I agree with you one hundred percent, Fernando. When I stand next to him..." She shuddered and glanced at the door she'd just come in. "My grandfather, Eagle Who Calls, was a tribal shaman. He walked the spirit world with the ancestors of our tribe. His spirit guide was a shy coyote and the two of them roamed the spirit realm asking questions and returning with answers that, many times my people didn't know needed to be asked." She smiled at the memories and Carmen nodded with understanding.

I didn't know Gail Redfox very well, but I'd heard Ruthanne talk about the wonderful stories she'd tell on some of their longer stakeouts. She was a natural born storyteller, and I was interested to see where she was going with this particular tale.

She acknowledged Carmen's encouragement with a nod of her own. "There were many times that I sat with Eagle Who Calls as he walked with his friend the shy coyote. One time, we sat next to the campfire. My grandfather was swaying and chanting, completely unaware of the physical world around him. As I sat staring into the fire, I felt a blackness descend on our campsite and I watched as a vile, obscene being formed within the smoke of our fire."

Carmen crossed herself while Gail continued. "Grandfather went into convulsions. I couldn't move and I watched as that cloud of evil swept toward me." She stopped and shook herself as though trying to get the image out of her mind.

Celia whispered, "What happened to you? What happened to your grandfather?"

I watched as Gail kept shaking her head back and forth in a slow, wide motion. Finally she seemed to gather herself. After taking in a deep breath and letting it out slowly she said, "He died. My grandfather died that night." She looked over at me. "I know it doesn't sound like something a professional law enforcement officer would say or believe, but I think he died because he was wrestling that demon to keep it away from me. Just before the smoke got to me, I saw a vision of a coyote leaping into the swirling mist, and then the evil was gone, but so was Eagle Who Calls." She let out a guttural sigh. "Anyway, when I stand next to Rudolfo, I see that image in the smoke, and I know the same spirit my grandfather wrestled with that night inhabits that demonio encarnado standing outside right now in handcuffs. That's why I had to come inside for a few minutes."

She seemed a little abashed and I wasn't sure what to say. That was a really strange story, but in a funny way, I knew exactly what she was talking about because I'd felt that same thing when Rudolfo was staring at me. We were silent for a while until Gail pulled her notebook and pen out of her back pocket. "Anyway, I'm not really sure why you guys are giving us the run around, but somebody here must know something about what happened the other night."

Fernando started to speak but Gail held up her hand. "I know, I know, we need to talk to Justíno, but we can't find him, he may be dead for all we know, and unlike my grandfather, I can't walk the spirit world looking for him."

No one offered any information so Gail continued to press. "Here's an easy question. Who is Gloria?"

Fernando glanced back at Carmen and Celia elbowed him in the ribs. He immediately turned back, but not before I saw the guilt flit across Carmen's face. I stepped over to the stove and put my hand on hers to still her frantic stirring. "Carmen, who is Gloria?"

A tear slid down her cheek. She quickly reached up to wipe it off. It was obvious she had more information than she was letting on and I waited quietly, wanting to let her know I wasn't going anywhere until she told us what we needed to know. After a long pause, she spoke so quietly I wasn't sure I'd heard her correctly. "I am."

I blinked several times trying to make sense of what she'd just said. "You? You made the 911 call that night?" Another tear appeared and I put my fingers under her chin so that I could look into her eyes. "Carmen, you know you're not in any trouble, right?"

She covered her eyes and began weeping, and I looked around with what I'm sure was a perplexed expression on my face. Gail walked over to put her arm around Carmen's shoulders and led her out into the empty bar so they could speak in private. Celia glared at me as she walked to the stove, picked up the spoon and took up stirring where Carmen had left off. "Papa, you'd better call Arny to come into work. It's almost time for the lunch crowd and now we're missing both Justíno and Carmen."

Fernando obediently took out his cell phone. He walked a short distance away and began calling in his employees. I studied Celia a minute. "So you guys honestly don't know what happened to Justíno? Do you at least know what your dad thought he could tell me?"

"No, I don't. Now if you don't mind, it's almost lunchtime."

I could tell I wasn't going to get any more information from anyone in the restaurant, not at this time of day anyway. At least we'd found out who Gloria was. When I stepped outside, Casey was loading Ratman into the back of a patrol car. Apparently Rudolfo had already been taken away because Ruthanne was on her cellphone and it sounded like she was letting Chuck know the two of them were on their way to the station. When she finished, the three of us wandered back into the bar area where our cold food awaited us at our table.

Casey pulled out her wallet and dropped a ten near her plate. Ruthanne and I did the same, then we all went back outside to regroup and wait for Gail. As we stepped into the brisk, fall air, Ruthanne walked to her car and popped the trunk. She rummaged around in her bags for a second before finally emerging with a squeeze bottle of hand sanitizer. She offered some to us and we all diligently slathered the stuff all over our hands. Ruthanne checked her watch. "Do you know what Gail's up to? We have to be at a briefing on this case in forty minutes."

"Yeah, Carmen says she's the one who called 911."

"Carmen is Gloria?"

I nodded. "Apparently. Anyway, that's what they're in there talking about. I didn't find out very much more except that they don't have any idea where Justíno is. I did however find out he's Fernando's nephew and all three of them are adamant that neither Rudolfo nor his brother are responsible for his disappearance. For some reason, I don't quite buy that."

Casey wiped the remainder of the sanitizer on her pant leg. "Kate called while you were inside. She wants us to meet her back at the racetrack. Are you ready to go?"

"Yup." Just as I turned to walk to our car, a white Chrysler pulled into the lot.

Ruthanne turned her back to the car and muttered. "Great, Emery is here. Just what we need."

I watched Captain Emery get out of his vehicle, tuck in his already immaculately tucked in shirt, pull a rag out of his car, wipe down his shoes, and straighten his perfectly knotted tie. I'd never worked for the man, in fact I hardly knew him. As I watched him, I realized his movements and body type were slightly effeminate. He was in good physical shape except his butt was a little rounder than it should have been and his narrow shoulders lacked any vestige of a manly, muscular build. None of that mattered to me as long as he could carry himself in a fight and treated his officers fairly.

He was friendly enough when he walked over to greet us. "Casey, Alex, good to see you both."

Casey shook his hand. "It's good to see you too, Sir. Alex and I were just leaving." I nodded a greeting, then followed Casey to her car. The two of us climbed in and drove out of the parking lot.

"So, did Kate mention why we're going back to the track?"

"She says she's taking Leslie slash Otto back there to get him to clarify some of his story. She thinks having you there might put him off his game." She chuckled, "Actually what she said was, having you there could put anyone off their game if you're in top form."

I smiled and wondered exactly what she expected me to do. Leslie's moronic comments were simply his attempts to make himself look cool in other people's eyes, but I'd be happy to help Kate if she thought listening to him insult my mother's sexual habits would do any good. When we pulled into the racetrack parking lot, I was surprised to see several detective vehicles pulled up next to the burned out barn.

When I got out, I heard voices inside the stall where they'd found the body. I stuck my head around the corner and saw Kate standing in the center of the room listening intently to Leslie who was wind milling his arms as he spoke. I sighed and stepped into the room, mentally preparing myself for the insults that were sure to fly.

Leslie didn't disappoint. As soon as he turned and saw me standing in the doorway, his lip curled into the sneer I'd grown to know and love so well. He motioned towards me with his chin and spoke to Kate. "See, Sergeant, not all species cull their young when they're born, this Neanderthal throwback is a perfect example of that."

I'd always felt sorry for Leslie. I'd never wanted to return his insults with insults because he had such an abysmally low self-esteem. It wasn't like my repartee with Tucker Jordan, the big biker whose girlfriend had shot off half his balls. Tucker just communicated with people through good-natured insults and actually loved when people insulted him back. Leslie on the other hand tried to hurt people in the same way other people had hurt him. I looked to Kate to see exactly how I was supposed to respond or what it was she wanted me to do. She was watching Leslie instead of me and although I could tell she was aware of me looking at her, she never returned my gaze.

Even though I wasn't inclined to bully the man, or, boy man, I guess would be a better description of the guy, I did have relatively well developed skills for rubbing people the wrong way. "Leslie, it's so good to see you again."

"Otto!"

"Otto?

"My name, you meat wallet. My name is Otto."

I wrinkled my nose. "Meat wallet? That's gross, even for you, Les. How would you like it if I told your mother you were going around calling women a meat wallet? For that matter, does she know you're not Leslie anymore? She'd probably be pissed to know that after twenty-four years of being Leslie her son decided to change the name she gave him when he came into this world."

His coloring was naturally a light shade of pink, and anytime he became upset or agitated he turned a lovely garnet color. He opened his mouth to further insult me but Kate grabbed his arm to turn him away from me and refocus him on what they'd been talking about. She pointed to the back of the stall. "Okay, Otto, you said you saw them standing back here somewhere?"

Leslie rolled his head around on stiff shoulders. "Yeah, there somewhere." He made a sweeping motion with his hand.

"Show me exactly where you saw them."

"Here." He took two steps forward and distractedly pointed to the ground.

"So you saw the woman standing right here?"

"Yeah."

Kate's gaze sharpened. "What woman?"

Leslie swung his arms in a wide circle. "What do you mean what woman? The fucking woman!"

"You were telling me about two men you saw come in here."

"Wha—? No, I mean...I saw that big goon in here. The one who's always with that rich ass lady."

Crossing her arms, Kate used her silence to get him to keep talking. It looked to me like he was gathering his story together, so I thought I'd lend a hand. "So, Leslie, you saw a big goon who looked like a woman with a rich ass? Am I getting this all down correctly?" I took out my pen and notebook, licked the end of my pen and poised it on the paper as though ready to write.

He charged over to me. Since he was a good head shorter than I he had to crane his head up to get in my face. "Get the fuck out of here, Wolfe. This is between me and..."

Kate walked over and stepped in front of me, which wasn't easy since Leslie and I were practically chest-to-chest. She pushed in and bumped me back. I took a couple steps backward and waited. "Otto, focus here. What did you see?" Kate sounded a little miffed.

Leslie grabbed a fistful of his hair and turned away. "The lady! I, I mean the big guy." He growled. "They said, they said..."

Kate stepped around so they were facing each other again. "Who said? Who said what?"

He swung his head back and forth as though looking for someone. "The guys! The fuckin'— "

"What guys, Otto?"

I took a step forward. "Yeah, Leslie, what guys?"

He whirled on me. "There was a lady!" He swung his arms around again. "I mean, the guy who's always with the lady!"

I lowered my eyebrows into my serious face. "Right, the lady with the rich ass."

"You fuck head! You're trying to mess me up! You're trying to mess up what they told me to tell ya!"

Once more Kate stepped in front of him but this time she put her arm around his shoulder and turned him away from me. "Otto, be honest with me, okay? Forget about Detective Wolfe for a second, in fact…" She turned to me. "Why don't you just leave, Detective? You're not doing anything except causing problems."

I knew she was trying to gain his trust and I thought it would be more believable if I resisted a little. "But…"

Casey, who'd been standing in the door turned to leave. "C'mon, Alex. She's right." I sighed as I followed Casey out, then when we were both out of their line of sight, we turned and put our ears to the wall to listen to what was being said inside.

Obviously, Kate must not have believed the story Leslie had given the detectives back at the station so she'd brought him here to try to trip him up. She started talking to him in her soothing, motherly manner. "Otto, you never really saw anything happen in here did you?"

"I did!"

"Let me tell you what I think happened. I think some people either paid you to tell us your story, or they told you that you could be part of their gang if you just showed up here and lied to us. Am I right?"

We didn't hear Leslie's reply but we did hear the shift in Kate's voice once again. She'd gone from ally to accuser, and now her voice held the growl I'd come to associate with just plain pissed. "Who are they, Otto? And don't you even dare lie to me. Those men may let you into their little gang, but I'll bury you so deep inside the Cimarron unit of the state prison you'll forget what the light of day looks like."

Both Casey and I snorted quietly. Lying to a cop is a crime, but one that'll get you a slap on the wrist at most and a dismissal from the judge at best. Apparently Leslie believed her because the next thing we knew he was spilling his guts. He's basically a coward at heart, and anytime anyone snarls at him he rolls over and exposes his belly in a pathetic act of submission. "There were three people. I didn't see two of them very well 'cuz they stayed back behind me, and every time I tried to turn around to look at them the big guy'd choke me. He was holding my collar closed around my neck like this."

I snuck a peek through the opening between the door and the wall. He'd bunched up the collar of his jacket in front of his neck and he twisted it to show what the man had done. Kate wanted to keep him talking. "All right then, what did he look like?"

"Ah, he was cool. Mean lookin'. I bet nobody messes with him." His voice held pure admiration. I guess any self respecting coward would look up to someone other people feared.

"Can you be a little more descriptive? Mean looking doesn't help us a whole lot."

"He had huge arms, and tats all over the place. There was a really great scar running from here to here." Unfortunately, I couldn't see where he was pointing. "Oh yeah, his ear was gone. I mean just gone! It was so cool."

Casey and I exchanged surprised glances. I tried to remember where I'd recently heard about a man who was missing an ear. Casey spoke quietly, "The hotel clerk said one of the people who rented that room was missing an ear. There's our connection."

We walked back to the parking lot to wait for Kate to come out. I leaned up against the hood of our car and stared out at the oval racetrack off to the left. "I'm gonna go look at the track, wanna come?" I pushed off the car and started walking. Casey hurried to catch up.

"Why are we going to look at the track?"

I shrugged. "I have no idea. I thought it might help to take a look around, see if I see anything that just doesn't look right or that might give us some kind of clue as to what's really going on here." I glanced back at the cars near the barn. "I wonder where all the detectives are. I only saw Kate there. Oh and Nate over in the corner of the stall. Kate probably told him to stay close but out of the way."

"I was wondering that myself. Maybe they're still sifting the dry crap off of all the stuff we pulled out of the horseshit in the barns. It's amazing what people have thrown there over the years. Syringes, knives, condoms, old horseshoes. I heard Nate even found an old necklace buried in one of his stalls."

The breeze shifted and I caught a whiff of the acrid scent of burnt wood and wet manure. We ducked under the three rail fence that ran the circumference of the track and walked to the center of the infield. I looked up into the enclosed part of the grandstands where Megan and I had sat with Gia towards the end of the last racing season. Most of the time she'd invite us up and by the time we got there she'd be entertaining some muckety muck from the city. My gaze dropped to the ground level bleachers where I preferred to sit and watch the race.

Nothing seemed out of the ordinary and I swiveled around until I was facing west. I gazed out over the expanse of the parking lot toward the complex of barns where the fire had taken place. "What the..."

Casey turned to look. "What?"

I took off jogging back to the barns with Casey falling into step next to me. "Someone's on the roof of that third barn. You go to the left, I'll go right." I lightly pushed her with my left hand then veered off toward the right side of the barn where the circular horse walkers were cemented into the ground. I realized it was possible I had seen one of the other detectives up on the roof checking for evidence, but the quick glimpse I got of the person gave me the distinct impression they weren't wearing any type of clothes typically worn by TPD detectives.

There was a block wall connected to the side of the building and I took a running leap and grabbed the top of the wall. I swung my leg around over the top and not very gracefully managed to pull myself into a standing position. I'd just reached up to grab the edge of the roof when I heard running footsteps coming my way. I plastered myself as close to the wall as possible hoping the small roof overhang would conceal me long enough for the guy to commit to getting off the roof.

He must have lain down belly first because the first thing I saw inching over the edge was a worn pair of old hiking boots. Next came the legs covered in a pair of army fatigues and tucked into the waistband was an unholstered Ruger semi-automatic handgun. I heard another set of pounding feet on the roof and heard Casey call out "Stop! Police!" Now there was no doubt in my mind that I wasn't dealing with one of the other detectives. He began to let himself down off the roof, but as soon as his feet hit the top of the wall he saw me. Startled, his eyes snapped wide and he jerked back, flailing his arms as he tried to catch his balance.

He hit the ground hard and I jumped down on top of him. I was hoping the force of the landing would knock the air out of him or stun him until I could get his arm into an arm lock but he was having none of that. He immediately twisted and punched me on the side of my head with a very hard fist. Fortunately for me I'd landed in the perfect position to bring my knee straight up into his groin. I must have surprised him, because as my knee connected with his manhood he squealed like a little piglet and rolled over into a fetal position with both hands belatedly protecting the family jewels. I picked up his shirt and retrieved the Ruger.

Casey poked her head over the edge of the roof. "Damn, he's fast for such a big guy." My eye was already swelling, and as I glanced up at her I gingerly felt my cheekbone to see if there was any major damage. Casey eyed my face and shook her head. "You grabbed him all by yourself? Did you get a look at how big that guy is?"

Actually, all I'd seen were his boots and legs, but come to think of it, the legs had resembled small tree trunks as they'd slid over the edge of the roof. Casey jumped from the roof to the retaining wall and from there she joined me on the ground. I removed the magazine from the Ruger, cleared the chamber and then shoved the handgun into my waistband. Casey pulled one of the man's hands out from under him and I knelt down and did the same to the other. We handcuffed him and sat him up against the wall of the barn.

I checked his pockets and found a wallet containing fifty dollars in cash and a New Mexico driver's license. In a zippered pocket on the inside of his baseball jacket I pulled out a badge case. When I flipped it open I found a private investigator's badge and an I.D. card from non other than...you guessed it, Stafford Limited. Completely taken off guard, I studied the man's face while I turned the wallet toward Casey so she could see what I'd just found.

She'd been right, the man was big with a weight lifter's neck, a large, square shaped head with a military crew cut, thick eye ridges covered by hairy eyebrows and a strong, clean-shaven jawline. The man sat with his knees pulled up into his chest apparently still trying for some form of protection or comfort of his manly parts. I rechecked the pocket where I'd discovered the badge case and found his cellphone. While I continued searching the guy's pockets, Casey walked to the other end of the barn to find Kate.

If I'd been interested in building a case against this guy for something other than punching me in the face, I wouldn't have been scrolling through the list of contacts on his phone. For some reason, I was still harboring the illusion that this guy just might have stolen the I.D. from an employee of Craig's company. When I reached the S's, and saw Craig Stafford's name and number, I knew things had just taken a very strange turn.

His P.I. license identified him as Jerry Dhotis. I knelt down to talk to him. "You know you wouldn't be in handcuffs if you had just stopped when she ordered you to. Oh, and punching me wasn't such a good idea either."

I heard someone walking around on the roof so I wasn't too surprised when Kate leaned out over the edge. "There are binoculars and listening equipment up here. Bring him around to the front where I can talk to him."

I felt the rock hard muscles in his arm as I reached down to help him up. Once he was standing, I self-consciously felt the left side of my face where he'd clocked me. Usually bad guys are proud of getting in a punch on a cop, but his pinched lips and concerned look told me otherwise. I thought I'd give him the benefit of the doubt. "You pulled your punch, didn't you?"

He nodded. "Yeah, I never hit women but I didn't get a good look at you on the way down and when you jumped on me it was just a natural reaction. Sorry about that. I realized my mistake just a fraction of a second too late." He nodded to his genitals. "Didn't seem to phase you much though." He took a tentative step and I guessed he was testing to see how much damage had been done.

"Does it still hurt? I felt things squish down there when my knee landed."

He let out a soft groan as he took another step. "You don't need to remind me. I used to play football, and sometimes I think I should wear a cup to work, but you're the first person to ever get me there. I've always managed to block the kick." We made our way around to the front, me supporting his arm and him hobbling uncomfortably one slow step at a time.

Kate had climbed down by the time we arrived. She watched him hobbling and raised her eyebrows. "Did he hurt himself when he jumped off the roof?"

I squinted and shrugged. "Kind of."

She put her hand on my chin and turned my face to get a better look at my eye. "Did he do that?"

For whatever reason, I really didn't want to see this guy go to jail. "That kind of happened during the fall, too."

She held my gaze. "Uh huh."

Leslie chose that moment to stroll around the corner of the barn. The excited glint in his eye took in everything, the big man in handcuffs, the swelling to the side of my face, the equipment on the roof that Casey was handing down to another detective on the ground. Suddenly his gaze jerked back to my swollen cheek and a slow, triumphant smile spread across his face. "You always think you're so tough." He motioned toward the man standing beside me. "He showed you."

As usual, the first time he opened his mouth he managed to irritate someone he wanted to ingratiate himself to. Jerry growled low in his throat. "I shouldn't have hit her, you little pissant, and did it even occur to you that I'm standing here in handcuffs? Who the fuck do you think put me in these?"

Leslie visibly deflated right before our eyes. He'd always looked up to tough men, had always tried to be one and much to his chagrin, always failed miserably. I thought back to a conversation I'd had with him one day after I'd picked him up and dusted him off after a particularly nasty beating by some neighborhood thugs. I'd offered him a ride home, but he'd flat out refused. He'd said, "You're so fucking ignorant, Wolfe. They always hit people they're testing for gang membership. They want to know if I can take what they give out. Well I took it, and next time, I'm in."

I happened to know that the next time they saw him, they put him in the hospital. And the time after that they left him hanging on a fence bleeding out from a stab wound in his side. What had been childhood bullying when he'd been a kid had turned into a deadly game as an adult. The problem was, he'd never grown into an adult. He was still that soft, pudgy little boy who wanted desperately to be a tough guy, to fit in.

Kate called out to Nate who was leaning against the hood of his car. "Nate, would you take Otto home? Before you let him go, cite him for lying to a police officer and interfering with a police investigation." She had another thought. "And make sure you use his real name."

Nate waved his acknowledgement and Kate shooed Leslie over to Nate's car. She then turned to Jerry and gave him the once over. Motioning to a bench beside the door to one of the stalls, she barked an order. "Sit."

True to his military bearing, he immediately stepped to the bench and sat. Kate then walked me a short ways away so we could talk. "Casey says he works for Craig. Did he confirm that?"

"No, but he has Craig's phone number in his cell." She held out her hand. I fished his phone out of my pocket and handed it to her. She located Craig's number, pushed send and put it on speaker.

It rang three times before Craig picked up. "Hey Jer, how's everything going on your end?"

Kate ended the call and handed the phone back to me. She took in a long breath and let it out slowly. When she looked at me, I could tell the wheels were turning overtime. "You probably already figured out that Otto was lying to us."

"Actually, I never knew what he'd told the detectives. I could tell by the way the conversation went today that whatever it was he'd said hadn't been the truth."

She turned and watched as Nate's car left the parking lot. "At first he told them that he'd been cutting through the parking area when he'd seen a man matching the description of Ms. Angelino's bodyguard carrying a body into the barn. He said another guy joined him. They were in there a while, set the barn on fire, then ran out to their car carrying shovels and took off."

"Do you have an identification on the body yet? Is it Mr. Myung's granddaughter?"

Kate shook her head. "No identification, but I do know the body belongs to a male who was shot execution style through the back of the head. The coroner puts the time of death at a few months ago. He can't get more specific than that until some of the tests come back from the lab."

I absently stroked my puffy cheek while I thought about all the pieces we were trying to tie together. "Do you think Leslie's in danger from the thugs who set him up with the fake story? He's a jerk but I don't want him to end up a dead jerk."

Kate shook her head. "I don't think so. He did give us one piece of very important information though."

"He gave us the connection between the Lithuanians and the fire. I just can't quite figure out the connection between me and the fire, other than my friendship with Gia." I remembered something Gia had said during her visit. "She said I should listen to you."

Kate laughed. "Why does she think you should suddenly start now?"

"I don't know. She's worried about something. She sent Shelley away to someplace safe. She said to pay attention to you because you have a lot of experience, and because you know when to go for the jugular."

Her head whipped up and her suddenly laser sharp eyes bored a hole into mine. I didn't look away because her reaction had caught me off guard just as my words had obviously taken her by surprise. She glanced back at Jerry. "Did he tell you anything?"

"No."

"And you don't think we should arrest him, do you?" She was the sharpest woman I'd ever met. Nothing escaped her notice and she factored in each piece of information into every decision she made.

"No, I don't."

"Why not?"

"Well... I don't know. Something's telling me we shouldn't. I will if you want me to, but I'd rather not."

"Let me see his I.D." I handed over his New Mexico driver's

CREDO'S FIRE

license and his New Mexico P.I. license. She studied them, then walked over to where Casey was waiting next to Jerry. I followed along wondering what she had planned. She stood in front of him, arms crossed, glare fully set in place. By the way he respectfully lowered his eyes I knew he recognized rank and authority when he saw it. "You work for Craig Stafford." It was a statement rather than a question.

"Yes Ma'am."

"Why did he have you up on that roof spying on us?"

Jerry raised he is eyes until his gaze met hers. When he didn't answer, Kate cocked her head and thought for a moment. She held up the two identification cards. "Your licenses are from New Mexico, so why did Craig bring you here? I know he has private investigators working for him here who are licensed to practice in Arizona."

This time, instead of meeting her gaze he looked down at Casey's feet. Once again Kate used the silence to gather her thoughts. "He doesn't know you're here, does he?"

Jerry pursed his lips and remained silent. Kate motioned to Casey. "Take off his cuffs."

Casey hesitated a second. Her eyes met mine and she raised her eyebrows silently asking me if I was ready for anything. I nodded. Our little exchange didn't escape Kate's notice and she took a step forward. "Listen to me," She read his name off of his driver's license. "...Jerry, I want your word as a man of honor that you won't get violent and that you won't run. Do I have it?"

"Yes Ma'am."

Casey motioned for him to stand up and then stepped around behind him with her handcuff keys. Once the cuffs were removed, Jerry brought his hands around in front and massaged his wrists before once again sitting down on the bench. Most of the time when a suspect has big arms and wrists, the cuffs tend to fit a little tight. In fact, I've had times where I had to use flex ties connected together instead of handcuffs just so I could get them all the way around a big man's wrists.

My pocket began to vibrate. I pulled out Jerry's cellphone, looked at it and handed it to Kate. "It's Craig."

She took the phone from me, glanced at the caller I.D, then handed it to Jerry. "Answer it."

They stared at each other a few moments before Jerry reluctantly took the phone from her. He pushed send and Kate reached over and hit the speaker button.

"Yeah?"

"Hey Jer, we got disconnected. Everything okay?"

"Yeah, I'm driving through the Narbona Pass on Highway 134 following up on that lead we talked about. You know, between Gallup and Farmington? My reception's not good."

"What'd you need?"

"I know I wrote down that lady's name and date of birth you wanted me to track down, but I can't find it. I remembered she lived somewhere near the pass, but that's about it. Can you text it to me?"

"You got it. I'll see you when I get back to Albuquerque."

Jerry glanced up at Kate before he asked Craig the next question. "When do you think you'll be back?"

"I'm not sure. Not for a few weeks anyway. Hey, I gotta run. I'll text that info to you right now. See ya." Craig disconnected and Jerry held the phone out to Kate. She didn't take it and he lowered his hand into his lap.

The wind kicked up a little dust devil in the courtyard. The twirling mini tornado circled round and round picking up leaves and tiny bits of paper before settling back under the sprawling canopy of a desert mesquite. Kate took out a business card and handed it to Jerry. "I want to know everything. Understand?"

Jerry fingered the edges of the card before looking up at her. "Yes, Ma'am. I believe I do."

I was a firm believer in littering the world with my business cards as well. You never knew when somebody might have some information that just might break a case. I took out one of my cards and handed it to him as well. "Here, I don't need to know everything, but if you get something you think might interest me..." I shrugged. He nodded and added it to his wallet along with Kate's card.

Kate turned to Casey. Take the tape out of the recorder and give him back his equipment."

Casey did as she was told. Jerry stood up and took the equipment from her. "What about my weapon?"

Kate tipped her head toward me. "He had a weapon?"

I blushed a little. "I guess I forgot to mention that particular detail."

She held out her hand and I retrieved the semi-auto from my waistband under my jacket and the clip from my pocket. I gave them both to her. After checking the slide to make sure it was empty, Kate flicked ten rounds out of the magazine, put them in her pocket and handed him the weapon and empty clip. He rammed the clip into the receiver and shoved the gun into his pants, nodded to the three of us and headed out of the yard. He got into a blue older model Dodge Durango and drove off. The three of us watched him go. Kate put both hands on her eyes and rubbed them up and down, moving outward to massage her temples and forehead as well. "Okay, neither of you heard any of that conversation. Do you understand?"

Casey and I looked at each other and then nodded to Kate who continued. "You will discuss this incident with no one." She glared specifically at me and I held my hands out to my side.

"What? If you say it didn't happen, it didn't happen." I had enough stray ends swimming around in my head and if I didn't have to factor in yet another set of details that was just fine with me. "Have you figured out who the guy without the ear is?"

"No, I've been doing some research to try to figure out who he is. Someone is bound to remember a person as disfigured as he is unless..." She trailed off into her own thoughts as she walked back to her car. Casey and I followed her out to the parking lot. We watched her drive out of the parking area then got in our own car and headed to the station.

CHAPTER 14

When we reached the parking garage, I took out my keys and walked over to my car. "I'll see you tomorrow, Case. There's something I want to follow up on." She waved her keys at me and disappeared into the stairwell on her way up to our office.

I drove to the downtown library and walked up to the customer service desk. A woman with straight black hair and pointy glasses watched me as I approached. It never ceased to amaze me how fashion that I thought was ugly when my mom was young tended to come back into style. "Can I help you?"

"I hope so. Do you guys have any yearbooks from the local high schools around here somewhere?"

"We most certainly do." Her friendliness lifted my spirits and I found myself returning her cheerful grin. "If you go to the third floor and take a right out of the elevator you'll come to our reference section where we keep yearbooks, almanacs, biographical sources, resources like that."

"Thanks a lot." Her directions took me straight to the area I wanted. Kate had said Craig was an old friend of hers, and Gia said Craig's dad knew her dad, which meant Craig had probably grown up in Tucson. If he was an old friend of Kate's it was just possible they went to school together. I knew Kate went to Conahey High so I searched through row upon row of yearbooks until I found the section containing those books. I wasn't exactly sure how old Kate was, but I knew she'd been on the department twenty-eight years and that she'd joined as soon as she'd turned twenty-one.

Being the math whiz I am, I whipped out my fingers and subtracted twenty eight from the current year, two thousand twelve, and figured she'd joined the department in nineteen eighty-four. If she joined when she was twenty-one, she had probably graduated from high school three years before that. I ran my fingers over the spines of the yearbooks until I came to nineteen eighty-one. I pulled it out and took it to one of the tables in the middle of the stacks. Several books lay scattered on the surface and I pushed them aside as I sat down and opened the yearbook to the index in the back.

It suddenly occurred to me that I didn't have a clue what Kate's maiden name was. "Damn." I started at the beginning of the names and stopped at the first Katherine I came to. "Pages twenty-two, thirty, and thirty-eight." I flipped to page twenty-two and located Miss Katherine Cover who turned out to be African American. "Nope." I went back to the index and settled in for a long, boring session of yearbook perusal.

I struck out with Katherine Deveroux, Catherine Gates, Katherine Hines, and Cathy Justman. My shoulders were getting tight from bending over the pages so I sat back in my chair and stretched, trying to work out the kinks centered around the base of my neck. "There has got to be an easier way."

I knew her husband's name was Thom Brannigan, and I thought about looking through old newspapers to find their wedding announcement, but I really didn't want to spend all afternoon going through page after page of old papers. I decided to walk back downstairs and find my new friend at the service desk. I waited in line to talk to her, and when it was my turn I quickly explained what I needed. Her face lit up with enthusiasm. "Oh sure, we have most of the old newspapers scanned into our database now. It's pretty easy to do a name search. What name are you looking for? And you say you want to find a wedding record?"

"His name is Thom Brannigan, and yeah, I'd like to know who he married."

Her hands flew across the keyboard. Ok, I have a few records here for a Thom Brannigan. The first one is an announcement for a wedding that took place in two thousand six." She glanced at me over the top of her glasses. I shook my head and she returned her attention to the screen. "The next one is an obituary."

"Nope, he's not dead."

She mumbled to herself. "Then I guess they wouldn't have buried him. Let's see, do you have an estimate of what year we're looking for?"

"I think it would be somewhere between, maybe, nineteen eighty-one and nineteen ninety-one?"

She used the mouse to scroll further down on the screen. "Here's one. Thomas Alistair Brannigan to wed Katherine Jessup O'Shea, March twenty third, nineteen eighty seven."

"That's it!" A brilliant idea occurred to me while I stood there watching her search their database. "Are the yearbooks on file too?"

She made a little mewling noise and shook her head. "No, not yet. I'm so sorry."

She seemed genuinely upset that her database had disappointed me. I guess I never realized how seriously librarians take their work, but now that I think about it, why shouldn't they? I smiled to show her it wasn't an issue. "No worries. I found the yearbook I need up on the third floor. I'll go grab it and finish what I started. Thanks a lot for your help."

When I got back to the table I'd been using there was a homeless man sitting in my seat looking through my yearbook. I sat down opposite him and pointed at the book. "I was reading that. Would you mind if I finished what I started?"

The man glanced up, then went back to slowly turning pages one at a time. I didn't have time for this. I reached into my pocket, pulled out a five-dollar bill, held it between both hands and popped it open. A slow smile spread across his sunburned face. Deep wrinkles crisscrossed his cheeks and spread out in a starburst pattern at the edges of both eyes. His voice was the guttural creaking of someone who doesn't speak very often. "I seen you at the corner."

I shook my head. "What corner is that?"

"I sell papers, I seen you drive by."

Now that he mentioned it, I did remember him sitting next to the streetlight in the median of La Cholla and Orange Grove selling papers to the drivers who had the misfortune of landing at a red light before they made it through the intersection. I drive by there every morning on my way to work and if I get stopped I usually give him a buck without taking a paper just to help him out. "I've seen you. You're usually way out in the county. What brings you downtown?"

He ignored my question. "I saw you sittin' here, lookin' through this, made me think bout that guy."

"What guy?"

"Every mornin', couple a weeks now. Same guy comes by 'bout five cars b'hind you. Gray Ford, four doors. Cracked windshield."

I shrugged. "I'm pretty regular about when I leave for work. He probably is too."

He reached over and took the five, then got up and left. As he walked away I noticed various library patrons wrinkle their noses at the vaporous cloud of noxious odor surrounding him. It wasn't unusual for homeless guys to come into a library to get warm so I didn't think much about him being here, but I filed away his information just for the heck of it.

I hadn't noticed anyone following me, but then again I hadn't been looking either. I thought back to Gia's warning and Mr. Myung's cryptic visit and realized I hadn't really been taking it too seriously. There's a time for everything and I decided maybe now was a good time to amp up my observation skills and become a little more aware of my surroundings.

I pulled the yearbook toward me and opened it to the index again. It didn't take me long to locate Katie O'Shea. "Hmmm, I never thought of her as a Katie." In fact, the more I thought about it, I decided she was definitely not a Katie. So now I knew I had the correct year, or at least, since she was a senior in this book, it was one of four yearbooks where I might find Craig Stafford. I looked at the S's but he wasn't there. I went back and pulled out the previous three years. I got lucky and found him during their junior year where they were both members of the National Honor Society and were both involved in student government.

It was interesting that Craig had left the school after his junior year and yet he and Kate had remained friends for the last twenty-eight years. I was about to close the book when a name jumped out at me from the names under the student government group photo. The advisor for the student council was a teacher named Gabriel Stafford. I flipped to the list of teachers and found that Gabriel had not only taught civics, but had also been the varsity football coach that year. I was curious to find out a little bit more about Coach Gabriel Stafford.

I know that football coaches of the larger high schools in the area are featured rather prominently in the local papers, so once more I made my way back to the help desk. "Is there a computer available where I can go through some of the old newspaper records myself?"

"Sure, right over there." She pointed to a row of computers on the north side of the building. I thanked her and strode over to commandeer a terminal. I typed in Gabriel Stafford, nineteen eighty, and Conahey High School. Entry after entry after entry popped up on my screen. Most of them were pretty boring. He'd been named coach of the year a few times and his teams had won several state championships. At one point, it looked like around nineteen seventy-eight, he'd received an offer to coach a major college football team but had turned it down stating, "My son has three more years of high school ball. When he's off to play in college, then maybe I'll reconsider." I almost closed out the computer when one particular headline suddenly caught my attention. It read; *The Fix Is In*. It was the subheading I was interested in. *High school football coach accused of involving players in point shaving scandal.*

Once I'd read the article, I opened each news story after that in succession. The final article was accompanied by a photo of Gabriel entering the state prison in Florence to serve out a five-year sentence for conspiracy to commit sports bribery along with a three-year sentence for contributing to the delinquency of a minor, which was apparently served concurrently with the five-year sentence.

When I'd finished reading, I sat back in my chair and contemplated what such a scandal had meant to a young man in his junior year of high school. To have his father, the coach of his high school football team, have such an ignominious ending after, from everything I could read, an exalted, almost deified twenty year coaching career would have been devastating, to say the least.

I thought about what Gia had said about her father and Craig's being friends. It wasn't difficult to put two and two together and guess Tancredo Angelino's involvement in the gambling part of the whole sordid mess. He'd never specifically been named in any of the newspaper articles, but there were oblique references to "a possible connection to organized crime..." and "Coach Stafford may have associated with mafia gambling cartels..." but never an out and out connection to the Angelino Family.

The library closed at five and when I glanced at my cell phone I saw that it was nearing time for them to give the announcement that everyone had to finish up what they were doing and get the heck out so the employees could go home at their regularly scheduled time. Just as that thought played out in my mind, the lights dimmed and a prerecorded announcement blared out of the P.A. system. *Right on time.*

I gathered up the books I'd been using and placed them on the cart with all the other unshelved materials. I used to try to put books back into their proper places but at one time I'd been reprimanded by a one hundred year old librarian who had told me it was just easier to do it themselves rather than try to fix all the shelving errors done by well-meaning people who insisted on reshelving their own books. I'm nothing if not trainable, especially where cranky old ladies are concerned, so I stacked the books on the cart and headed downstairs. My new best librarian friend gave an enthusiastic wave on my way out, which I returned just as enthusiastically before heading down to the parking garage to make my way home to Tessa and Jynx.

As I drove, I kept an eye on my rearview mirror just in case I happened to see a gray Ford with a cracked windshield following me home. Nothing jumped out at me so I felt reasonably safe pulling up into my driveway and heading inside.

CHAPTER 15

The following morning I went straight to the archived records section of the Pima County Court Reporters office to find the transcripts from Gabriel Stafford's trial. The records were on microfiche and the woman who was in charge set me up in front of a microfiche machine and gave me basic instructions on how to use it and how to find the records I was looking for. It took me about an hour, but I finally located the transcripts and began the lengthy process of scrolling through each page to find the information I needed.

Apparently, against his attorney's advice, Gabriel had agreed to testify on his own behalf. Throughout the proceedings he steadfastly maintained his innocence. Several times during the trial, the prosecuting attorney asked about the gambling operation Stafford was involved with. Every single time, the answer was that there was no gambling operation until the prosecutor, who was by all intents and purposes a relentless bulldog with very sharp teeth, harangued him into somewhat of an answer.

It went like this:

Prosecutor: *The proof is incontrovertible! Your own son has testified that* *on one occasion you ordered him to drop the football if he got anywhere near the end zone! Are you calling your own son a liar!*

His own son? So Craig had testified against his father. Interesting. I noticed that the court reporter had added exclamation marks to the prosecutor's questions, something that would never be done today, but which made it so much easier to actually hear the testimony in my mind as I read.

Stafford: *No, he must have simply misunderstood my instructions.*

Prosecutor: *Misunderstood? Misunderstood a man who has coached hundreds if not thousands of young men over a career which spanned twenty-two years? I don't believe a man with your coaching record would be in the habit of giving confusing instructions to his players, do you Mr. Stafford?*

Stafford: *I already told you! They misunderstood!*

Prosecutor: *Your son and seven other boys misunderstood the same instructions? Seven? My original question still stands, Coach Stafford! Why did you pay those boys to throw games? Who paid **you** to throw games?*

Stafford: *No one! I did not...I cannot—*

Prosecutor: *You cannot? You cannot what? Divulge who paid you? Are you afraid your mafia friends will take issue with your testimony? Is that it Coach? Are you a coward who's afraid to tell the truth in a court of law?*

Stafford: *There are no mafia friends! You're putting words in my mouth!*

Prosecutor: *Your son isn't afraid! He testified that you and Tancredo Angelino know each other. That on several occasions he waited out in your car while you went into the Angelino home! Your son is not a coward, Mr. Stafford, but I submit that you are!*

Stafford: *My son is a fool! He knows nothing! He is a fool!*

I read to the end, but the back and forth just continued in the same vein. I removed the microfiche from the machine and searched through the other cartridges pertaining to the case until I came to Craig's testimony. As I read through the transcript, one thing became very clear. Craig had a seventeen year old's feeling of righteous anger against his father. As far as he could see, again, from an angry, hurting teen perspective, his father had brought humiliation and derision down upon his family and deserved to spend the rest of his life in prison.

I glanced through the rest of the testimony, but there was nothing more of any value that I could see. I wondered briefly where Craig and the rest of his family had gone after the trial since he hadn't been in Kate's senior yearbook. I also wondered where Gabriel Stafford was now. By all counts, if he served his full sentence, he should have gotten out of prison in nineteen eighty-five or eighty-six.

I thought it might be interesting to speak to Mr. Stafford, so my next step was to return to my office and do a little computer work to see if I could locate him through some cyber snooping. When I reached my office I turned on my desktop and fired up Google. My search didn't turn up anything I didn't already know. I tried the White Pages and came up empty again. I checked the police department database and didn't find anything there either. I finally checked the Arizona Department of Corrections database. "Bingo."

"Bingo, what?"

I looked up as Casey set her briefcase down on her desk, pulled out her chair and sat. I wasn't sure where I was going with my search, in fact I really didn't know why I was looking into Craig's background in the first place, so I thought I'd just keep my research to myself for a while. "Oh, nothing. Just found some info I've been looking for. How's your day going?"

"I went over to the hospital to talk to Marcos. He's really a mess."

"Have Ruthanne or Gail come up with anything new on Jason's case?"

"No, but Marcos has managed to raise enough money to bond Jason out. He's going there this afternoon to do all the paperwork and pick him up."

I returned my attention to the Department of Corrections database. Gabriel Stafford was listed as deceased three years after he went to prison. The computerized record didn't show if he'd been killed, had committed suicide or whether he had simply died of natural causes. I wondered if I needed to make a trip out to the Florence prison to find the records. It was possible I could get a helpful records clerk to look up the answer over the phone, but I wanted to get that information when no one else was around. It was also possible I was on a wild goose chase.

I swiveled around in my chair and stared out the big plate glass window behind my desk. Our offices were on the second floor and we had a killer view of the block wall of the Fire Station and the brick wall surrounding St. Augustine's Cathedral. I needed to start putting together all of the pieces of the puzzle I'd gathered so far, because they were still scattered in disjointed fragments in my mind and frankly, they were starting to drive me crazy.

Kate came striding into the office and as she stepped into her cubicle she called out over her shoulder, "Casey, Alex, you're with me. Nate, you go to University Hospital and wait with the patrol officers who've been stationed there." When she found what she needed she headed back out the office door.

Casey and I grabbed our gear and hurried after her. We reached the elevators at the same time as our lieutenant and captain. They both had businesslike expressions and when they nodded at us, we simply nodded back. All except Kate, who adjusted the strap of her briefcase as she spoke. "Do we know anything else?"

Lieutenant Lake shook his head. "No, uniform is holding the scene until we get there. I don't need to tell you this could morph into quite a mess." The three of them simultaneously turned and studied me. Since I didn't have a clue what was happening, I was slightly insulted that they'd finger me for causing a mess I knew nothing about, or, if I was reading them correctly, hadn't actually happened yet.

The elevator door opened and we joined Assistant Chief Robards who moved to the side to make room for us. The two commanders and Kate all greeted him with a brisk nod, "Chief." It's customary to drop the word "assistant" when addressing one of the four assistant chiefs on the department. I always tried my hardest not to come into any kind of contact with them and so I never had a reason to call them anything, let alone say something to one of them in an elevator.

Casey, who treats most commanders with the utmost respect, gave a quick nod, and murmured, "Sir." Then she turned to face the front of the elevator. We rode down in silence. When the elevator doors opened we all made a beeline for our cars. I had taken about two steps when Kate called out, "Alex, you're with me. Casey, follow us in your car."

Casey glanced at me, then nodded. "Yes, ma'am."

Curious, I followed Kate to her car and climbed in the passenger seat. When she slid behind the steering wheel I asked, "What's goin' on?"

Kate was quiet as she waited for the cars in front of her to exit the garage. When it was our turn, she pulled in behind Lt. Lake who was following behind the Captain. It appeared the assistant chief was heading in a different direction, possibly to the hospital where Kate had told Nate to go and wait. Kate was all business. "There's been a shooting at the Angelino residence. We don't know much yet because uniform had just reached the scene when the chief got the notification and called me. There are apparently several dead or wounded."

Numb, I stared out the windshield and watched the city slide by as we drove toward Gia's neighborhood. I couldn't bring myself to ask if she knew who had been hurt or killed. Kate tuned her police radio to the midtown frequency and we listened as uniform officers set up a perimeter around the neighborhood in case anyone involved in the shooting had run away on foot. They were calling in one of the K9 units from home since they usually worked the night shift and hadn't come into work yet.

"Alex."

I glanced over. "Yeah?"

Apparently she'd been talking because she seemed slightly annoyed. "I know you didn't hear what I just said, but I need you to pay attention right now. You are to stay with me unless I tell you otherwise. I'm not sure exactly what we're going to find, but remember, the brass is going to be on scene. None of them are happy about your friendship with Gia. The press is going to be there also, and the best advice I can give you right now is to remain completely detached and professional." I nodded, not really concentrating on what she was saying. "Alex." I looked over at her again. "Detached and professional. For both your sake and for Gia's."

I took in a deep breath and let it out slowly. "Okay, I got it. Detached and professional, but if she or Gabe are dead, I'll hunt down the S.O.B.'s who shot them and—"

The biting edge to her voice brought me up short. "Those are the types of comments you have to keep to yourself. If you let yourself indulge in that type of talk, and the wrong people hear you, then this could very well be a career ending event for you."

We turned a corner into the neighborhood. My eyes were riveted on the road ahead as I tried to get a glimpse of what was happening at the house. My breath caught as we pulled around the last curve and I saw the bloody aftermath of the shooting. Bullet holes riddled the wall surrounding the property and bodies lay in the street. Several police cars, lights still flashing, were parked at haphazard angles around the perimeter. When we pulled to a stop, I could see a pool of blood streaming out of the gateway that led into the inner courtyard. My mind stumbled a little as it tried to make sense of the blood draining out of the beautiful courtyard I knew to be full of marigolds and peonies and a little cumquat tree.

I took in a shaky breath and followed Kate as she strode over to the first body. I didn't recognize the man and mentally counted to myself. *One.* One who wasn't Gia or Gabe. We walked to three other bodies, all of them strangers. "Two, three, four." Kate glanced back at me, her eyes lowering into a puzzled look. I hadn't realized I'd started counting out loud.

I shook my head and began to walk to the gate. Casey joined me while Kate overtook us and stepped through the archway first. The river of blood had come from a short man in a pinstriped suit whom I recognized as one of Gia's bodyguards. I knew him from the racetrack and whenever I'd passed him he'd always been friendly enough. He was lying flat on his back with his head pointing toward the home. His left arm had been blown mostly out of its socket, probably at close range by a shotgun judging from the extent of the damage. The blast had severed his brachial artery and his heart had pumped the majority of his blood out of his body. That accounted for the large puddle we'd seen coagulating in the archway. I muttered to myself. "One point three gallons."

Casey stood from where she'd been squatting next to the body. "What?"

It surprised me that she'd heard. "One point three gallons of blood in his body. Looks like he lost every last drop."

Kate moved toward the front door and we followed, careful not to kick any of the shell casings littering the ground or to step in any blood. The beautiful carving of the Angelino crest that had been centered on the huge entry door had been blown into a mass of splinters. The part of the door where the knob should have been was completely missing. The captain, lieutenant and two officers were standing in front of the door talking to a patrol sergeant who was in the middle of his narrative when we walked up. "We let paramedics go in, but made 'em leave as soon as they were done. The house is secured. We've got cops at every entrance but the big guy there," He motioned into the house. "Said nobody's talking to anyone until some..." He pulled out his notepad. "Detective Wolfe gets here. We've got a body upstairs and another witness there too, but just as we were getting ready to move everybody out and start talking to witnesses I got a call from Chief Robards. He said to freeze the scene, and wait." He shrugged. "So we're waiting."

I stepped to the right of Kate so I could see into the doorway to see what big guy they were talking about. Gabe stood just like I'd pictured him in Kublai Khan's court. He had his arms crossed, legs spread and feet planted firmly on the terrazzo tile of the entryway. He was oblivious to the uniform officer standing beside him.

When Gabe saw me, he motioned with a tilt of his head to come in. I started forward and heard Kate growl softly behind me so that only I could hear. "Alex."

I glanced back at her and remembered her saying she didn't want me to go anywhere without her. I nodded and she followed me up to the door. Gabe uncrossed his arms. "I'll take you to Ms. A."

Lt. Lake, who'd come in behind us put his palm on Gabe's chest to stop him. "I'm sorry, sir. You need to stay here until the detectives get your statement." Gabe pushed the lieutenant's hand aside and started down the hall. Both the lieutenant and the officer grabbed one of Gabe's arms, but before any kind of fight broke out, Kate stepped in.

"That's really not necessary, Lieutenant. Gabe, I'm sure Ms. Angelino expects you to cooperate fully with the police. I think she has enough problems here without seeing you go to jail. Can you point Alex and I to where she is?" As she spoke, she pulled two pair of gloves out of her jacket pocket. She handed one pair to me and we both tugged them on.

"She said she didn't want nobody but Alex."

Relief flooded through me when I heard him say that. If Gia was giving orders it meant she was still alive. Both Kate and I looked at the lieutenant, waiting to hear what he wanted to do. He let go of Gabe's arm and motioned for the officer to do the same. "You two go on up. The fewer people in the crime scene the better. We'll wait here with..."

He glanced at Kate who supplied him with the name he was looking for. "Gabe."

Kate and I started down the hallway. I leaned into her and whispered. "What about the captain? He looked like he wanted to come in too."

"Let him wait. They mostly just get in the way anyway. Let's go see what we have."

I raised my eyebrows in surprise. That definitely didn't sound like the Kate I knew. Unless someone was unprofessional, crooked, or an idiot, Kate was a rules and procedures kind of gal the entire way. She respected the rank if not always the person, and expected the same from the people who worked for her.

She motioned with a sweep of her hand. "After you."

Gabe called after us. "Ms. A's at the top of the stairs."

I nodded thanks and made my way to the end of the hall. Bullet holes tracked across the wall where someone had shot a sweeping pattern straight through one of Gia's priceless masterpieces. I could only hope it was a copy and she had the original stashed away in a museum somewhere like the Da Vinci hanging at the end of the hall. She'd once laughed at me when I'd recognized the name Leonardo at the bottom the painting and had jumped away because I was afraid I'd accidentally destroy a priceless antique.

Judging by the pattern of the bullet holes, I assumed that someone had fired through the window, but when I checked, none of the hall windows were broken. Kate saw my puzzled look and tapped on the window with her fingernail. "Bulletproof. Would you expect anything less?" She was right, I should have realized that. Normally I would have studied the angle of entry on the holes in the drywall, but today I just wanted to make sure Gia was all right.

I continued down the hall, careful not to step on any evidence as I went. Kate mimicked my steps exactly so as not to contaminate an already very messed up crime scene. Another uniformed officer stood at the corner where the hallway opened up into the family room. He pointed to a set of stairs to my left. I'd been in Gia's home many times, but this was the first time I'd ever been invited upstairs. That was her father's domain and I guessed it was also where Gia and Shelley had their respective bedrooms.

The officer was guarding two of Gia's bodyguards who were seated on the sofa in the middle of the room. As Kate and I passed, I leaned close to one I recognized and spoke quietly. "I see bullet holes and blood spatter on the wall, but no bodies. Why aren't there any bodies in the house?"

His answer was quiet as well. "Only two made it inside. Once the shooting stopped we picked 'em up and tossed 'em out the back door." He shrugged. "Didn't want 'em bleedin' all over the place."

Kate groaned. I was pretty sure she was contemplating the destroyed crime scene the homicide detectives were going to have to deal with. We started up the stairs and followed them around to the right where they took a ninety-degree turn at the top. When I climbed the last three steps I saw Gia sitting with her back against the wall holding the hand of a very old, very dead man whom I could only assume was her father. The front of his striped pajama shirt was riddled with bloody holes. He'd fallen straight back and his free hand was flung up and over his head. His other arm was thrown out to the side and his fingers were wrapped around what looked like a Thompson submachine gun.

I turned around and saw a bloody pattern of holes in the panels of dark wood that graced the semi-circular walls of the stairwell. There was also a large smear where someone had bounced into the wall and slid down onto the landing. Mr. Angelino had obviously hit whoever had been coming up the stairs. Unfortunately, the other guy had hit his target as well.

I stepped over to Gia who didn't seem to know I was there. Her head was resting against the wall and her eyes were closed, giving her a frighteningly dead appearance herself. She held a Sig Sauer P-229 .40 caliber semi automatic handgun in her lap. The slide was locked back, most likely meaning the weapon had been fired until empty. The ground around the body was littered with spent .45 caliber casings, which had probably been fired from Mr. Angelino's Tommy Gun. I didn't see any .40 caliber casings near where Gia sat propped against the wall. Kate must have been looking for them as well because after a few seconds she pointed to a spot near the stair railing. "There." Several .40 caliber casings lay scattered about. Two had actually come to rest on the wide flat baluster running along the top of the landing.

I knelt next to Gia and slipped my arm around her shoulders. "Gia, it's Alex." When she didn't move I gave her shoulder a slight squeeze. "I am so, so sorry." With my free hand, I carefully picked up the .40 caliber and handed it back towards Kate who took it and then stood to go look around the rest of the upstairs rooms.

On the way, she handed the pistol to a uniformed officer who was standing quietly in the middle of the hallway. "Here, secure this until the homicide dicks arrive." He pulled out a pair of rubber gloves and after he'd wrestled his hands into them he took the pistol from her. She nodded at him and continued down the hallway.

When I had first knelt down beside her, Gia didn't move, but after a few minutes she brought her father's hand up to her cheek and held it there. Her face slowly crumpled as she leaned forward and put her forehead onto her father's shoulder. She began sobbing quietly and I rubbed her back, thinking about all the inane things a person is supposed to say at a time like this. I've always had a difficult time coming up with the right platitudes to say to someone who's lost a member of their family, and this particular case was especially vexing. I couldn't say what a great guy he'd been because from everything I'd heard, he been a ruthless, megalomaniac bastard. I finally settled on some mind numbing clichés. "I know you're going to miss him. I'm here to help you any way I can."

Kate came back and knelt beside me. She touched my back to get my attention. When I looked over at her, she pointed first to Gia, then to an open door off to our right. I nodded that I understood and leaned down close to speak directly into Gia's ear. "Gia. I'm very sorry for your loss." I paused to gather my thoughts. "Unfortunately, pretty soon the detectives are going to have to come in here and begin their investigations. I think it'd be better if we went into one of the bedrooms and let them do what they have to do."

She took in a deep breath and let it out slowly, obviously gathering herself to say goodbye to her father one last time. Wiping her eyes with her sleeve as she sat up, she reached out to caress her father's cheek and whispered, "I love you, Daddy."

Leaning back against the wall again, she finally made eye contact, first with me, and then with Kate who was waiting patiently for me to get her into the bedroom. Gia visibly straightened before pushing herself to a standing position. Resolutely, she took in the bloody stairwell and sighed. "Believe it or not, Alex, I would rather he go out with his Tommy Gun in his hands than from that bloody Alzheimer's that was stealing him away from me one memory at a time." Her face crumpled once more before she regained her composure.

I took her arm and led her into the bedroom Kate had indicated. As I started to close the door, Kate braced it open for a second. "Ms. Angelino. I'm going to have the crime scene people come and look at your father. You'll be hearing quite a bit of noise as they move about the stairwell."

Gia pointed a shaky hand at the bureau. "Would you bring a cigar over for me, Alex? They're in the top drawer."

Kate cleared her throat. "Ms. Angelino?"

"Yes, yes, do what you have to do. Please ask Gabe to come up as well." To me she said. "I need to get out of here. I need to pack some clothes and leave, now."

Kate had just stepped out into the hallway and was pulling the door shut behind her when she heard Gia's plans. She stopped and pushed the door open again. "I'm sorry Ms. Angelino, but I'm afraid you'll have to stay here until we get your statement."

Gia's gray eyes flashed. "I said I'm leaving, immediately."

Kate stepped into the room and shut the door. "Ms. Angelino. I'm going to go down now and get my tape recorder. I promise you that Alex and I and one other detective will be the only ones to take your statement, and we'll do it right now so that you can leave... immediately." Kate's steel matched Gia's perfectly as the two women glared at one another. Kate finally continued. "But—you *will* stay here until we're through." The two women's faces could have been carved in granite. I honestly had no clue which one was stronger or more powerful and I just stood back and watched these two immutable forces collide.

The horror of the past hour had taken a lot out of Gia. Her stiff spine and erect posture began to flag and she reached back to pull a chair close enough so that she could sit. As Gia wearily lowered herself onto the cushion, Kate nodded and left the room. Soon after she left I could hear people ascending the stairs. Cameras began to whir as picture after picture was taken of the macabre scene. We sat silently waiting for Kate to return. When the door finally opened and she stepped inside, we could see the ever-faithful Gabe standing guard with his back toward us, his hands clasped in front ready for anything.

Kate pulled up a chair next to Gia and sat while I stepped over to the window to see what was happening outside. The window opened onto the backyard where two tarps covered what I assumed were the bodies of the men the Angelino bodyguards had tossed out into the dirt. Crime scene techs and detectives were busy taking measurements, photographing the scene, and collecting evidence. Casey walked out the back door and knelt next to one of the bodies. She lifted the tarp and studied the man's face, then carefully lowered it again. She repeated her inspection of the second dead guy. As she stood, her gaze traveled up to the second floor window where I was standing. She pointedly looked at me for a second, then reached up and swiped at her ear. She let the hand holding her notebook casually drop and point at one of the bodies.

Just to make sure I understood, I reached up and covered my right ear, then made a slashing motion down my cheek to the edge of my mouth. She nodded. So, one of the men was the guy who was missing an ear. That didn't make much sense. He was apparently friends with the Lithuanians, and yet Bill Silverton, Gia's attorney, had bonded out the Lithuanians.

The door opened and Ruthanne stepped into the room. The fact that she was the homicide detective interviewing Gia was great, but I wasn't sure why she was here. "I thought you were temporarily reassigned from homicide to Jason's case with Gail.

Ruthanne pulled a rolling desk chair over next to Kate. "They pulled me in to help with the interviews on this case." She set the tape recorder on her knee. "Ms. Angelino, I don't know if you remember me. I'm Detective Stahl. We met at Alex's house once, and then one other time when Alex was in the hospital. I wonder if we could go ahead and take your statement."

Gia shook her head. "No. You'll have to contact my attorney, Mr. Silverton and bring him upstairs."

Kate pursed her lips and stood. "I'm sorry, Ms. Angelino, but we've already broken just about every rule in the book on this case and I'm not willing to contaminate the crime scene any more by bringing another set of footprints and fingerprints into the house. I noticed some back stairs behind a door in the third bedroom on the left."

Anger flashed in Gia's eyes, but as she rose and began to speak, Kate held up her hand to silence her. "Like it or not, this is a crime scene Ms. Angelino. I wasn't snooping through your private living quarters like some petty voyeur. I was thinking we could meet Mr. Silverton downstairs and then go somewhere quiet for the interview."

The two women glared at one another while Ruthanne and I watched. I finally decided to break the gridlock. "Where do the stairs lead?"

The two women answered simultaneously. "Down to the garage."

I glanced out the window. "The news media's at the perimeter tape in the back yard. It looks like about fifteen or twenty of them standing around gawking and waiting for a story."

Ruthanne confirmed what I suspected. "There's a ton of them out front too. Is there a limo in the garage where we can sit and do the interview?"

Kate nodded. "It didn't look like anyone got into that part of the house. Let's go." She opened the door and elbowed Gabe to the side so we could leave. Gia narrowed her eyes and stayed rooted to the spot. When Kate realized we hadn't followed, she turned, allowing no hint of her frustration to show on her face. "Ms. Angelino, do you have a better idea?"

A headache had begun throbbing in my left temple. I reached up and massaged the area hoping these two could somehow come to a consensus so we could get on with our investigation. Ruthanne's boss, Sergeant Logan, stood at the top of the stairs and was watching as his detectives processed the scene. Mr. Angelino's body had been covered by a tarp, I assumed so that Gia could exit the scene without having to look at it again. When Kate glanced at Logan, he motioned her over to where he was standing. She must have been having the same type of headache I was because she mirrored my movements exactly.

As soon as Kate walked over to Logan, Gia regally swept down the hall and entered the third door on the left. Ruthanne, Gabe, and I quickly followed. Gabe passed all of us and hurried to open what I assumed was the door leading to the back stairwell. Gia strode through the door and I called after her. "Gia, wait." She stopped on the top step without turning towards me. I slipped past her and drew my Glock. "I know Kate has already been down here, but I can only assume you and your father were targeted for assassination and I really don't want to run into any surprises with you leading the way."

Gabe reached to a holster hanging on the back of the railing and pulled out a weapon as well. Ruthanne turned and put her hand on his chest. "Whoa there. If we run into other cops and you have that gun out, there'll be major problems." She unholstered her weapon. "Put it away and I'll cover the rear, not that I think it needs covered, but like Alex says, no surprises. Besides," She tapped the barrel of his gun with a manicured fingernail. "Now that I know about that little gem, it's evidence." I watched her, once again thinking this entire crime scene had been contaminated way before the police ever arrived and it was getting progressively worse as we went along.

Gabe stared at Gia's back, probably hoping she'd give him some kind of direction. The pulse in my temple ramped up a notch. "Gia. Tell him to put his gun away."

I wasn't sure she'd even heard me until she nodded slightly and barely waved her hand back in Gabe's direction. He holstered his weapon and we began our descent. When we were half way down, the door at the top of the stairs opened once more and Kate joined the procession. "I told Nate to bring Mr. Silverton around to the garage. He's going to meet us there."

When we reached the garage, I did a quick circuit around the perimeter checking in cars and closets for anyone hiding where they shouldn't be. Once I'd finished, Kate pulled Ruthanne and I aside. "Apparently no one from the Angelino household are talking, and my guess is neither Gia nor Gabe are going to say anything either. Alex, you stay here while Ruthanne and I interview them in the limo one at a time." She held an evidence box out to Ruthanne. "Here. If that new bulge under Gabe's jacket is any indication, he's re-armed himself. Take his weapon into custody."

Taking the flat box from Kate, Ruthanne quickly folded the cardboard into shape, then walked over to where Gabe was holding the limo door open for Gia. I went with her in case there were any issues. When Gabe shut the door, Ruthanne took some rubber gloves out of her pocket, pulled them onto her hands and then motioned toward the hood of the car. "Please step over there. I'm going to reach inside your jacket to take your weapon." Gabe looked at me. I simply raised my eyebrows and nodded. He held his arms out to the side and Ruthanne reached in and secured his weapon. She then held his jacket open. "No extra clips?"

He shrugged. "I guess not."

It was obvious no one was going to tell us anything. What was also obvious was that they didn't expect nor did they want the police to do much more than catalogue the evidence and move on. I'm sure if the neighbors hadn't called us, we never would have heard about the shooting in the first place.

We all turned when the side door opened and Nate ushered in Gia's attorney. Kate motioned to the far side of the limo. "Mr. Silverton, I'm Sergeant Kate Brannigan. We've spoken a few times on the phone. We'd like to proceed with the interviews in the limo. Gia's already seated inside and the three of us can join her now." Kate motioned to Ruthanne. "This is Detective Stahl. She and I will be conducting the interview." She turned to Nate. "Did you already pat him down?"

Nate nodded. "Yes, ma'am. Do you need me in here? Sgt. Logan asked me to come back when I was done."

"No, go ahead." She opened the limo door and waved for Silverton to get in. "After you." Ruthanne climbed in after him and Kate pulled the door shut once she'd gotten in as well.

As expected, the interviews were short and to the point. Both Gia and Gabe officially declined to give a statement, and when Kate and Ruthanne had climbed out of the car, Gabe got in the front seat and inclined his head as though listening to instructions from Gia. I watched him nod, then reach into the center console and pull out yet another handgun, which he slipped into his shoulder holster without even a glance toward us. He touched something on the steering wheel and the garage doors slowly opened upward. Outside, two black SUV's were parked and running to either side of the garage. One pulled in front of the limo and when Gabe drove out of the garage the second pulled in behind. An officer lowered the crime scene tape that had been stretched across the driveway, and the three vehicles drove through the throng of reporters like Moses parting the Red Sea.

As the media rushed back to crowd into the tape the officer was once more securing across the drive, I thought I saw a brief glimpse of Craig standing slightly behind one of the cameramen who had his shoulder camera up and in place ready to film what was sure to become the story of the decade. "Kate, is that Craig out there?"

She turned toward the direction I was looking. When she didn't say anything I glanced over at her, wondering what was going through her mind. I thought I'd try to fish for a little information. "Do you want me to go get him and bring him over? He is working as a consultant after all."

Chuckling, Kate turned and put her arm around my shoulder. "Yes he is, but I think he can stay out there for a while."

"How long have you guys been friends?"

"Quite a while. Why?" She paused long enough to push the button that closed the garage door. We stood and watched it few moments before walking back to the stairwell.

"Just curious, I guess. Did I tell you Gia mentioned that her dad knew his dad?"

Kate stopped dead in her tracks. Her eyes bored into mine while she tried to decipher exactly what I was getting at. I stared back, trying to gauge her reaction to my question. "No, I don't think you mentioned that little fact. Why do you think she mentioned it, and why did you tell her we were using Craig as a consultant?"

Best to put a good face on it before I gave away the little bit of side research I'd been doing on her. "I didn't. She already knew he was helping you. I'm not exactly sure how, but that doesn't surprise you, does it?"

She continued to stare at me and I began to get nervous. As hard as I tried to stop it, I could feel a blush moving up my neck toward my face and I turned and started up the stairs hoping she hadn't noticed. Fat chance of that.

"Alex."

"Yeah, boss?" I kept climbing until I felt her hand grab my shoulder.

"What are you fishing for?"

"Fishing? I'm not fishing for anything." I swiveled around on the step and tried for my most innocent expression. "I'm just making small talk, that's all. Why would I be fishing? I mean, what would I be fishing for? What's to fish for?" I knew I was babbling and I shut my mouth to keep from digging myself any deeper.

Her eyes narrowed and I knew she knew that I knew more than I was saying. "Anything else you might have forgotten to tell me?"

"Nope." I thought about Craig's dad going to prison but I was sure Kate already knew about that. I decided to change the subject as I started to climb the stairs again. "Have we gotten any identification on the body in the barn? Oh, did Casey tell you the guy without the ear is one of the dead shooters here?"

"*What?*" Kate's voice reverberated through the stairwell. She pushed her way past me to stand on the step above looking down at my surprised expression. "I haven't seen Casey since we got here." She thought for a second. "And neither have you for that matter so how in the hell do you know the identification of any of the bodies here and why the hell didn't you see fit to give me that little tidbit of information?"

"I...well, I guess I just assumed you already knew."

Kate growled as she climbed the stairs two at a time and disappeared into the bedroom and then out the door into the hallway.

As I stared at the doorway, I realized my problem wasn't the body in the barn or the fire or even the murder of Tancredo Angelino. My problem was figuring out how each of the players figured into the picture as a whole. Who were the good guys and who were the bad? I slowly walked into the hallway and began cataloguing everybody into two columns. Who was I absolutely sure was a good guy? Casey. No question there. Megan wasn't really involved in any of this so I guess she didn't count. Ruthanne was in the same category as Megan since she was just at this scene on loan from Jason's case, but I put her on the good guy side anyway. I tried to come up with some more people but came up short.

Gia and Gabe I was never sure about even though I considered Gia one of my closest friends. Kate I usually trusted one hundred percent but for some reason this case had her rattled and I needed to find out why. I stepped over Tancredo's body and headed down the stairs. I ran into Nate on the landing. He was taping number cards on the wall next to each bullet hole. I mentally put him into the good guy column. Not a lot of experience, but a good guy just the same.

The bad guy column filled up pretty fast. All the Lithuanians, maybe Craig but I really wasn't even close to being sure which column he should go into. Leslie obviously went into this column, and so did the guy with one ear. I suddenly thought about Mr. Myung, and mentally pushed him onto the good guy side.

Casey found me just as I entered the family room. "Kate wants you to look at the other dead guy outside to see if you recognize him from the alley."

I followed her through the kitchen and out the back door. I heard what sounded like hundreds of flash cameras going off as the media snapped my picture. "What the hell?"

"Hey Detective Wolfe! How about an interview for tonight's news?"

"Detective Wolfe, are the Angelinos dead?"

"What can you tell us about your relationship to Gia Angelino? Is she dead or alive?"

Andy Duval from Channel 9 tried to make himself heard over all the rest. "Hey Alex! Why did Gia come visit you the other night? What can you tell us about that?"

My head shot up as I tried to find Andy in the crowd. Kate was kneeling next to one of the bodies and without looking up she whispered. "Don't react, Alex. Whatever they say, don't even flinch."

I stepped over to the body and picked up the tarp covering the face. Casey stood behind me to block the body from the prying cameras with extra zoom capabilities. I spoke quietly to Kate. "How did he know Gia was at my house? Are they following me?"

She didn't answer. "Do you recognize this one?"

I knew him immediately. "Yeah. I only got a glimpse of him, but he's the second man who jumped into the alley. He didn't come into the restaurant with the family. He's one of the ones who tried to block my escape at the other end of the alley." Lowering the tarp, I stared at the back of the house. "Kate. Are...they...following me?" Anger was slowly creeping its way up my spine. I turned to look at her. She was watching me with piercing brown eyes, trying just as hard as me to put the pieces together. Without knowing who the players were, I was sure she was having just as difficult a time as I was. She grabbed my arm and pulled me into the kitchen.

Her silence was a little unnerving and I forgot all about the media's questions. When she finally spoke, I could hear the uncertainty and distrust in her voice. "When was Gia at your house?"

I thought maybe it was about time to fill her in on a few things. I took a deep breath and let it out slowly, not really looking forward to her reaction. "The same night Mr. Myung came to visit?"

Kate slammed her hand down onto the countertop. "Jesus, Alex!" She spun in place, paced to the stove and back to me again. When she shoved her finger into my chest my anxiety level shot up another notch. "There's a lot of shit going on right now. I'm juggling disjointed pieces of information, missing pieces of vital intelligence, and stumbling around in the dark a lot of the time and it's scaring the hell out of me. When the Lithuanians tried to grab you, I couldn't figure out what was happening. I still don't know what's happening but I'll tell you this. You damn well better let me know when someone like Gia or Mr. Myung comes to see you. You aren't completely in the information loop on this one, Alex, but let me tell you the shit is hitting the fan and I need every scrap of information I can gather."

A rattled Kate really scared me. I tried to remember everything Gia had said that night. "I didn't tell you about Gia because she didn't say very much. Well wait, that's not true, I did tell you that she'd said I should listen to you. Remember? She said you knew when to go for the jugular."

"And Mr. Myung?"

"He didn't tell me anything except that he thought I might be in danger and he started teaching me some martial arts. He said anything I could learn might help me if I ever got into a fight."

"What kind of danger?"

"I don't know, something about shadows and darkness. It didn't make much sense."

The sound of someone brushing up against the door between the kitchen and the dining room distracted her. As she walked over to it, she put her finger to her lips and then motioned for me to move across the floor to the area in front of the stove. When she pulled the door open, Nate, who was leaning against it with his back to us, practically fell into the room. She took one look at him, then stepped into the dining area and looked around. She waved to the lieutenant who was standing at the other end of the room talking with Sgt. Logan. "I'll be right there to brief you, Jon. Give me a few more minutes."

She dragged Nate with her as she came back in and shut the door. Nate stepped back when she turned angry eyes on him. Her hands went to her hips and rested there while she waited for him to explain himself. He swallowed hard and sent a pleading look my way. I'm sure my quizzical expression didn't help him gather his flagging courage. I was starting to wonder if maybe I'd put him into the good guy column a little prematurely. He swallowed again and then tried to explain. "I wasn't eavesdropping. I came down the stairs and the L.T. was standing close to the door and it seemed like he was trying to listen to what was being said in here. When he saw me watching him, he moved over to talk to Sgt. Logan. I heard the two of you talking in the kitchen and decided to stand in front of the door to make sure you had some privacy."

Okay, he was back solidly in the good guys column, but now I wasn't so sure about Lieutenant Logan. Kate reached up and rubbed her eyes, using her fingers to massage them while she rocked her head side to side trying to loosen overly tight shoulders. She let out a big sigh and turned toward the dining room door. "Both of you go on back to the office or do whatever it is you have going on. I need to brief the lieutenant on what I know about this fiasco." When she left the kitchen, I realized I needed to catch Casey to get a ride.

When I turned to hurry out to the backyard, I was surprised to see her standing with her back to that door as if she was guarding this entrance in the same way Nate had been protecting us from unwelcome ears in the house. As soon as I opened the door and stepped onto the porch, the media, who'd finally settled down after Kate and I had gone inside, started buzzing with activity again. Casey turned to look at me and shook her head. "Weirder and weirder, Alex."

"Can I catch a ride with you? I think Kate's gonna be here a while."

"Yeah, my car's out front."

Nate fell into step with us as we walked around the side of the house. The media in front was just as obnoxious as the ones out back.

"Hey Alex. How about a statement?"

"Can you tell us anything about who was killed? Were Tancredo and Gia Angelino in that limo that left a little while ago?"

"Why all the secrecy?"

I looked back to the house hoping to see the Captain coming to rescue me. I was relieved to see the next best thing. The lieutenant and Kate came out the front door and walked over to the yellow crime scene tape where the lieutenant held up his hands asking for quiet. Once the media's attention had been drawn away from the three of us, we ducked under the tape and hurried to our cars. Nate jumped in his and drove off. As Casey and I opened our doors, I just happened look up in time to see Craig following the path that led around to the back of the house.

"Now that's interesting." I closed car door and started jogging towards the house. I heard Casey's door slam and knew she was following right behind me.

"What's interesting?" Her voice jiggled a little as she ran.

I didn't have time to explain so I held up a finger to let her know I'd tell her when I could. We rounded the corner into the back yard in time to see the kitchen door close. I hurried over and pulled it open, catching Craig as he was about to go through the other door into the dining area. When he heard me come into the kitchen he turned and adopted an innocent, sheepish expression.

I decided two could play at that game. I plastered a smile on my face as I walked toward him and held out my hand to shake. "Craig. Good to see you again. I guess Kate called you in because of the gang connection on the case."

He nodded. "She did. Do you know where I can find her?"

"Right here." Kate strolled through the door and pinned him with an icy glare. My guess was she'd seen Casey and I jogging back to the house and had followed to see what was up. I stepped behind Craig and placed myself between him and the dining room door.

Craig, the consummate undercover professional, didn't even break a sweat. "There you are, Kate. I've been looking all over for you."

Kate held her hands out to her side. "Here I am."

"I thought maybe if you gave me a walk through of the scene I could probably fill in some of the blanks for you." The guy was good, I'd give him that much.

Kate surprised me by smiling and taking his arm. "Come on outside and I'll tell you what I can. This is still an active crime scene," She paused for effect, "And the Angelino's private residence. The fewer people who go traipsing through their home, the better."

He allowed her to guide him out the back door. "Of course, whatever you say. Hopefully I can identify some of the players for you."

We followed them outside and as Kate led him around to the front of the house I motioned to two cops who were shooting the breeze next to the bodies. One of them, a rookie judging by his demeanor, hurried over to see what I wanted. I reined in my temper before I spoke. "Why did you just let that guy waltz right through the door like that?"

A blush spread up his neck, painting his face a bright crimson. "He badged us as he walked through the yard. He's a detective, right?"

"Wrong. Did you check the badge to make sure it was legit?"

He guiltily crossed his arms. "No, ma'am."

I pointed to the tarps. "Did he look at the bodies?"

He seemed a little relieved with that question. "No, ma'am, he didn't."

I nodded. "Okay, listen. Nobody goes through that door without you checking their identification. Got it?"

"Yes, ma'am."

Casey and I glared at the other officer before making our way back to her car. She'd been a training officer when she'd worked uniform patrol and I knew she had a soft spot for rookies. She grinned. "I'm glad you didn't take that kid's head off. It was a rookie mistake, one I'll bet never happens again on his watch."

"I was really more pissed at the other guy, Jenks, who was standing there with his thumb up his ass while Craig walked right through the crime scene. He's been on the department for more than twenty years, you'd think by now he'd know better."

She shook her head in disgust. "Time on doesn't necessarily mean competent. He's been a sluggard ever since I first came on the department." We walked back to her car and had to push our way through the onslaught of microphones the media was shoving into my face. Kate had warned me months ago that having a friendship with the head of the ruling mafia crime family was going to cause all kinds of problems and now her words were beginning to bear out. We managed to make it into our car without me punching anyone in the face and I considered that quite an accomplishment. Casey did a three-point turn without intentionally running down any reporters and we drove back towards the downtown area.

CHAPTER 16

Two days later, as Casey and I were driving out of the parking garage, Ruthanne came on the radio and asked us to meet her behind the bank at Twenty Second and Alvernon. She was already there by the time we arrived. Her vehicle was backed into a parking space at the rear of the lot and as Casey pulled up beside her Ruthanne rolled down her window so we could talk. Gail was sitting in the passenger seat holding a large cup of coffee that looked really good right about then. I was still running on less than five hours of sleep thanks to Mr. Myung's second visit in the wee hours of the morning.

Ruthanne shook her head. "That was one hell of a scene the other day. Thank God Gia had so much security there or she'd a been dead meat." I felt the heat rise in my cheeks and chose to look out my window instead of biting her head off. She must have realized her mistake because she began to backpedal. "I didn't mean it like that, Alex. I'm sorry. I haven't really taken off my detective hat and that just popped out."

I mumbled into the window, "Don't worry about it."

Casey poked me on the arm. "C'mon, Alex. Normally, something like that would be just another part of our conversation and you wouldn't think twice about it. It slipped out, give her a break."

She was right and I knew it. I took a deep breath and turned to face the three of them. Ruthanne raised her eyebrows and I nodded to let her know it was okay. I didn't really want to talk about the shooting, and since Gail was here, I guessed that wasn't why they'd asked us to meet up with them. Casey must have thought the same thing. "So what's up?"

Ruthanne and Gail exchanged glances. After a few seconds, Gail spoke up. "We wanted to bounce something off you guys. Something about Jason's case just doesn't feel right." She stopped and focused on the parking lot behind Casey and me. "Isn't that Kate's car?"

Both of us turned as Kate pulled into the space next to us. Casey backed up so she and Ruthanne could open their doors to get out and we all met Kate in front of her car. She leaned against the hood and propped one foot up behind her on the grill. "I heard Ruthanne call you two over to talk." She looked at Gail. "Mind if I listen in?"

Gail and Ruthanne looked at each other again and when Ruthanne shrugged, Gail repeated what she'd told us so she could bring Kate up to speed. "I was just saying, something about Jason's case doesn't feel right." She looked down at her shoes and then back up at Kate. "The reason we asked these guys to meet us out here is because we needed to bounce something off of them and...well, it might not be exactly politically correct as far as the department's concerned."

Kate smiled. "Anything you say will stay right here. You know me well enough to realize I'm not the type to go running my mouth off about things."

"Well, it's just that Captain Emery is keeping a very close eye on everything Ruthanne and I do. It seems like we can't turn in a circle without him asking why we're doing it."

Kate nodded. "I can understand that. It's a fairly high profile case since Jason is Captain Buelow's son."

Shaking her head, Ruthanne put in her two cents. "No, it's more than that. Every time one of us comes up with an idea, he makes it seem like we don't know what we're doing. Other detectives have told us that he belittles our investigative techniques behind our backs and actually makes fun of us when he's around the guys in the unit."

When Kate didn't say anything, I spoke up. "He knows you're one of the best detectives on the department, Gail. Why's he being such a jerk?"

Casey took a piece of bubble gum out of her pocket and began to unwrap it. "He's insecure."

Ruthanne snorted, "Emery? He's the most conceited Captain on the department. Never has a hair out of place, always checking himself in the mirror when he walks by. I don't think that's his problem."

Kate folded her arms across her chest. "Actually, Casey's right on the mark." She looked each one of us in the eye. "Look, I'm going to talk about something that could get me into hot water if it ever got back to the department." All of us nodded, indicating that we realized this was an off the record conversation. "He didn't want the two of you on this case. He has a couple close detective friends. He fought to give them this assignment because if it's handled right, it would have been quite a feather in their cap. Assistant Chief Robards more or less forced you guys on him." She paused for a second, then continued. "So, you all know Captain Emery's gay, right?"

The other three nodded but I'd never been around him enough to really know one way or the other. Kate stopped to gather her thoughts. "There are a lot of gay men on the department who are completely secure in their sexuality. He's not one of them. He's a little effeminate, and knows it, and to be honest, he's intimidated by strong women. You two scare the heck out of him. Add to that the fact that he couldn't bring his buddies onto the case, and you've got a situation just like you described. He's insecure, so he's going to make life miserable for the two of you."

"I know. That's what's so frustrating." Gail's voice rose a few decibels. "This is an incredibly important case and he can't get past the fact that he's stuck with two very competent women who know what the hell we're doing. I don't want to screw up this case because he's playing games. Honestly, Kate? I don't think Jason did it, but both times I've said that to him, he completely shuts me down. He's not willing to listen to my reasoning. He's already made up his mind that Jason's guilty as sin."

Something wasn't adding up. "Wouldn't you think that since he's gay he'd be more inclined to keep an open mind about the possibility that Jason, another gay man, might not have gone to a homophobic bar and raped a woman?"

Ruthanne shook her head. "No, it's almost as though he has to prove his manliness by distancing himself from the fact that Jason is gay."

If there was one thing I admire about Kate, it's that she rides a case to its proper conclusion, regardless of the implications politically or personally. She reached over and put her hand on Gail's shoulder. "Make sure you don't let his insecurity dictate the parameters of the case. If you think Jason is innocent, prove it beyond any doubt. Luckily, neither of you have to work for Emery once this case is wrapped up. So, what exactly is it that makes you think Jason is innocent?"

We all watched as a patrol car drove into the lot and pulled up to the drive through ATM. Ruthanne must have known the officer because she waved at him before turning back to answer Kate's question. "Unfortunately, his alibi is pretty weak. He and Marcos drove up to a nightclub in Phoenix, The Sistah's Club. They'd never been there before and didn't know anyone, didn't particularly talk to anyone. Gail and I went up there and asked around. It's a big club and no one remembered seeing either one of them there."

Gail took up the narrative. "My biggest problems are the people at Fernando's. No one can really describe Jason. Two of the three people who originally said they saw him couldn't pick him out of the line-up. Fernando told Alex that we should speak to Justíno, but no one has seen him and when Alex and Casey went to his apartment it was a torn up bloody mess."

"Here's the real kicker." Ruthanne glanced around at all of us as she spoke. "Two years ago, vice arrested the victim for prostitution but she was never charged."

When Kate heard this she nodded. "Which suggests they either turned her for information or let her go in exchange for help sometime in the future. What did the Vice guys say?"

"Dario Santana was the arresting officer. He doesn't remember her, but his notes say they released her and put in the paperwork to use her as a C.I. They never actually got around to it." When Gail finished speaking, she motioned to Ruthanne who picked up the story again.

I interrupted before she could begin. "What's the victim's name?"

Ruthanne pulled a notebook out of her back pocket. "She gave her name as Sally Jessup. We've been trying to talk to her again but we haven't had any luck finding her."

Everyone was quiet while we thought about the case. Finally Kate asked. "Okay, where's the smoking gun? You said Emery was convinced Jason did it. Why?"

Both Ruthanne and Gail shook their head while Gail answered. "That's the fly in the ointment. Sally said he used a condom and a condom was found buried in the trash right outside the front door. It had a small amount of Jason's semen in it and vaginal fluid from Sally on the outside. They got her DNA when they did the rape kit on her."

Casey scratched her head. "Ouch."

"Ouch is right. You guys haven't been able to talk to Jason because he lawyered up, right?" Kate asked absently, not expecting an answer. "I'd suggest talking to Marcos again. Find out if Jason even uses condoms, and if he does, find out what brand. I know Marcos isn't being helpful at all, but let him know how important this is. And you absolutely have to track down Sally Jessup and Justíno. Without them, you don't have a case, whether it was Jason who raped her or somebody else."

Ruthanne turned to Casey and I. "Marcos won't talk to us. He made that perfectly clear, but maybe if you guys tried..."

Casey glanced at Kate who shrugged. Apparently she didn't care who got the information as long as we got it. We finished our meeting and Kate said she was going back the office. Ruthanne and Gail left to work on finding Sally and Justíno and when Casey and I got back into the car, she asked. "Where to?"

"I'd like to go back to the hotel where the Lithuanians stayed. Maybe Angel or the hotel owner can tell us where to find this Sally Jessup."

"Have you ever heard of a hooker named Sally?"

"That's what's bothering me." I reached into the back seat and grabbed her briefcase. I pulled out the notebook where she kept the names of all the known hookers, drug addicts and dealers she ran into during the course of her various investigations. Sometimes I thought she kept better intelligence than the detectives in the Special Investigations Unit. "Okay, let's see." I thumbed through every page and every mug shot she had. "Nope, no Sally, let alone a Sally Jessup. Let's see if Angel can give us any help."

A short time later we pulled into the hotel parking lot. The owner was outside emptying the trash bags from individual garbage cans into a large rolling container. He greeted us when we walked up. "Detectives! Long time no see."

"Yeah, what, two days?" There were maggots crawling in and out of the larger container and I walked over to take a peek. A dank stench hit me full in the face. "Ugh, what the hell do you have in there? That's disgusting."

"I know, right? The garbage pick up is Friday. Last Sunday, some schmuck dumped a bunch of old meat into one of my cans after he checked out. I didn't discover it until the maggots started crawling out. Pretty disgusting, huh?"

"No body parts?" I really hoped he'd already checked, because I certainly didn't want to.

"No, just some old meat he had in the fridge. They were still wrapped in the paper from the grocery. People do that, check in for a few days, go to the store to buy some food so they don't have to eat out all the time. I let 'em use the barbecue over there by the pool." He pointed to a large fenced in swimming pool in the center of the lot. I expected it to be full of green sludge, but the water actually looked sparkling clear. It would have even looked inviting if it wasn't seventy degrees out and probably forty-five in the water. He began pushing the fly and maggot infested barrel around to the side of the hotel complex where there was a three-sided bricked-in containment area for the dumpsters. He wheeled the container onto a small platform, strapped it tightly against some pipes and hit a button that raised the platform high enough that when it tilted backwards, the container dropped all the garbage into the dumpster.

When he'd finished, he held his hands away from his body and we followed him back to his office where he immediately disappeared for a few minutes, presumably to wash the stench off his hands. He came out drying them on a paper towel. "Okay, so how can I help you today? Those men haven't been back since you guys were here the last time."

Watching him dry his hands made me feel like I had some maggoty goo on me and I involuntarily wiped my hands down the front of my pant legs. "I know you get a lot of hookers coming and going around here. Have you every heard of somebody named Sally Jessup?"

I was surprised when he didn't even try to deny the type of clientele his hotel catered to. "Nope, never heard that name come up."

"Is Angel still hanging around here?"

He pointed off to the right. "Yeah, she's in room sixteen. She's pretty fucked up most of the time. Pays the going rate on the room though, so I let her stay."

"Do you know if she has a john with her right now?"

He shook his head so Casey and I walked over to the last room on the right side of the first floor. We listened a second. Everything was quiet. Too quiet really. I knocked several times, each time progressively louder in case she was in some kind of drugged stupor and needed a little extra stimulation. In the meantime, Casey had gone back to get the master key from the owner. When she returned, she unlocked the door and gave it a shove. As the door swung open, both of us leaned around the corner of the doorframe to see if Angel was inside. The curtain was pulled closed so it was too dark to really make out who the person lying on the bed was. I stepped inside slowly. "Angel? It's Detective Wolfe. Are you okay?"

I reached to the side and pulled on the little string that opens the curtains. Sunlight streamed into the room making it easy to see why Angel hadn't come to the door. She lay sideways on the bed, wide eyes moving back and forth as though she had front row seats to her own private tennis match. Now that I could see her lips moving, I realized she was also mumbling something very softly to herself.

Casey pulled on some gloves and handed me some as well. She felt for a pulse on the side of Angel's neck. "Really slow, but steady." She pointed to a syringe that was partially covered by a pillow. "She probably just now shot up." She retrieved the syringe, then walked over and set it on the filthy, grime encrusted windowsill.

I held Angel's chin to see if I could focus her at all. "Angel. Look at me." Her gaze tracked across the room and lit on my face for a second. I saw that little ghost of a smile I'd seen the last time we'd spoken. "Can you talk to me?"

Her voice was dreamy and disjointed when she answered. "Can...always...talk. Don't always want...to."

I let go of her chin. "Angel. We're looking for a hooker named Sally Jessup. Do you know her?" I repeated it in hopes that some of my words might penetrate the heroin haze. "Sally Jessup?"

She giggled and started quietly singing what sounded like a nursery rhyme, the kind little kids might sing while they jumped rope. Her voice was barely above a whisper. "You saw her, you saw...her. Said you'd seen her naked, naked, said you'd seen her naked."

Casey and I exchanged frustrated looks. I pulled off my gloves and headed for the door. "This is getting us exactly nowhere. C'mon, it was a stupid idea. Let's head back to the station.

Angel seemed to be stuck in a repeating reality. "You saw her, you saw...her. Said you'd seen her..."

Just before Casey pulled the door shut, a picture flashed through my mind. "Oh damn." I pushed the door open again and returned to the bed. I pulled on another set of gloves while I listened to her singsong voice.

"...naked, naked, naked."

I grabbed her face between my hands and made her focus. "Angel, does Sally have a street name?"

A sloppy smile spread across her face. She whispered. "Naked..."

I shook her head a tiny bit. "Focus here a minute. What is Sally's street name?"

Her eyes started to close, which was typical of a heroin addict on a high. I'd known them to actually go to sleep mid-sentence or while they were bringing food up to their mouth to eat. I yelled so loud she actually jumped. "Angel!"

Her eyes cleared slightly and she whispered something I couldn't hear. I really didn't want to get any closer, but apparently the feedback loop in her brain had her repeating everything she said and the second time around she spoke a little bit louder. I was pretty sure I knew what she was going to say, so I was finally able to catch her whispered words. "She's naked, naked, naked, Tanya's naked now."

I let go of her face and straightened up. Casey raised her eyebrows, silently asking if I'd been able to hear what Angel had said. I nodded. "She said, Tanya's naked now." I stared at her to see if the penny would drop. The only reason I understood what Angel meant was because we'd talked about Tanya the last time I'd seen her. I repeated the name to Casey one more time. "Tanya? Remember, Ruthanne showed us those pictures of the hooker who was beaten to death a few days ago?"

It was obvious when the light bulb went off. She straightened up and looked over at Angel. "The guy left her naked. He beat the shit out of her, then left her lying naked on the street where everyone would see her."

I reached behind my back and pulled my radio off my belt. "I'm gonna call the paramedics. She's too wasted and I don't feel right leaving behind her like this."

It took the paramedics another forty-five minutes to get Angel packed up and ready to transport. By the time they'd driven out of the parking lot, a small but enthusiastic crowd of rag tag onlookers had gathered. I'd been standing by the door to Angel's room talking to a toothless meth addict. Well, to be perfectly accurate, he wasn't exactly toothless, but he was definitely tooth challenged. He'd filled me in on pretty much everything I had absolutely no interest in. Casey had been sitting in the car doing paperwork so I said my goodbyes and climbed into the passenger seat. "Did you call Ruthanne and Gail to tell them what we found out?"

She shook her head. "No, you're the one who figured it out so I thought you should be the one to let them know."

My phone was shoved way down into my pocket. I had to unbuckle the seatbelt I'd just fastened, straighten my leg until it was shoved up against the floorboard and root around in the front pocket of my Dockers. In the meantime Casey had pulled out into traffic and had to swerve suddenly to avoid an old man who had pulled into our lane with about two inches to spare between his rear bumper and the hood of our car. I quickly retrieved the phone and refastened my seatbelt. "Jeez, be careful, would ya?"

Ruthanne answered her phone on the first ring. "What's up, Alex? You have some good news for me? Please tell me you solved the case."

"Well not exactly. In fact, I think I just made it more complicated for you. We tracked down a hooker we know named Angel. She said that Sally Jessup's street name was Tanya."

"No shit? As in the Tanya who ended up getting her face bashed in?"

"Yeah, and I had another thought, too. You might want to check her DNA against the blood you collected from Justíno's apartment. We were assuming it was his, but what if it was Tanya slash Sally's blood instead?"

"I'll call the lab and have them check it out. I tried to talk to Marcos again but he's still refusing to cooperate. He says we're just trying to railroad Jason and doesn't want anything to do with us."

Marcos and I had grown close over the last year or so. I'd met his somewhat quirky group of friends, and to my amazement, I actually liked them. "Do you remember when we met Roddy, Marcos' blue friend at that nightclub he took us to?"

"How do you forget meeting a man who had his entire face and neck tattooed blue with small lizard scales etched into his skin with yellow ink?"

I laughed. "Did you know, when I was shot, Roddy came to the hospital to see me? Several times as a matter of fact. Honestly, he was the person who broke through. I could talk to him, to this blue guy who, if it weren't for Marcos, I would have just walked by him on the street thinking he was nothing more than another weirdo."

"I know. Marcos has sure opened my eyes about what really constitutes strange. But what does that have to do with seeing if he'll talk to you?"

"It doesn't really. I was just thinking that Marcos accepts everyone just how they are. Not only accepts, but genuinely likes them. I think that's a great gift, that's all. And I think it'll hurt a lot if he refuses to talk to me, if I lose his friendship simply because I wear a uniform. That now, to him, all the people in blue," I laughed at the vision of Roddy with his blue face, "well, everyone except Roddy, are his enemies." I took a deep breath, embarrassed that I'd just said all that when we were in the middle of working a case. "So, anyway, Casey and I will go see if he'll talk to us."

"You can try, but he's pretty adamant he never wants to see any of us ever again. Hey, it'll be all right, Alex. Try to convince him we're not here to railroad, Jason. We're just trying to uncover the truth. Sorry, but I've gotta run, the L.T.'s waiting to talk to Gail and me. Talk later, and let us know how it goes with Marcos." She disconnected before I even had a chance to say goodbye. I checked the phone to make sure she'd actually hung up, then let Casey know what she'd said.

Traffic on this particular road had slowed to a crawl. There didn't seem to be anything out of the ordinary. I didn't see any accidents, there shouldn't have been any construction going on and when we came to a complete stop I wondered aloud what was going on. "Can you see what's happening up there?"

"No." She opened her door and stood on the running board to get a better look. "The traffic light's malfunctioning. It looks like it's stuck on red for us and yellow for the other direction."

We inched forward as drivers figured out how to move through the intersection safely. As we sat there, I was vaguely aware of the line of cars coming toward us who'd had to fight the light in the opposite direction. Casey, who had phoned in the malfunction to commo, was impatiently tapping the steering wheel. I glanced down at her fingers, then quickly looked up again. "Isn't that Kate's car coming this way? I thought she said she was heading back to the office."

The department frowned on decorating our vehicles with anything that might convey a political statement or personal beliefs. The brass made the occasional exception, and two weeks ago we'd been allowed to tie a black ribbon with a blue stripe through it to our antennae to honor an Arizona officer who'd been killed in the line of duty. Kate hadn't taken hers off yet and as the car approached, I studied the antennae to make sure it was her. Casey must have seen it at the same time I did. "That's her all right. I'll bet somebody called her for a cup of coffee or something."

I didn't think too much about it until several cars later I saw Craig Stafford drive by in a gray four door Ford sedan with a cracked windshield; the same description the homeless guy had given me of the car that he'd seen following me. So it had been Craig tailing me. What was up with that? I turned in my seat and watched him follow Kate's car around a corner. "That was Craig in that Ford. What the hell..." It wasn't until I recognized the blue Dodge Durango that drove by minutes later that little alarm bells really began to go off. "Case—"

"I saw." We were blocked in by cars to both the front and rear, with a raised median to our left and a sidewalk to our right. Casey swiveled her head in every direction trying to figure out a way to get clear. By the time she maneuvered the car around to follow the three of them, they were nowhere in sight. Casey hit the steering wheel hard. "Shit."

"It's probably nothing. I think we're starting to get a little paranoid." Trying to convince her was one thing, but trying to convince my little gnome was a whole other proposition. I pulled out my phone. "Do you think we should call her?"

Casey glanced at the phone and then shook her head. "No. Like you said, she's a big girl with a lot of experience under her belt. If she needs us, she'll call."

Even though I agreed with her, I stared at the phone trying to quell the growing apprehension I felt building inside me. "Kate was rattled."

"What?" She looked at me as though I'd just spouted Shakespeare.

"Something has Kate off balance. Something's...oh I don't know." I put my phone away and motioned for her to turn around. "Let's just get back to the station. It's been a long day, I'm tired and I just want to go home, heat up some mac and cheese and curl up with a good book."

CHAPTER 17

The cheese on the macaroni had melted to a perfect, stringy mess. Normally, I'd just boil the macaroni from the box, drain it, stir in the butter and the powdered cheese and hotdogs and, voilà, a gourmet feast. Tonight I was feeling a little antsy. Instead of pacing around my kitchen waiting for the noodles to cook, I had taken out the block of Asiago cheese I had left over from the last time Terri had come with Casey to cook her special mushroom Asiago chicken recipe, and had begun to shred. When I finished that, I'd pulled out the Colby Jack and shredded that as well. I'd fried up two Hebrew National hotdogs, chopped them up into little bite-sized pieces and thrown them in as well. I was just sitting down on my sofa with my Kindle when my cell phone rang in my bedroom.

I didn't recognize the ring so I reluctantly set my bowl up high enough so Tessa couldn't reach it and padded in and grabbed the phone off my dresser. The call was from a blocked number. I almost didn't answer it, but then I thought about that afternoon on the road with Casey and pushed send. "Hello?"

"Is this Detective Wolfe?"

"Who's this?"

"First, I need to know who I'm speaking to."

The voice seemed somewhat familiar, and I was silent while I tried to put the inflection with a face. "Okay...I'll play. This is Alex Wolfe. Now who's this?"

"Jerry Dhotis. Look Detective, I know this is gonna sound...well, just hear me out. There's something you need to know, but I've got to fill in some background for you first."

I waited for him to say more, then decided he needed a prompt. "Okay..."

I guess that was all he needed because he started right in. "I've worked for Stafford Limited for about four years now. About six months ago, I began noticing some," He searched around for the right word. "Irregularities."

"What kind of irregularities?"

"That's not important. Look, Craig hired me because I'm retired Special Forces. You catching me on that roof was just plain dumb luck on your part. I'm good, Detective. And, as my commanding officer once told me, I'm honest to a fault. Honor and integrity mean everything to me."

"Hold on, Jerry. Why are you telling me all this?" I walked back into the living room, grabbed my mac and cheese and began eating while he talked.

"Because I want you to understand why I opened my own investigation on Craig. He's always hated organized crime. That was one of the reasons I joined his group, because I hate them just as much as he does. Until about six months ago, that is."

When he stopped talking, I heard an airplane in the background. It was loud enough that I guessed he was somewhere down south near the airport. I forked some noodles into my mouth. "Go on."

"I was always privy to everything Craig was into, until one day, he received a phone call he said he had to take in private. That had never happened before, and I thought it was strange, but nothing worth losing any sleep over, until it began happening most every time he talked on the phone. We'd always worked as a team. If we had to meet up with a source, we went together. I'm a curious person, Detective, and when he began going to meet people on his own, I wanted to know why. I followed him and photographed the man he was meeting with. I ran the pictures through our facial recognition software. The man was Donatas Puniskis, a mid-level lieutenant in the Andrulis Mafija."

"Jerry, let's get back to my original question. Why are you telling me all this now?" The cheese fairly dripped off the noodles. I was in heaven.

"You'll understand why in a minute. Andrulis Mafija translates into the Andrulis Mafia, one of the most brutal crime syndicates ever to come out of Lithuania." I choked on a noodle and began coughing into the phone. "Detective? Are you okay? What's happening?" Jerry sounded genuinely concerned and I would have been touched if I'd been able to breathe.

I took in a long breath through my nose and continued to breathe slowly until I thought it was safe to speak again. I finally choked out in a hoarse voice, "I'm okay. Really."

"Yeah, okay, anyway, I know for a fact that the Andrulis Mafia is moving a branch of its syndicate to the United States. They've partnered with a Korean mafia group called Jug-eom. Their goal is to take over all the organized crime here in the states."

Some of the puzzle pieces were falling into place. "So, now they're targeting the Angelinos, and she's in an all out war, then. How does Craig fit into all of this?"

"I don't know." He was beginning to sound agitated. "Listen to me, please. I've been following Craig, keeping an eye on him. About three hours ago, he was in a parking lot. It looked like he was waiting for someone. After about a half an hour he became super nervous, pacing back and forth. He got a phone call which ramped him up even more. After the call, he started punching and kicking whatever was around him—trashcans, tires. Then he called someone. When he finished, he took off in his SUV. I tailed him and eventually realized he'd targeted your sergeant's car and he was following her. Someone deliberately cut me off in traffic and by the time I got around the car, I'd lost the two of them."

I excitedly waved my fork in the air. "We saw you! Casey and I saw the three cars earlier. You passed us on Campbell. We were stuck in traffic." I was already shoving my holster into the waistband of my pants. "Where did you lose them?"

"I'm at Country Club and Valencia right now. I'm going to keep looking but I'm worried about what he's up to and I could use some help."

I was already out the door. "I'm on my way." I hung up and hit auto dial for Kate's cell phone. It rang once and her voicemail kicked in. I punched the end button. "Shit." There was no quick way to get to Craig's location from where I lived. I drove like a bat out of hell, making it to Valencia in about twenty minutes. I didn't see Jerry's Durango so I began cruising the neighborhoods, watching for anything out of the ordinary, hoping that something unusual would catch my eye and give me a clue about where Kate might be. "She's probably home right now having dinner with her husband." I realized I was talking to myself, but I listened anyway. I grabbed my phone again, found Kate's home phone number and hit send."

Thom picked it up on the third ring. "Hello?"

"Hi Thom, Alex Wolfe here. Is Kate around?"

"No, she probably had to work late. Have you tried the office?"

That was another place I hadn't checked before I came tearing out here on a wild goose chase. "No, I'll do that now. Thanks." I hung up and dialed her work extension. It rang until the answering machine picked up.

I continued driving the back streets and alleys. The area I was in was more industrial than residential. Huge warehouses dotted large tracts of land, some with manicured lawns and flowered walkways, some more utilitarian, mostly made out of cement with incline ramps going up to large roll-up doors. Still other buildings sat in open fields strewn with weeds, obviously abandoned. Many of them had large For Lease signs posted on the doors or on chain link fences that surrounded entire factory or storage complexes. Luckily, I wasn't running into any traffic because it was after seven and the streets were deserted. I hoped to hell Kate hadn't come out here to meet someone by herself. That wasn't like her.

It felt like I was driving in circles because all of the buildings were pretty much alike, except for their upkeep, until I came to a block where there were two or three factory buildings that sat right in the middle of several acres of open land. The only way to get to them was to drive up a long, completely exposed one-lane dirt road. I parked and stared at the buildings for a few minutes, waiting to see if there was any type of movement around the grounds. Everything was completely still. There weren't even any rabbits moving through the desert scrub brush. I drove forward slowly, watching the buildings the entire time. When I came to an intersection, I turned right, wanting to completely circle the tract of land hoping to be able to see all four sides of the complex. I was currently looking at a six-foot block wall that enclosed the back yard of the storage facility.

I still didn't see any movement or anything out of the ordinary. At the next intersection I turned right again. I drove to the middle of the block and stopped. I'd always trusted my subconscious, and as I stared at the wall, I knew that something odd had caught my attention. Unfortunately, I didn't have a clue what it was. I reached into the back seat and pulled out a pair of opera binoculars from my briefcase. They'd been a gift from my mother back when she'd tried to set me up with a visiting tenor from London or some such place. Needless to say, the tenor went home to England and I got to keep the binoculars.

I got out of the car and propped my arms on the roof to steady myself. I focused on the back right corner of the wall, then slowly tracked left. When I reached the left corner, I switched directions and moved the viewfinder to the right, slower this time. Just before I reached the end, I saw what I was looking for. There, sticking up about a foot over the wall, was the tiny bit of motion that had tickled my subconscious. At this distance, it could have been anything; a bird hopping along the cement blocks or a branch from a tree behind the wall. Luckily for me, my mother had been trying to impress the opera singer and had spared no expense when she'd purchased the binoculars. I adjusted the zoom function to increase the magnification. The powerful little buggers zoomed in so close I found myself staring at the pock marked surface of a single cement block. I moved the lenses in large sweeping motions to try to orient myself along the wall.

It took a while, but I finally located the charcoal capstones along the top and tracked along them until I came to what I was looking for.

Barely visible, a black ribbon with a blue stripe was fluttering in the light breeze blowing across the desert floor. I happened to know the ribbon was attached to the antennae of a metallic blue Ford Taurus that had either been driven inside the compound by Kate, or had been hidden there by somebody else. I fervently hoped it was the former.

I took out my cellphone and texted Jerry. *Gry & wht bldg on 2 acres at Brosius and Bonny Ave. Blck wall in bck.* I hoped that was enough because I wasn't inclined to wait for him. I put the binoculars back in my car and locked it before taking off at a jog across the desert toward the back wall. When I reached it, I piled up several blocks that were lying scattered on the ground, climbed up on them and slowly stuck my head over the capstones.

I watched for at least a minute trying to see if anyone was waiting in the loading area behind the factory. Nothing moved so I slipped over the wall and into the yard. I checked the hood of Kate's car. It felt cool and I guessed it had been here a couple of hours. Now I really wished Casey and I had tried to find the three cars after they'd disappeared. I quickly ran to the back of the factory building, hugging the wall as I went. There was a large capacity dumpster in my way, and as I skirted it I came face to face with Craig's Dodge Durango and two brand new shiny black Escalades. I'd been unable to see them from the point where I'd come over the wall. I crept in front of the cars intending to peek in the windows when I almost tripped over a body lying on the ground next to the Durango's front tire.

I didn't recognize the man, but judging by the awkward angle of his head, I knew I wouldn't be having coffee with him any time soon. Directly in front of the vehicles was a gray metal door propped open by a man's loafer. I looked back at the body and sure enough, the guy had one loafer and one blue and gray argyle sock on his other foot. The second I slipped in the door I heard arguing from somewhere in the interior of the building. The door had opened onto a dark hallway. I turned right and quietly walked forward with my left hand skimming along the drywall hoping to feel an opening in the inner wall where I could see deeper into the interior of the warehouse. Several old, discarded boxes littered the floor. I stepped around one and found another body lying partially covered with cardboard. I quickly checked for a pulse. The guy was deader than a doorknob.

The arguing escalated and the need to see what was happening became more pressing. I continued down the wall and finally came to a corner. I peeked around and could see light filtering into the hallway from a rolling door that was propped open in the up position. I edged toward it trying to make as little sound as possible. When I reached the opening, I inched my head around until I could see into the cavernous interior of the warehouse. I stifled a gasp as I saw Kate and a young oriental woman, each sitting in a straight-backed chair with their hands tied behind them and their feet lashed to the chair's spindly front legs.

Boxes the size of hay bales were stacked one on top of the other in neat five-foot squares. They lined the perimeter of the warehouse, which seemed to be about the size of half a football field. A metal, second floor walkway hung about twenty feet in the air and wound around the perimeter wall. There was a short, four-foot railing that ran the full length of the walkway. Unfortunately, the crosshatch flooring was constructed out of contractor grade expanded metal, which made it difficult to see up into the walkway area from where I was standing.

I studied the entire layout of the building, then brought my attention back to where Kate and the woman were sitting in the middle of the room. I took in a long, shaky breath, trying unsuccessfully to calm my nerves. There were four men in the center near the two women. One oriental man waited off to the side, while two men in business suits stood with their backs to me. Craig was pacing back and forth in front of them, arguing about something that had him extremely agitated. The man on the right held some kind of submachine gun lazily at port arms across his chest. I looked back at Kate and found her staring at me, the only indication that she'd seen me was a slight crinkling at the corners of her eyes.

A noise off to my right startled me and I quickly knelt and tried to blend into the shadows. I'd lost my night vision by looking into the bright lights of the warehouse and it took me a minute before I could see in the dark again. As my sight gradually returned, I strained to see what had caused the noise. About five feet from the other side of the opening, someone else was using the shadows to hide. I froze while I worked out my options. Very slowly, the man came closer until I recognized the compact figure of Mr. Myung.

We stared at each other until he raised his fingers in a peace sign, pointed to his eyes and then up towards the walkway in the warehouse, once to the right and once to the left. Two guards then, up on the walkway. Not good. I nodded understanding. He raised his hand palm forward telling me to wait. I watched, completely awed as this seventy-year-old man grabbed onto a vertical electrical conduit and begin to climb until he disappeared into the darkness.

I slid my head along the wall trying to catch a glimpse of the guard on the walkway to the right. I couldn't see anything until he slowly paced forward, keeping a wary eye on the happenings below. I knew it was coming, but his sudden disappearance surprised me all the same. I assumed as soon as Mr. Myung had finished with that guard he'd head over to take care of the other, so while I had some extra time I tuned into the discussion taking place in the middle of the floor.

Craig was now standing in front of the man on the left gesticulating wildly. "You said no cops would get hurt. You gave me your word! First your fucking goon squad tries to kidnap that detective to lure Gianina Angelino out into the open. Fail! You completely destroy the Angelino residence in a hail of bullets and only manage to kill one ninety-year-old man! Epic fail! All of your people on the raid are dead and Gianina is still very much alive!" He paced back to the oriental woman, pulled her head back by her hair and stuck his finger in her face. "Then! Then you join up with the Jug-eum to get to Myung. What the fuck? I've told you from the beginning, I don't care about Myung and I don't care about this bitch."

He released the fist full of black hair and stormed back towards the man. "All I care about," His volume increased twofold. "Is destroying the Angelino Crime Family. That's why you called me in the first place you dumb fuck!" Apparently that was going too far. The man on the right stepped forward and bashed Craig in the side of the head with the butt of his gun.

Craig went down, dazed but not unconscious. As the goon raised the gun to hit him again, the man on the left reached out and stopped him with a hand on his arm. The goon stepped back into his earlier position. Craig slowly pushed to his feet. He spoke much quieter now, his voice breaking as he pleaded with the man. "You gave me your word. No cops hurt or killed." He pointed towards Kate. "I lured her here knowing you gave your word, Puniskis. I lured her as bait because you promised me Gia Angelino on a platter. You said Gia would come for her just like she would have come for the detective, and now you say you can't afford to let her live?"

Puniskis? I thought back to the Lithuanians in the coffee shop. Their last name had been Puniskis. I watched the man on the left lift his shoulders and heard him say. "I lied."

Out of the corner of my eye I saw an AK-47 falling from the upper walkway on my left. Other people saw it as well. "Uh oh." I really didn't think that was part of the plan. In the short amount of time it took for the rifle to hit the floor, I kept my eyes on the walkway, expecting a body to follow the gun. Instead, Mr. Myung vaulted over the second story railing. I took that as my cue to move.

All eyes were on Mr. Myung as he fell to the floor and landed like a cat, legs flexed and fingertips barely brushing the floor. I ran as fast as my legs could move, repeating to myself the target point Mr. Myung had been drilling into my head the last few mornings. *Side of the neck, side of the neck, side of the neck.* In the time it took me to get to the guy on the right, he'd had time to raise the AK-47 and point it at the oriental whirlwind who'd already begun devastating the ranks of Puniskis' men who were rushing in from the sides where they'd been waiting out of my sight. As the man tried to find a target on the wildly spinning and kicking Myung, I leapt into the air, tucked my fist next to my waist palm up, and punched the big guy directly on the side of his neck with all the force I could muster. I really didn't expect it to work, but the man dropped into an unconscious heap.

My momentum carried me beyond where the men had been standing. My body was twisting from the force of my strike and as I pivoted, I caught a glimpse of Puniskis reaching into his jacket to get a gun while Craig was jumping at him from five feet away. My feet hit the ground running and without slowing I leapt at the seated women with my arms stretched out to the side. My forearms hit both of them in the chest and they and their chairs crashed backwards onto the floor. I skidded on my stomach just as bullets snapped over our heads. I turned and grabbed the backs of both chairs, dragging them across the floor and behind some pallets where I hoped to quickly cut their bindings and get back into the fight.

The room had erupted into total chaos. I dug in my pocket for my folding knife, all the while watching as bodies went flying right along with the bullets. Out of the corner of my eye I saw Jerry run into the room from the side hallway, swing a pole at the gun arm of one of the goons and then finish him off with a crack to the head. The oriental woman screamed at me. "Untie me! I can help him! Untie me!" I quickly cut the cords around her hands, then sliced through the ones holding her feet to the chair. Once free, she bounded up and ran toward Puniskis who seemed to be indiscriminately shooting in every direction. Kate and I both watched her leap into the air and smash the side of his head with a very powerful, well-timed flying kick. Puniskis' head snapped sideways and as he went down, she followed with a second, deadly blow to the side of neck.

Completely absorbed in the fighting, I jumped up to go help, but as I took my first step, Kate yelled. "Alex!"

"Oh, yeah, sorry!" I quickly turned and grabbed my knife from where I'd dropped it on the floor. I'd slashed the bindings on the other woman so fast I'd caused some small cuts on her wrists and legs so even though I was quick, I made very sure I didn't cut Kate. When I finished, I looked up to see a gaggle of Korean men run into the building. As both Kate and I raced toward them, Jerry decked the first man in line with a powerful roundhouse punch. Kate plowed into the second guy and before I could claim my prize, Mr. Myung charged past me and delivered a double kick to the third man's chest and neck. As he turned to help Kate, who was punching the man she'd taken to the ground, he glanced at me with a fire in his eyes and a quick nod of approval. *Was that a wink I just saw?* He actually seemed to be enjoying himself.

His confidence bolstered my own fighting spirit and I turned and kicked the man Jerry was fighting squarely between the legs. The man dropped. Jerry grinned and shook his head as he ran and slammed shut a door that had just opened to allow several new men and women into the building. I couldn't help but wonder where the hell all these people were coming from.

As Jerry and the two Myung's took on this new threat, Kate and I put our shoulders into one of the pallets and slowly shoved it in front of the door. Out of the corner of my eye I watched Mr. Myung's granddaughter and another Asian woman exchange quick punches and a variety of kicks. I thought the Asian woman was winning until the granddaughter leapt into the air, kicked over the other woman's head and then, as the woman ducked, quickly followed up with straight kick directly into her opponent's windpipe. The lady was dead before she hit the ground.

I spun in a circle looking for my next target and to my surprise, there was none. Just when I thought we had everything under control, several gunshots sounded in the hallway. We all exchanged puzzled looks and then ran in the direction of the shots. To our surprise, Gabe and several of his men came skidding into the warehouse, weapons drawn and ready for a fight. Everyone froze, scanning faces to identify friend or foe. Finally, Gabe lowered his weapon and signaled for his men to do the same. Gabe motioned to Kate. "Some guy with a thick accent called Ms. A and said he was holding you. She sent me to come get you, but..." He motioned around the room with his gun.

I watched as the granddaughter walked up to Mr. Myung. He pulled her into a long, heartfelt embrace, holding her for a very long time. When they finally separated, they stepped over to stand in front of Kate and me. Mr. Myung indicated the woman with a wave of his hand. "My granddaughter, Myung Kyung-Soon." The woman, who carried herself with a regal bearing, gracefully inclined her head. Breathing heavily, both Kate and I returned the gesture. Mr. Myung then bowed with his back straight and his arms held rigidly at his side. "Sergeant Brannigan. My granddaughter and I must leave, immediately. Thank you for your help in restoring her to my family. I owe both you and Detective Wolfe my life." Without waiting for a reply, they quickly turned and left through a side door.

As sirens wailed in the distance, Gabe lifted his chin towards me.

"We gotta go, too, Alex." With that, he turned and jogged back toward the hallway with his men following close behind.

Kate surveyed the room while she stood with her hands on her hips looking none too happy. She finally turned angry eyes on me. "Okay, Alex. Were you following me or did you just happen to be in the neighborhood?"

"Neither. How about you? Were you out here playing hero all by yourself?" I was more than slightly pissed off myself.

She at least had the grace to blush. She let her arms fall to the side and walked over and toed one of the bodies littering the floor. "Craig phoned and said he knew where the granddaughter was being held. I called Mr. Myung and told him where I was supposed to rendezvous, then drove here myself and waited for Craig. He snuck up behind me and pulled a gun, took mine and forced me into the warehouse."

I looked over to where Jerry was kneeling next to Craig. There was a perfectly round hole where a bullet had caught him square in the temple. "Why would you trust a man like that? You knew he was after the Angelinos, and I *know* you were suspicious."

She brought her eyebrows down low. "How did you know he was after the Angelinos?"

I shrugged. "A little research," I paused for effect. "Katie O'Shea." I grinned when the fire ignited behind her eyes.

CHAPTER 18

I didn't get home until after midnight. Apparently Tessa and Jynx hadn't waited up for me because when I walked into the bedroom they both raised their sleepy heads off my pillows long enough to give little wags before laying back down and once again falling fast asleep. "Some noble companions you two are. Can't even wait up long enough to greet me at the front door when I come stumbling home after a long day at the office." I pushed Tessa towards the center of the bed, kicked off my shoes and fell fully clothed onto the rumpled sheets she'd already warmed for me. I don't remember pulling up the blanket, but I was snuggled deeply under the covers the next morning when Casey came knocking on my door.

"Alex? You in there? Wake up. I've been trying to call you for the last hour or so. Alex?"

"I'm coming, I'm coming, jeez. What's the rush?" Falling asleep fully clothed has it's advantages. It didn't matter who happened to stop by, I could answer the door without having to worry about whether or not I was decent. I pulled open the door and blinked bleary eyes at Casey who stood on my doorstep holding two cups of Circle K coffee and a bag I fervently hoped contained some kind of gooey, chocolaty donuts. "What time is it anyway?" I stumbled to my sofa and lay down, hoping she'd go away so I could sleep a little longer.

"Ten thirty-eight. Kate said to let you sleep for a while, and I did, but I think we need to go find Marcos and see if he'll talk to us. Word around the department is the Chief is pressing for Captain Emery to take Jason's case to the Grand Jury because the media is starting to say we're stalling because he's Beulow's son. And get this." She opened the bag and poured four donuts of various shapes and sizes out onto my coffee table. She picked up a cruller and quickly took a bite. "Nate was out drinking with some buddies last night and guess who else was at the bar?"

I put my arm over my eyes and mumbled. "No clue."

"Captain Buelow. Nate said he was drunker than snot and talking up a blue streak to whoever would listen about how macho his son is. Nate said every other word was stud, or he-man, and macho. Stuff like that."

I sat up and nabbed a chocolate croissant. "No kidding? That's about as weird as it gets."

"No, actually it gets even weirder. Nate said Buelow actually sounded proud of the fact that his son has so much," She held up two fingers on each hand and wiggled them. "Aggressive testosterone that he'd actually forced himself on a woman. That asshole was proud of the fact that his studly son had raped a woman!"

The croissant tasted wonderful, and as I took a sip of coffee I thought about how convenient it would be to set up an I.V. drip and mainline enough caffeine to get my brain working again. "So he's an asshole. Is anybody actually surprised by that?" I shoved the rest of the pastry into my mouth and headed for my bedroom. "I've gotta jump in the shower and change my clothes. Could you let the dogs out to do their thing for me?"

I glanced over my shoulder in time to see Casey tear the last of her cruller in two and feed each of the dogs a piece before taking them through the kitchen and out the back door. The heat of the shower began to lull me to sleep again so I turned the water down to an almost cold spray to try to wake myself up. When I'd finished, Casey and I said goodbye to Tessa and Jynx, grabbed the coffee and the last two donuts and headed out to her car.

Twenty minutes later we were standing in front of Marcos' front door waiting for him to decide whether or not to let us in. He must have decided in our favor because he gave one last scowl and turned to go back into his living room, leaving the front door open in an obvious invitation to enter. He threw himself down on the sofa and sat with his arms crossed over his chest and his thick black eyebrows pulled down low over his eyes. "What do you want? I already told Ruthanne she can go fuck herself. I have nothing to say to any fucking cop, ever again."

I pushed a blue and gray striped recliner closer to the sofa and sat. Casey walked around behind him pretending to admire the various pieces of art he had hanging on his walls. I knew she was actually taking herself out of the conversation for now. Out of sight out of mind as the saying goes. I leaned forward and rested my forearms on my knees. "How's Jason?"

Jason walked into the living room from the kitchen. "Jason is fine. What are you doing here, Detective? I already told the other cops I'm not talking to anybody without my lawyer."

"I wanted to try to get some information from Marcos. Not everybody is convinced you're guilty. If you're innocent, and I think you are, we need to be able to prove it. So far, all we have is the evidence that's stacked up against you. I'd like to ask Marcos some questions that, depending on the answers, might help your case."

The two of them sat quietly until Jason reached over and squeezed Marcos' knee. "She might be able to help. We need to do something because I'm beginning to think even my lawyer thinks I did it. What do you think? I'd like to have at least one other person in my corner besides you and mom."

Marcos rubbed his eyes with the palms of his hands. "I can't believe we're going through this." He dropped his hands to his lap and sighed. "Fine. What do you want to know?"

"Let's start at the beginning. I know you've already answered some of these questions, but humor me, okay? Tell me about the night of the rape. Where were you, who did you talk to, what did you do?"

"That night, Jason and I went to The Sistah's Club, a nightclub in Phoenix. It was our three-month anniversary and we mostly just wanted to be by ourselves. We ate dinner, we danced, and we came home. We really didn't talk to anyone and we didn't see anyone we knew. That was the whole reason we went to Phoenix. To be anonymous and alone."

"So there's nobody who can corroborate your alibi? You must have told someone you guys were going to Phoenix."

He shook his head. "I told Maddie it was our anniversary, but going to Phoenix was kind of spur of the moment. We decided to go that afternoon, and we went."

"Okay, then, moving on. I understand a condom was found at the scene. What brand does Jason use?"

Marcos gave me a frustrated look and waved towards his partner. "He's right here, why don't you ask him?"

"Because I can't. He invoked his Miranda rights and I can't ask him any questions."

Jason sat forward. "Listen, for right now, just talking to you, I take back what I said. I don't need my attorney here. I need help and I'm getting desperate. I want to talk to you."

I glanced up at Casey who had turned and was staring at me. She shook her head, then reached into her pocket, pulled out her Miranda card and read it to Jason. When she finished, she said. "Now having been advised of these rights and understanding these rights, will you answer our questions?"

Jason nodded. "For right now, with you two, yes."

I sighed. "Jason. I want you to understand. If you give us any incriminating information, both Casey and I will be put on the witness stand and we'll have to testify against you."

He looked down at his hands which were clasped tightly in his lap. He was pressing them together so hard his knuckles were a creamy white. He consciously let go and shook them, obviously trying to relax. "Okay. I understand. I could be fucking myself. But I'm innocent, so anything I say should help. What do you want to know?"

I sat back and studied him. "Well, I guess we can begin with my last question. Do you use condoms, and if so, what brand?"

He got up and disappeared into the bedroom. When he came back, he was holding a box of Rough Rider studded condoms. "This isn't the box I've been using. When the detectives searched our condo, they took my other box, but this is the type I usually use."

"When was the last time you used one?"

"Last night."

I smiled. "I mean before the night of the rape. See, one of your big problems is that the condom they found at Fernando's had some of your sperm on it. Any idea how that happened?"

He stood up and began to pace. "Jesus, I have no fucking clue. I've never had sex at Fernando's."

"So I'm asking you again. When was the last time, before the night of the rape, you used a condom?"

Marcos broke in. "Probably a couple days before. We were at his parents' house. His dad was supposed to be out of town so we had come to visit with his mom. She went to the store to get some steaks, and we decided to climb into their hot tub while she was gone. One thing led to another. Jason's pretty paranoid about STD's, so we climbed out of the hot tub, he put on a condom and..."

I held up a hand. "Okay, I get the picture. Did you both use a condom or just Jason?"

Marcos shrugged. "Just Jason."

"All right, so what happened then?"

"His father came home from his trip early and caught us. The old man went fucking ape shit and threw us out."

I rubbed my face wondering why Marcos would have sex at Jason's parents' house when he knew his father was about as homophobic as a person can get. But honestly, I figured that was his business and decided to move on. "You said you've never had sex at Fernando's. Have you ever been there before?"

He nodded. "Yeah. You need to understand something. I knew I was gay when I was in the sixth grade. Can you imagine a little eleven, twelve-year-old Catholic kid who has a macho asshole for a father, knowing he prefers little boys to little girls? I didn't come out to my mom until my junior year of high school. She was pretty cool about it, but we both agreed there was no way we were going to tell my father. When I went to college, one of my best friends was a lesbian. Cheryl.

We both had homophobic parents, so we decided to move in together and pretend we were a couple." He chuckled as he thought back to that time. "It worked, too, until one day about a year ago Cheryl and I went to my parents' house for dinner. Everybody but mom got pretty shit-faced, and Cheryl accidentally let the cat out of the bag."

Marcos added his two cents. "The fucker tried to disown him, but his mom wouldn't let him. Jason couldn't go home anymore and the lease was up where he and Cheryl had been living. She moved back to Pennsylvania with a new girlfriend and Jason was living on other people's couches until we met and he moved in."

Other people's childhoods always made me appreciate my own, slightly skewed upbringing. "You said you'd been to Fernando's before? Why? From what everybody says, that place is dangerous for anybody who's gay."

"Because Cheryl knew someone who worked there. We'd go hang out as a couple. Nobody questioned it." He held up his arm and flexed his muscles. "I'm a body builder, a gaybro. A gay guy who likes traditionally manly interests. Sports, fishing, outdoors. I fit in there pretty well, especially with a woman on my arm."

"Have you ever met the victim before?"

"No."

"Do you have any idea why she'd say you raped her?"

"None."

Casey stepped around to the front of the sofa. "Do you think your mother would talk to us without your father knowing?"

He picked up his phone. "Absolutely. She can't stand the asshole either, but she's too afraid of him to leave. You want me to call her?"

Casey shook her head. "Not right now, but I might ask you to call her another time." She looked at me to see if I had any more questions. When I shrugged, she said, "Can you think of anything else, and I mean anything, that might help us figure out who raped Sally Jessup?"

I thought of another question just as he was shaking her head. "The victim gave her name as Sally Jessup, but do you know anyone named Tanya Rodriguez?"

His head snapped towards me and he blinked twice before answering. "What?"

Both Casey and I suddenly had our attention riveted on Jason. I knew he'd heard the question and didn't bother repeating it. He stood up and began pacing and then suddenly punched the bedroom door so hard he put his fist through it. "Fuck!"

Marcos had gone a pasty white. Casey and I exchanged surprised looks and I raised my eyebrows wondering if she wanted to field this particular line of questioning. She nodded. Walking over to where Jason was standing, she casually leaned against the wall and crossed her arms. "I'll take that as a yes. Is there something we need to know about?"

His answer was strong and immediate. "No."

Marcos got to his feet. "No? What do you mean, No?"

Jason got right up into Marcos' space and growled, "No." Picking up his jacket he angrily strode out the door, leaving Casey and I thoroughly puzzled and Marcos obviously upset.

Marcos rushed out after him. "Jason. Where're you going? Hold up! I'm coming with you."

Casey ran her hand through her short-cropped hair. "That was interesting. I think we need to go talk to Kate about some things."

I nodded. "Yup."

CHAPTER 19

Casey didn't say much on the drive back to the office. I knew her thought process and realized the best way to help her think was to shut up until she was ready to talk. When we walked into the office, she immediately put her head into Kate's cubicle. "We need to talk." She looked around at all the detectives seated at their desks. "In private."

Kate nodded and led us into the lieutenant's office. She closed the door once Casey and I had entered and taken our seats. "Okay, what's the matter?" She walked around and sat in the lieutenant's chair on the other side of the desk.

Casey licked her lips. I hadn't seen her this agitated in a while. Her eyes were focused on the floor, but not on a single spot. Her gaze was darting this way and that as she tried to pull together several thoughts into one coherent idea. Kate glanced at me but I wasn't sure what Casey had put together. I'd obviously either missed something or just hadn't connected the dots. I shrugged at Kate and turned back to Casey. Kate sat back in her chair and clasped her hands over her stomach, waiting.

Casey sat up straighter in her chair. "Kate." She stopped a second, shaking her head before forging on. "I think we might have a problem."

When Casey didn't continue, Kate nodded slowly. "Go on."

"I can't prove it yet, but I think Jason was set up." She ran her hand through her hair, obviously agitated about something.

Neither Kate nor I were particularly surprised by that little revelation. Kate prompted her again. "By?"

Casey looked her squarely in the eye. "By—."

My cellphone interrupted her mid-sentence. I quickly pulled it out "Sorry, sorry, I should have turned it on silen..." I trailed off as I saw the caller identification. When Fernando had given me Justíno's phone number, I'd programmed it into my phone so I could put the little piece of paper he'd written on into evidence. I looked up at Kate. "Justíno."

She flicked her fingers towards my phone. "Answer it." She pulled a recorder out of the lieutenant's desk drawer, set it near me on the desktop and turned it on.

I pushed send. "This is Detective Wolfe."

A man whispered hurriedly into the phone. "Detective, this is Justíno Cabrera."

"Justíno, my partner is here with me. I'm going to put you on speaker."

"No! Just you. Tío said I could only trust you."

I put it on speaker anyway. "Your Tío, your uncle, that's Fernando Cabrera?"

"Sí. He told me to call you, but if they know I did, they'll kill me y mí familia. But what they did, I can't live with myself. I told Tío what happened, and he said I could trust you."

"What who did, Justíno?"

"I worked for them once. I needed money and I muled for them. That's why they came to me, I think. They brought her to my apartment and fucked her up. They said if I didn't say I saw that guy, you know, come out of the bathroom that night, they'd do the same to me. When they left, I ran. Mí Hermana, she was hiding me, but Tío came and found me."

"You said they came and fucked up a woman. Who came?" There

was silence on the other line for quite a while. Kate motioned for me to prompt him again. "Listen, you can trust me. A young woman is dead. You saw them beat her to death."

He began sobbing. "I know...I can't get it out of my head. She kept screaming for me to help her and I didn't. Oh God, I didn't."

The sobbing intensified and I tried one more time to get him to give us the information we needed. "Please, help her now. Who killed that young woman, Justíno?"

He practically wailed the names. "Adolfo and Enrique."

"What are their last names?" Even though I knew the answer, I needed him to say the name for the recording.

"Aguilar."

"Did they tell you why you had to say you saw the man come out of the bathroom?"

"No. They said I had to, and I couldn't go to the police because they'd know. They'd know if I did. Adolfo said they had connections, and if I told the polícia anything but what they said, they'd know."

Casey put her fingers to her eyes and rubbed them, then looked at Kate who was watching her intently. I looked back at my phone. "Where are you now? I'd like to come talk to you in person."

"No! I can't."

The screen showed that he had ended the call. Kate reached over and clicked the recorder off. We sat silently a minute, then Casey began to speak. "Let me just lay some things out to see what you think, okay?"

We both nodded, but when she started to speak, we heard Gail Redfox's voice out in the office. "Where's Kate? Or how about Casey or Alex?"

Kate held up a finger. "Hold that thought, Case." She got up and opened the door. "We're in here, Gail." Kate waived her in. "What's up?"

"Ruthanne is down in the lobby with Jason and Marcos. The front desk officers had to handcuff Jason and then they called us. He keeps screaming he's going to kill him and Marcos is so upset he's not making any sense." She looked directly at Kate. "Ruthanne said to come get you."

When Kate got up to go with Gail, Casey said, "Kate. Wait." She quickly recapped what was on her mind. "First, only one out of three witnesses can pick Jason out of a photo line-up, and Jason just told us he'd been to Fernando's before so that could account for that one person. Second, Jason just told us that the last time he used a condom was at his parents' house. Third, his homophobic father came in, caught him and Marcos in the middle of having sex, became enraged and threw them out. I can't prove anything, but that *could* be where the condom at the restaurant came from if Buelow or whoever he hired to set up Jason planted it there. Fourth, Nate overheard Captain Buelow bragging about Jason's manly qualities at a bar. Buelow even went so far as to allude to the fact that Jason was a he-man because he'd raped a woman."

I suddenly realized where she was going with this. "Whoa."

Kate held up a finger telling me to shut up. "Go on, Case."

She motioned to the tape recorder. "Just now, it seemed to me like Justíno was saying Adolfo and Enrique had a mole on the department. Add to all that, the fact that there are rumors that Captain Beulow," She stopped, probably trying to find just the right words. Casey was nothing if not precise. "Entertains himself with hookers. And finally, when Alex asked Jason if he knew someone named Tanya Rodriguez, he flipped out. It made me wonder if Jason had maybe overheard his dad talking about, or to Tanya." She shook her head. "I can't prove that part yet, it's just speculation. Anyway, now, right after Alex mentions Tanya, Jason is here screaming he wants to kill someone." She shrugged. "Maybe someone like his dad?"

The ticking of the clock on the lieutenant's desk was the only sound in the room for several seconds. Kate slowly leaned back onto the desk. "Casey." She waited until Casey was once more looking directly at her. "You do realize what you're saying don't you?"

Casey nodded. "Yes, Ma'am. I think Captain Buelow paid Adolfo and Enrique to set up his son. He wanted—no—he needed his son to be his version of what a man should be, even if the only way for that to happen was if he could brag that his son had so much testosterone he'd actually raped a woman. I think when he walked in on Jason and Marcos having sex, something snapped."

Gail had left the door open when she'd walked in and Kate reached over and pushed it shut. "All three of you, you listen to me. *I* am going to be the one to handle this from here on out. This could be a career ender, and if something falls out, it's gonna be on me."

I snorted. "Fat chance. I'm not leavin' you to take a fall for us."

Kate shocked me when she grabbed me by the collar and pushed me up against the wall. "You listen to me. This is my case now, and you'll keep your mouth shut. Understand?"

I glared back at her a second, and then nodded. She let go of my collar and opened the door. "Let's go." I straightened my collar and we all followed her to the elevator and waited for it to arrive. When the doors opened, we stepped in and rode down to the main lobby in silence. There is an interior staircase in the middle of the atrium, and as we exited the elevator, I saw Captain Buelow standing off by himself next to the stairs looking smug. Captain Emery stood next to Ruthanne looking confused and Assistant Chief Robards was speaking with Jason. Another detective had taken Marcos over by the window to wait until the whole mess got sorted out. Kate and Gail both walked over to join Jason and company.

I decided I wanted to wipe that smug look off of Beulow's face so I stepped over and stood next to him. We both watched what was happening with Jason and the Assistant Chief. I motioned their way. "Jason seems pretty upset."

Beulow crossed his arms. "Yeah, he's always been hotheaded."

I nodded. "I wonder why Marcos is here with him." I put my hands in my pockets and rocked back and forth on my heels. "I know him from the hospital. He's gay as gay can be." I turned to look at Buelow. "You think maybe he has a thing for Jason?"

He turned angry eyes on me. "My son wouldn't let that faggot anywhere near him."

"Oh yeah, that's right. Your son's the one who raped that woman. Sometimes I think rapists just have too much testosterone, ya know?"

"You got that straight." The smugness reappeared on his face.

"You have a hot tub at your place, don't ya? I love hot tubs."

He turned and studied me, his face morphing into tight mask of suspicion. "What are you getting at, Wolfe?"

I shrugged, then leaned in and whispered, "Do the names Adolfo and Enrique ring any bells?" One minute I was on my feet, the next I was sprawled on my back, the side of my head ringing from where he'd sucker punched me. I looked up and saw his face had contorted into a grotesque snarl. He grabbed his holstered weapon and even though I reached for mine, I could tell I was going to be a millisecond too late. The barrel of his semi-auto pointed at me and I heard two gunshots, one right after the other. I grunted in anticipation, knowing full well exactly how it felt to be shot. What I didn't expect was for him to crumple to the ground with blood oozing from his white uniform shirt. I quickly looked behind me and saw Casey in a perfect weaver's stance, weapon drawn and pointing straight at Beulow.

CHAPTER 20

It had been one month to the day since Casey had shot Captain Beulow, or should I say ex-captain, current inmate Beulow. Marcos and Jason had invited everyone to something called an ABC party at The Backdoor to celebrate Jason's full exoneration. They'd invited Kate as well, but she'd declined. Casey, Ruthanne, Kathy and I had arrived early and were waiting in the parking lot for the others to get there. When Casey had shot Beulow, she'd been given administrative leave and both of us had been told not to talk to anyone about Jason's case. Since the investigative portion was over now, this was the first time we'd had a chance to talk to Ruthanne and Kathy about what had happened.

Kathy leaned back on the seat of her Harley and crossed her arms. "It turns out Captain Beulow has been playing dirty for a very long time." I harrumphed, and she looked at me and nodded. "I know, you've been trying to tell people that for a while now, but he must have had something on some pretty high up commanders because most of what he's done over the years has been effectively hushed up. Apparently, when he was the commander of the Vice Unit, he'd have the officers long-form certain hookers instead of arresting them, then he'd contact the hookers and make a deal in exchange for sex. Tanya was one of them. When he hired Adolfo and Enrique Aguilar to arrange the set up at Fernando's, he put them in touch with her. We don't think he meant for them to kill her, but Beulow's still going to be charged for her murder under the felony murder rule."

Another car pulled into the lot and Casey moved out of its way before commenting. "But why would he set up his own son? Did he really think making his son into a rapist would up his macho factor with the other guys? That it would make him appear less gay? That's just sick."

Ruthanne chimed in. "It is, and he is."

The whole Buelow thing didn't really surprise me, but there was one detail about the barn fire I still hadn't heard. "Okay, so who was the body in the barn, and how did that relate to the Angelinos?"

The lights in the parking lot began winking on one by one as the sun went down behind the Tucson Mountains. The sunset was a beautiful strata of orange and yellow ribbons topped with layers of vibrant fuchsia and cerulean blue. Ruthanne gave a low whistle. "I don't know of anywhere else in the world that gets the incredible sunsets we do." She sighed as the final colors faded into the early evening sky. "Anyway, Alex, after we finished Jason's case, I was assigned to help with that one. The kid who was buried in the barn was named Jerome Sinclair. He was a sixteen-year-old runaway from Boston. We have some evidence linking him to the Andrulis Mafia, that Lithuanian group that tried to kidnap you. We haven't figured out how he died yet, but we think they buried the body there a few months ago as part of a multi-pronged attempt at framing and/or eliminating the Angelino Crime Family. When nobody found it, they decided to draw attention to it by burning down the barn. It was all part of an elaborate set-up that fell apart when you and Kate messed up their plans in the warehouse."

Kathy smiled and patted me on the back. "Congratulations by the way. I heard you two were gonna get medals of valor for that until someone decided it was just better to keep the whole affair low profile. Ya just gotta love the higher ups, don't ya?"

"Don'cha just?" I knew there was no way I'd ever get a medal for anything I did on this department, but I was definitely pissed that they'd screwed Kate out of her medal too. We all turned and watched as Megan pulled into the lot, followed by Maddie in her funky little 1960's Volkswagen. When they joined us we all made our way over to the blinking neon backdoor sign. When we walked through the door, I stopped dead in my tracks. "What the hell?"

Semi naked bodies filled the room. Single saw us and came traipsing over wearing nothing but a black garbage sack. "Hey! Glad you could make it, but you're kinda over dressed."

I looked down at my jeans and sweatshirt, then back at the people in the room. Marcos caught sight of us and came running over. He tried to grab me in one of his mega-hugs but I pushed him away. "Marcos! What the hell?" I waved at his not quite clad body and couldn't help but stare. He was totally naked except for bright yellow caution tape that he'd wrapped around his nether regions.

He paraded around all of us, grinning mischievously. "What? I know I told you it was an ABC party, so why are you guys dressed like that?"

Casey, who'd turned a bright red laughed. "Nate told us it meant Ale, Brown Ale and Cask Ale, but…"

Jason, who had a bunch of leaves judiciously taped to various parts of his body, joined us. "ABC party! Anything but clothes, ladies. Join us!"

I slowly turned to the other women and grinned....

THANK YOU FROM THE AUTHOR

If you enjoyed this book, please take a minute of your time to leave a review. Your opinion is important to me and to other readers and I appreciate the help getting the word out. If you didn't like it, please feel free to send me an email from the contact page on my website and I'll be happy to chat with you about it.

ALSO BY ALISON NAOMI HOLT

Mystery

Credo's Hope - Alex Wolfe Mysteries Book 1

Credo's Legacy – Alex Wolfe Mysteries Book 2

Credo's Fire – Alex Wolfe Mysteries Book 3

Fantasy

The Spirit Child – The Seven Realms of Ar'rothi Book 1

Duchess Rising – The Seven Realms of Ar'rothi Book 2

Mage of Merigor

Psychological Thriller

The Door at the Top of the Stairs

"If you don't like to read, you haven't found the right book."
J.K. Rowling

Alison, who grew up listening to her parents reading her the most wonderful books full of adventure, heroes, ducks and puppy dogs, promotes reading wherever she goes and believes literacy is the key to changing the world for the better.

In her writing, she follows Heinlein's Rules, the first rule being *You Must Write*. To that end, she writes in several genres simply because she enjoys the great variety of characters and settings her over-active fantasy life creates.

There's nothing better for her than when a character looks over their shoulder, crooks a finger for her to follow and heads off on an adventure. From medieval castles to a horse farm in Virginia to the police beat in Tucson, Arizona, her characters live exciting lives and she's happy enough to follow them around and report on what she sees.

She loves all horses & hounds and some humans...

For More Information
www.Alisonholtbooks.com
ANHolt@Denabipublishing.com

ACKNOWLEDGMENTS

Editor: Harvey Stanbrough
http://harveystanbrough.com
Cover Art: Kat McGee
https://daringcreativedesigns.com

Alison Naomi Holt

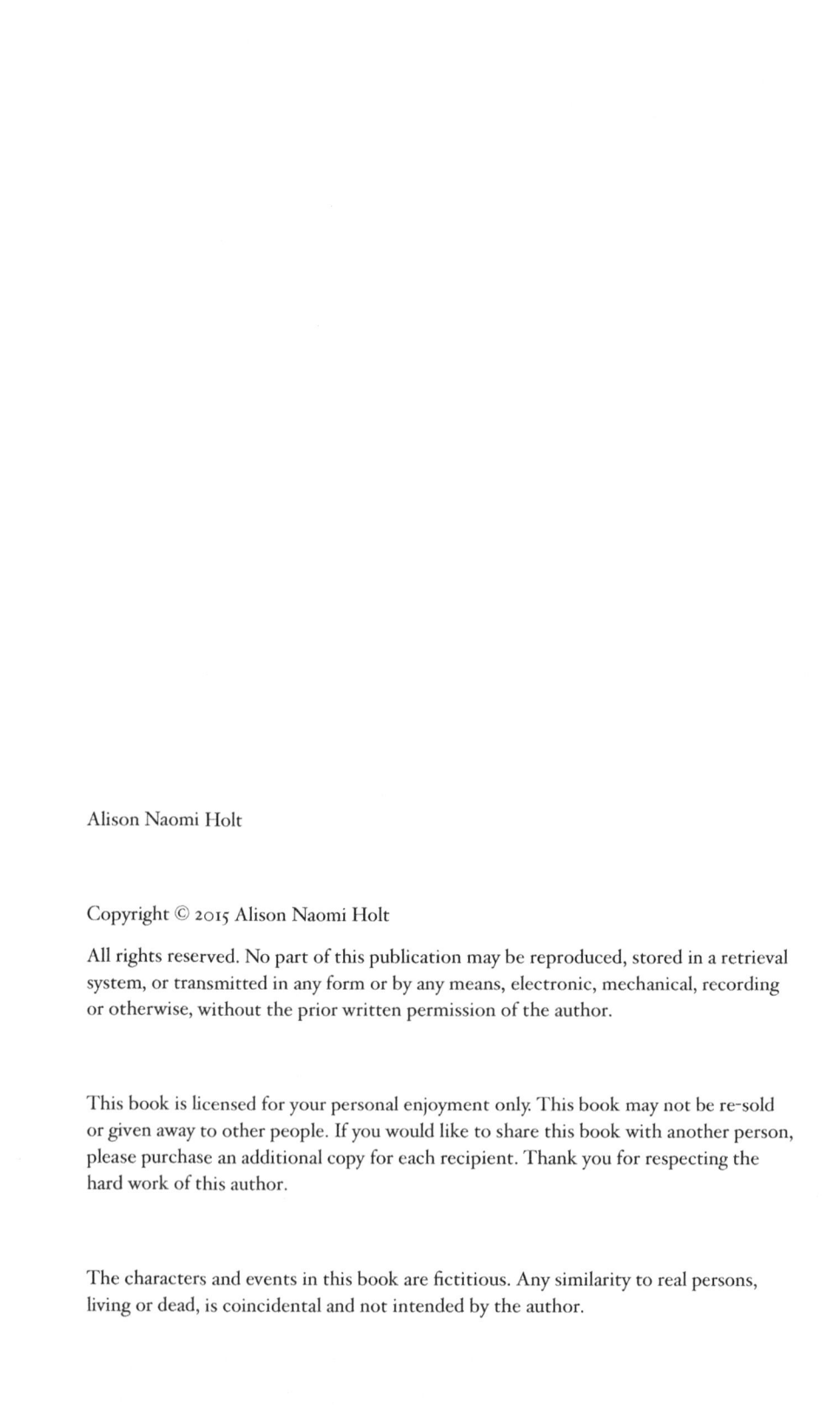

Copyright © 2015 Alison Naomi Holt

All rights reserved. No part of this publication may be reproduced, stored in a retrieval system, or transmitted in any form or by any means, electronic, mechanical, recording or otherwise, without the prior written permission of the author.

This book is licensed for your personal enjoyment only. This book may not be re-sold or given away to other people. If you would like to share this book with another person, please purchase an additional copy for each recipient. Thank you for respecting the hard work of this author.

The characters and events in this book are fictitious. Any similarity to real persons, living or dead, is coincidental and not intended by the author.

Made in the USA
Monee, IL
05 April 2021